THE WICKED DEEP

SHEA ERNSHAW

SIMON AND SCHUSTER

First published in Great Britain in 2018 by Simon and Schuster UK Ltd
A CBS COMPANY

First published in the USA in 2018 Simon Pulse, an imprint of
Simon & Schuster Children's Publishing Division

3 5 7 9 10 8 6 4 2

Simon & Schuster UK Ltd
1st Floor,
222 Gray's Inn Road
London WC1X 8HB

www.simonandschuster.co.uk
www.simonandschuster.com.au
www.simonandschuster.co.in

Simon & Schuster Australia, Sydney
Simon & Schuster India, New Delhi

A CIP catalogue record for this book is available from the British Library.

PB ISBN 978-1-4711-6613-6
eBook ISBN 978-1-4711-6614-3

Typeset in the UK by M Rules
Printed and bound by CPI Group (UK) Ltd, Croydon, CR0 4YY

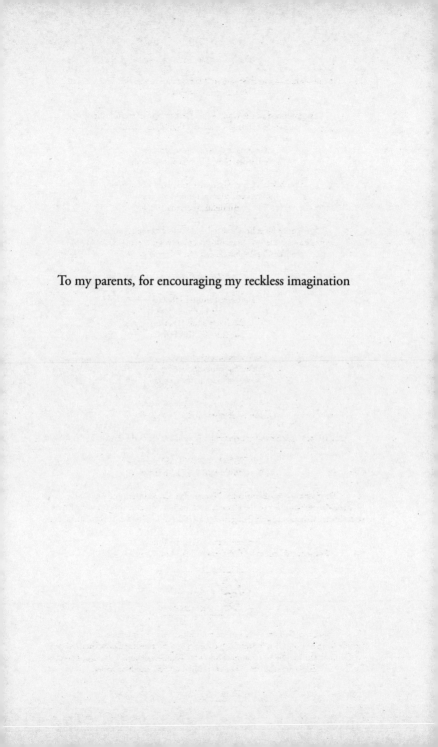

To my parents, for encouraging my reckless imagination

If there is magic on this planet, it is contained in water.
—Loren Eiseley

THE SEA

Three sisters arrived in Sparrow, Oregon, in 1822 aboard a fur trading ship named the *Lady Astor*, which sank later that year in the harbor just beyond the cape.

They were among the first to settle in the newly founded coastal town, and they strode onto the new land like thin-legged birds with wavy caramel hair and pastel skin. They were beautiful—too beautiful, the townspeople would later say. Marguerite, Aurora, and Hazel fell in love often and typically with the wrong men—those whose hearts already belonged to someone else. They were coquettes, temptresses, and men found them impossible to resist.

But the townspeople of Sparrow found the sisters to be much more: They believed them to be witches, casting spells on the men to make them unfaithful.

And so at the end of June, when the moon was nothing but a thin shard in the overcast sky, stones were tied to the sisters' ankles, and they were dropped into the ocean just beyond the cape, where they sank to the bottom and drowned. Just like the ship they arrived on.

ONE

I have an old black-and-white photograph taken in the 1920s of a woman at a traveling circus floating in a massive tank filled with water, blond hair billowing around her head, legs hidden by a false mermaid's fin made of metallic fabric and thread to look like scales. She is wispy and angelic, with thin lips pinched tightly together, holding her breath against the icy water. Several men stand in front of the glass tank, staring at her as if she were real. So easily fooled by the spectacle.

I think of this photograph every spring, when murmurs begin to circulate through the town of Sparrow about the three sisters who were drowned beyond the maw of the harbor, past Lumiere Island, where I live with my mother. I imagine the three sisters floating like delicate ghosts in the dark shadows beneath the water's surface, mercurial and preserved just like the sideshow mermaid. Did they struggle to stay above the waterline two centuries ago, when they were forced into the deep, or did they let the weight of each stone carry them swiftly to the cold, rocky bottom of the Pacific?

A morning fog, somber and damp, slides over the surface of the ocean between Lumiere Island and the town of Sparrow. The water is calm as I walk down to the dock and begin untying the skiff—a flat-bottomed boat with two bench seats and an outboard motor. It's not ideal for maneuvering in storms or gales but fine as a runner into town and back. Otis and Olga, two orange tabby cats who mysteriously appeared on the island as kittens two years back, have followed me down to the water, mewing behind me as if lamenting my departure. I leave every morning at this time, motoring across the bay before the bell rings for first period—Global Economics class, a subject that I will never use—and every morning they follow me to the dock.

The intermittent beam of light from the lighthouse sweeps over the island, and for a moment it brushes across a silhouette standing on the rocky western shore atop the cliff: my mother. Her arms are crossed in her knobby camel-colored sweater wrapped tightly around her fragile torso, and she's staring out at the vast Pacific like she does each morning, waiting for someone who will never return: my father.

Olga rubs up against my jeans, arching her bony back and raising her tail, coaxing me to pick her up, but I don't have time. I pull the hood of my navy-blue rain slicker up over my head, step into the boat, and yank the cord on the motor until it sputters to life, then steer the boat out into the fog. I can't see the shore or the town of Sparrow through the dim layer of moisture, but I know it's there.

Tall, sawtooth masts rise up like swords from the water, land mines, shipwrecks of years past. If you didn't know your way, you could run your boat into any of the half-dozen wrecks still haunting these waters. Beneath me lies a web of barnacle-crusted metal, links of rusted chain trailing over broken bows, and fish making their homes in rotted port-holes, the rigging long since eaten away by the salty water. It's a grave-yard of ships. But like the local fishermen chugging out through the dreary fume into the open sea, I can navigate the bay with my eyes pinched shut against the cold. The water is deep here. Massive ships used to bring in supplies through this port, but not anymore. Now only small fishing boats and tourist barges sputter through. These waters are haunted, the seamen still say—and they're right.

The skiff bumps against the side of dock eleven, slip number four, where I park the boat while I'm in class. Most seventeen-year-olds have driver's licenses and rusted-out cars they found on Craigslist or that were handed down from older siblings. But instead, I have a boat. And no use for a car.

I sling my canvas bag over my shoulder, weighted down with textbooks, and jog up the gray, slick streets to Sparrow High School. The town of Sparrow was built where two ridges come together—tucked between the sea and mountains—making mudslides all too common here. One day it will likely be washed away completely. It will be pushed down into the water and buried beneath forty feet of rain and silt. There are no fast-food chains in Sparrow, no shopping malls or movie theaters, no Starbucks—although we do have a drive-through coffee hut. Our small town is sheltered from the outside world, trapped in time. We have a whopping total population of two thousand and twenty-four. But that number increases greatly every year on June first, when the tourists converge into town and overtake everything.

Rose is standing on the sloping front lawn of Sparrow High, typing on her cell phone. Her wild cinnamon-red hair springs from her head in unruly curls that she loathes. But I've always envied the lively way her hair cannot be tamed or tied up or pinned down, while my straight, nut-brown hair cannot be coaxed into any sort of bouncy, cheerful configuration—and I've tried. But stick-straight hair is just stick-straight hair.

"You're not ditching me tonight, are you?" she asks when she sees me, tenting both eyebrows and dropping her cell into her once-white book bag that's been scribbled with Sharpie and colored markers so that it's now a collage of swirling midnight blues and grassy greens and bubblegum pinks—colorful graffiti art that has left no space untouched. Rose wants to be an artist—Rose *is* an artist. She's determined to move to Seattle and attend the Art Institute when we graduate. And she reminds me almost weekly of the fact that she doesn't want to go alone and I should come with her and be her room-mate. To which I've skillfully avoided committing since freshmen year.

It's not that I don't want to escape this rainy, dreadful town, because I do. But I feel trapped, a weight of responsibility settled firmly over me. I can't leave my mother all alone on the island. I'm all she has left—the only thing still grounding her to reality. And perhaps it's foolish—naive even—but I also have hope that perhaps my father will return someday. He'll magically appear on the dock and stroll up to the house as if no time has passed. And I need to be here in case he does.

But as our junior year comes to an end and our senior year approaches, I'm forced to consider the rest of my life and the reality that my future might be right here in Sparrow. I might never leave this place. I might be stuck.

I'll stay on the island, reading fortunes from the smeared remains of tea leaves in white porcelain cups just like my mom used to before Dad vanished and never came back. Locals would steer their boats across the harbor, sometimes in secret under a ghost moon, sometimes in the middle of the day because they had an urgent question they needed answered, and they'd sit in our kitchen, fingers tapping on the wood-block table, waiting for Mom to tell them their fate. And afterward they'd leave folded or crumpled or flattened bills on the table just before they left. Mom would slide the money into a flour tin she kept on the shelf next to the stove. And maybe this is the life I'm destined for: sitting at the kitchen table, the sweet scent of chamomile or orange lavender tea settling into my hair, running my finger around the rim of a mug and finding messages in the swirling chaos of leaves.

I've glimpsed my own future in those leaves many times: a boy blowing in from across the sea, shipwrecked on the island. His heart beating wildly in his chest, his skin made of sand and wind. And my heart unable to resist. It's the same future I've seen in every cup of tea since I was five, when my mom first taught me to decipher leaves. *Your fate lies at the bottom of a teacup*, she had often whispered to me before shooing me off to bed. And the idea of this future stirs inside me whenever I think about leaving Sparrow—like the island is drawing me back, my fate rooted here.

"It's not ditching if I never said I'd go," I say in response to Rose's question.

"I won't allow you to miss another Swan party." She shifts her hips to the side, looping her right thumb around the strap of her book bag. "Last year I was stuck talking to Hannah Potts until sunrise, and I won't do it again."

"I'll think about it," I say. The Swan party has always served a double purpose: the start of the Swan season and also the end-of-the-school-year bash. It's a booze-fueled celebration that is an odd mix of excitement to be free of classes and teachers and pop quizzes, blended with the approaching dread of the Swan season. Typically, people get way too smashed and no one remembers any of it.

"No thinking, just doing. When you think about things too long, you just talk yourself out of them." She's right. I wish I wanted to go—I wish I cared about parties on the beach. But I've never felt comfortable at things like this. I'm the *girl who lives on Lumiere Island*, whose mom went mad and dad went missing, who never hangs out in town after school. Who would rather spend her evening reading tide charts and watching boats chug into port than chugging beers with people I barely know.

"You don't even have to dress up if you don't want to," she adds. Dressing up was never an option anyway. Unlike most locals in Sparrow, who keep a standby early 1800s costume tucked away in the back of their closet in preparation for the yearly Swan party, I do not.

The warning bell for first period rings, and we follow the parade of students through the main front doors. The hallway smells like floor wax and rotting wood. The windows are single-pane and drafty, the wind rattling the glass in the frames every afternoon. The light fixtures blink and buzz. None of the lockers close because the foundation has shifted several degrees off center. If I had known another town, another high school, I might find this place depressing. But instead, the rain that leaks through the roof and drips onto desks and hallway floors during winter storms just feels familiar. Like home.

Rose and I don't have first period together, so we walk to the end of A Hall, then pause beside the girls' bathroom before we part ways.

"I just don't know what I'll tell my mom," I say, scratching at a remnant of Blueberry Blitz nail polish on my left thumb that Rose made me paint on two weeks back at her house during one of our movie nights—when she decided that to fit in as a serious art major in Seattle she needed to watch classic Alfred Hitchcock movies. As if scary black-and-white films would somehow anoint her as a *serious* artist.

"Tell her you're going to a party—that you actually have a life. Or just sneak out. She probably won't even notice you're gone."

I bite the side of my lip and stop picking at my nail. The truth is, leaving my mom alone for even one night makes me uneasy. What if she woke up in the middle of the night and realized I was no longer asleep in my bed? Would she think I had disappeared just like my dad? Would she go looking for me? Would she do something reckless and stupid?

"She's stuck on that island anyway," Rose adds. "Where's she going to go? It's not like she's just going to walk out into the ocean." She pauses and we both stare at each other: Her walking out into the ocean is precisely what I'm afraid of. "What I mean," Rose corrects, "is that I don't think anything will happen if you leave her for *one* night. And you'll be back right after sunrise."

I look across the hall to the open doorway of my first-period Global Economics class, where nearly everyone is already in their seats. Mr. Gratton is standing at his desk, tapping a pen on a stack of papers, waiting for the final bell to ring.

"Please," Rose begs. "It's the biggest night of the year, and I don't want to be the loser who goes solo again." A slight lisp trails over the word "solo." When Rose was younger, she talked with a lisp. All her *S*s sounded like *Th*s. In grade school, kids used to tease her whenever a teacher asked her to speak out loud in front of the class. But after regular visits to a speech therapist up in Newport three days a week during our first years of high school, suddenly it was like she stepped out of her old body and into a new one. My awkward, lisping best friend was now reborn: confident and fearless. And even though her appearance didn't really change, she now radiated like some beautiful exotic species of human that I didn't recognize, while I stayed exactly the same. I have this sense that someday we won't even remember why we were friends in the first place. She will float away like a brightly colored bird living in the wrong part of the world, and I will stay behind, gray-feathered and sodden and wingless.

"Fine," I relent, knowing that if I skip another Swan party she might actually disown me as her only friend.

She grins widely. "Thank God. I thought I was going to have to kidnap you and drag you there." She shifts her book bag higher onto her shoulder and says, "See you after class." She hurries down the hall just as the final bell chimes from the tinny overhead speakers.

Today is only a half day: first and second period, because today is also the last day of school before summer break. Tomorrow is June first. And although most high schools don't start their summer session so early, the town of Sparrow began the countdown months ago. Signs announcing festivals in honor of the Swan sisters have already been hung and draped across the town square and over storefront windows.

Tourist season starts tomorrow. And with it comes an influx of outsiders and the beginning of an eerie and deadly tradition that has plagued Sparrow since 1823—ever since the three Swan sisters were drowned in our harbor. Tonight's party is the start of a season that will bring more than just tourist dollars—it will bring folklore and speculation and doubt about the town's history. But always, every year without fail or falter, it also brings death.

A SONG

It starts as a low croon that rolls in with the tide, a sound so faint it might just be the wind blowing through the clapboard shutters, through the portholes of docked fishing boats, and into narrow cracks along sagging doorways. But after the first night, the harmony of voices becomes undeniable. An enchanting hymn sailing over the water's surface, cool and soft and alluring. The Swan sisters have awakened.

TWO

The doors of Sparrow High are flung open just before noon, and a raucous parade of students is set loose into the sticky midday air. Shouts and whoops of excitement echo across the school grounds, scattering the seagulls perched along the stone wall that borders the front lawn.

Only half the senior class even bothered to show up for the final day, but the ones who did tear out pages from their notebooks and let the wind carry them away—a tradition to mark their freedom from high school.

The sun sits lazy in the sky, having burned through the morning fog, and it now seems defeated and weary, unable to warm the ground or our chilled faces. Rose and I stomp down Canyon Street in our rain boots, jeans tucked inside to keep them dry, with our coats unzipped, hoping the day will brighten and warm the air before tonight's all-night bash, which I am still not entirely thrilled to attend.

On Ocean Avenue we turn right and then stop at the next corner, where Rose's mom owns a shop that sits like a little square cake with white-painted brick walls and pink eaves—and where Rose

15

works every day after school. The sign above the glass door reads: ALBA'S FORGETFUL CAKES in pale pink frosting–swirled letters on a cream-colored background. Yet the wood sign has started to collect a greenish brine that will need to be scrubbed away. A constant battle against the salty, slimy air.

"I only have a two-hour shift," Rose says, hoisting her book bag over to the other shoulder. "Meet at nine on the dock?"

"Sure."

"You know, if you had a cell phone like a normal person, I could just text you later."

"Cell phones don't work on the island," I point out for the hundredth time.

She blows out an exasperated breath. "Which is catastrophically inconvenient for me." As if she were the one who has to endure the lack of cell service.

"You'll survive," I say with a smirk, and she smiles back, the freckles across her nose and upper cheeks catching the sunlight like constellations of golden sand.

The door behind her whips open with a fluttering of chimes and bells clanking against the glass. Her mom, Rosalie Alba, steps out into the sunlight, blocking her gaze with a hand as if she were seeing the sun for the first time since last summer.

"Penny," Mrs. Alba says, dropping her hand. "How is your mother?"

"The same," I admit. Mrs. Alba and my mom were friends once, in a very casual way. Sometimes they'd meet for tea on Saturday mornings, or Mrs. Alba would come out to Lumiere Island and she and my mom would bake biscuits or blackberry pie when the thorny blackberry bushes began to overtake the island and my dad would threaten to burn them all down.

Mrs. Alba is also one of the only people in town who still asks about my mom—who still cares. It's been three years since my father disappeared, and it's as if the town has forgotten about him entirely. Like he never lived here at all. But it's far easier to endure their blank stares than it was to hear the rumors and speculation that spun through town in the days after he vanished. *John Talbot never belonged here in the first place*, people had whispered. *He abandoned his wife and daughter; he always hated living in Sparrow; he ran away with another woman; he went mad living on the island and waded out into the sea.*

He was an outsider, and he had never been fully accepted by the locals. They seemed relieved when he was gone. As if he deserved it. But Mom had grown up here, gone to Sparrow High, then met my father at college in Portland. They were in love, and I know he never would have abandoned us. We were happy. He was happy.

Something far stranger happened to him three years ago. One day he was here. The next he wasn't.

"Will you give this to her?" Mrs. Alba asks, extending her palm where she's holding a small pink box with white polka-dot ribbon.

I take it from her, running the ribbon through my fingertips. "What flavor?"

"Lemon and lavender. A new recipe I've been experimenting with." Mrs. Alba does not bake ordinary cakes for ordinary cravings. Her tiny forgetful cakes are intended to make you forget the worst thing that's ever happened to you—to wipe away bad memories. I'm not entirely convinced they actually work. But locals and summer tourists devour the tiny cakes as if they were a potent cure, a remedy for any unwanted thought. Mrs. Potts, who lives in a narrow house on Alabaster Street, claims that after eating a particularly decadent chocolate fig basil cake, she no longer could recall the day her neighbor Wayne Bailey's dog bit her in the calf and made her bleed, leaving a scar that looks like a spire of lightning. And Mr. Rivera, the town postman, says he only vaguely recollects the day his wife left him for a plumber who lives in Chestnut Bay an hour's drive north. Still, I suspect it might only be the heaping cups of sugar and peculiar flavors in Mrs. Alba's cakes that for a brief moment allow a person to think of nothing else but the intermixing earthiness of lavender and the tartness of lemon, which not even their worst memories can rise above.

When my father vanished, Mrs. Alba began sending me home with every flavor of cake imaginable—raspberry lime tart, hazelnut espresso, seaweed coconut—in hopes they might help my mother forget what had happened. But nothing has broken through her grief: a stiff cloud not easily carried away with the wind.

"Thank you," I say, and Mrs. Alba smiles her wide, toothy grin. Her eyes are like pools of warmth, of kindness. And I've always felt comforted by her. Mrs. Alba is Spanish, but Rose's father is true-blooded Irish, born in Dublin, and Rose managed to get all her father's features, much to her displeasure. "See you at nine," I say to Rose, and she and her mom vanish into the shop to bake as many forgetful cakes as they can before the tourists arrive tomorrow morning by the busload.

* * *

The eve before the start of Swan season has always felt burdensome to me. It's like a dark cloud I can't shake.

The knowing of what's coming, the death that creeps up over the town like fate clawing at the door of every shop and home. I can feel it in the air, in the spray of the sea, in the hollow spaces between raindrops. The sisters are coming.

Every room at the three bed-and-breakfasts along the bay front is booked solid for the next three weeks until the end of Swan season—which will come on midnight of the summer solstice. Rooms facing the sea go for twice what can be charged for the rooms facing inland. People like to push open their windows and step out onto their balconies to hear the beckoning call of the Swan sisters singing from the deep harbor.

A handful of early tourists have already found their way into Sparrow, dragging their luggage into lobbies or snapping photos of the harbor. Asking where to get the best coffee or hot cup of soup because their first day in town usually feels the coldest—a chill that settles between the bones and won't go away.

I hate this time of year, as do most locals. But it's not the influx of tourists that bothers me; it's the exploitation, the spectacle of a season that is a curse on this town.

At the dock, I toss my book bag onto one of the bench seats inside the skiff. All along the starboard side, dotted into the white paint are scrapes and dings like Morse code. My dad used to repaint the skiff every spring, but it's been neglected for the last three years. Sometimes I feel just like that hull: scarred and dented and left to rust since he vanished somewhere out at sea.

I place the small cake box onto the seat beside my bag, and then walk around to the bow, about to untie the front line when I hear the hollow *clomp* of footsteps moving down the dock behind me.

I'm still holding the bowline when I notice a boy standing several feet back, holding what looks like a crumpled piece of paper in his left hand. His face is partly obscured by the hood of his sweatshirt, and a backpack hangs heavy from his shoulders. "I'm looking for Penny Talbot," he says, his voice like cold water from the tap, his jaw a hardened line. "I was told I could find her down here."

I stand up fully, trying to see his eyes, but there is a shadow cutting over the top half of his face. "Why are you looking for her?" I ask, not entirely certain I want to tell him that *I* am Penny Talbot just yet.

"I found this up at the diner . . . the Chowder," he says with an edge of uncertainty, like he's not sure he's remembered the name right. The Chowder is a small diner at the end of Shipley Pier that extends out over the water, and has been voted Sparrow's "Best Diner" for the last ten years in the local *Catch* newspaper—a small print paper that employs a total of two people, one of which is Thor Grantson because his father owns the paper. Thor is in the same class as me. During the school year, local kids overtake the Chowder, but in the summer months we have to share the worn stools along the bar and the tables on the outdoor deck with the horde of tourists. "I'm looking for work," he adds, holding out the limp piece of paper for me to see, and then I realize what it is. I posted a note on the cork bulletin board inside the Chowder nearly a year ago, asking for help maintaining the lighthouse out on Lumiere Island, since my mom had become nearly incapable of doing anything and I couldn't manage on my own. I had forgotten about posting it, and when no one ever came looking to fill the position, and the scribbled, handwritten note was eventually buried beneath other flyers and business cards, I made do.

But now, somehow this outsider has found it among the clutter of papers tacked to the bulletin board. "I don't need the help anymore," I say flatly, tossing the bowline into the boat—and also inadvertently revealing that I am indeed Penny Talbot. I don't want an outsider working on the island—someone who I know nothing about. Who I can't trust. When I had posted the listing, I had hoped a laid-off fisherman or maybe someone from my school might have responded. But no one did.

"You found someone else?" he asks.

"No. I just don't need anyone now."

He scrubs a hand over his head, pushing back the hood that had shrouded his face, revealing stark, deep green eyes the color of the forest after it rains. He doesn't look like a drifter: grimy or like he's been showering in gas station bathrooms. He's my age, maybe a year or two older. But he still has the distinct look of an outsider: guarded and wary of his surroundings. He clenches his jaw and bites his lower lip, looking back over his shoulder to the shoreline, the town twinkling beneath the afternoon sun like it's been sprinkled with glitter.

"Are you here for the Swan season?" I ask, flattening my gaze on him.

"The what?" He looks back at me, a measure of hardness in every move he makes: the twitch of an eyelash, the shifting of his lips before he speaks.

"Then why are you here?" He obviously has no idea what the Swan season is.

"It was the last town on the bus line." This is true. Sparrow is the final stop on a bus route that meanders up the coast of Oregon, stopping in several quaint seaside villages until it meets a dead end in Sparrow. The rocky ridgeline blocks any roads from continuing up the shore, so traffic has to be diverted inland for several miles.

"You picked a bad time to end up in Sparrow," I say, unhooking the last rope but holding on to it to keep the skiff from drifting back from the dock.

He pushes his hands into his jean pockets. "Why's that?"

"Tomorrow is June first."

By his stiff, unaltered expression, I can tell he really has no idea what he's just stumbled into.

"Sorry I can't help you," I say, instead of trying to explain all the reasons why he'd be better off just catching tomorrow's bus back out of here. "You can look for work at the cannery or on one of the fishing boats, but they usually don't hire outsiders."

He nods, biting his lip again and looking past me to the ocean, to the island in the distance. "What about a place to stay?"

"You can try one of the bed-and-breakfasts, but they're usually booked this time of year. Tourist season starts tomorrow."

"June first?" he echoes, as if clarifying this mysterious date that obviously means something to me but nothing to him.

"Yeah." I step inside the boat and pull the engine cord. "Good luck." And I leave him standing on the dock as I motor across the bay toward the island. I look back several times and he's still there, watching the water as if unsure what to do next, until the final time I glance back and he's gone.

THREE

The bonfire throws sparks up into the silvery night sky. Rose and I scramble down the uneven trail to Coppers Beach, the only stretch of shore in Sparrow that isn't bound in by rocks and steep cliffs. It's a narrow length of speckled white and black sand that ends at an underwater cave that only a few of the bravest—and stupidest—boys have ever attempted to swim into and then back out of.

"Did you give her the forgetful cake?" Rose asks, like a doctor who's prescribed medication and wants to know if there were any ill side effects or positive results.

After returning to Lumiere Island, after showering in the drafty bathroom across the hall from my bedroom then staring at my small, rectangular closet, trying to decide what to wear to tonight's event—finally settling on white jeans and a thick black sweater that will keep out the night's chill—I went into the kitchen and presented my mom with Mrs. Alba's forgetful cake. She had been sitting at the table staring into a cup of tea.

"Another one?" she asked drearily when I slid the cake in front of her. In Sparrow, superstition holds as much weight as the law of gravity or the predictability of the tide charts, and for most locals

Mrs. Alba's cakes have the same likelihood of helping Mom as would a doctor's bottle of pills. So she obediently took small bites of the lavender and lemon petit four, careful to not spill a crumb onto her oversized tan sweater, the sleeves rolled halfway up her pale, bony forearms.

I don't think she even realized today is the last day of school, that I just finished my junior year of high school, and that tomorrow is June first. It's not like she's completely lost all sense of reality, but the edges of her world have dulled. Like hitting mute on the remote control. You can still see the picture buzzing on the TV; the colors are all there, but there's no sound.

"I thought I saw him today," she muttered. "Standing on the shore below the cliff, looking up at me." Her lips quivered slightly, her fingers dropping a few crumbs of cake onto the plate in front of her. "But it was just a shadow. A trick of the light," she amended.

"I'm sorry," I told her, touching her arm softly. I can still hear the sound of the screen door slamming shut the night my father left the house, recall the way he looked walking down the path toward the dock, his shoulders bent away from the spray of the sea, his gait weary. I watched him leave on that stormy night three years earlier, and he never came back.

He simply vanished from the island.

His sailboat was still at the dock, his wallet on the side table by the front door of the house. No trace. No note. No clues. "Sometimes I think I see him too," I tried to console her, but she stared at the cake in front of her, the features of her face soft and distant as she silently finished the last few bites.

Sitting beside her at the kitchen table, I couldn't help but see myself in her: the long straight brown hair, same liquid blue eyes and tragically pale skin that rarely sees the sun in this dreary place. But while she is polished and graceful with ballerina arms and gazelle legs, I have always felt knock-kneed and awkward. When I was younger, I used to walk bent forward, trying to appear shorter than the boys in my class. Even now, I often feel like a puppet whose master keeps pulling all the wrong strings so that I fumble and trip and hold my hands clumsily out in front of me.

"I don't think cake is going to fix her," I tell Rose as we walk single file down the path lined with dry grass and thorny bushes. "The memory of my dad's disappearance is so solidified in her mind that no amount of local remedies will strip it out."

"Well, I don't think my mom has given up yet. Today she was talking about a new mixture of bee pollen and primrose that she thinks might help unsnag the worst of memories." We finally reach the beach and Rose hooks her arm through mine, our feet kicking up sand as we make our way to the bonfire.

Most of the girls are wearing long, layered dresses with low necklines and ribbons tied in their hair. Even Rose has on a pale green gown made of lace and chiffon that sweeps across the sand when she moves, dragging bits of driftwood and shells along with her.

Olivia Greene and Lola Arthurs, best friends and the rulers of Sparrow's social elite, are dancing on the other side of the bonfire when we enter the crowd, obviously already intoxicated, which is no surprise to anyone. Their hair is an identical shade of gothic black with short, severe bangs, dyed and trimmed just two weeks ago for the Swan season. Normally, their locks are bleached white—long and beachy. Which will probably return in a month, when the Swan season is over and they aren't feeling the need to dress like death. But Olivia and Lola love the dramatic, love dressing up, love being the center of attention at any social gathering.

Last year they pierced each other's noses in defiance of their parents—Olivia's is a silver stud in her left nostril, Lola's is a hoop through the right. And their nails are painted a matching macabre black, a perfect complement to the hair. They spin in circles beside the bonfire, waving their arms in the air and lolling their heads from side to side as if to mimic the embodiment of a Swam sister. Although I doubt the Swan sisters ever did anything so idiotic-looking two hundred years ago.

Someone hands Rose a beer and she in turn hands it to me to take the first sip. On weekends, sometimes we'll sneak beers or a half-finished bottle of white wine from her parents' fridge then get buzzed while stretched out on her bedroom floor listening to music—lately it's been country hits, our most recent obsession—and flipping through last year's yearbook, speculating about who's going to hook up this year and who might be inhabited by a Swan sister come summer.

I take a swig and look through the crowd at all the faces I recognize, at people who I've gone to school with since grade school, and I have the sharp thought that I hardly know any of them. Not really. I've had passing conversations with a few: *Did you write down the chapters we're supposed to read tonight in Mr. Sullivan's third-period history? Can I borrow a pen? Do you have a cell phone charger I can use?* But to call any of them friends wouldn't just be a stretch, it would be an all-out lie. Maybe it's partly because I know most of them will leave this town eventually—they will go off to college and have lives far more interesting than mine. We're all just passing ships; no point forming friendships that won't last.

And while Rose is not exactly climbing the social hierarchy at Sparrow High, she at least makes an effort to be friendly. She smiles at people in the halls, starts chatty conversations with her locker neighbors, and this year Gigi Kline, cheerleading captain for our struggling basketball team, even invited her to try out for the squad. They were friends once—Gigi and Rose—in elementary school. Best friends, in fact. But friendships are more fluid in grade school; nothing feels as permanent. And though they aren't exactly close anymore, Rose and Gigi have remained friendly. A tribute to Rose's kind nature.

"To the Swan sisters!" someone shouts. "And to another fucking year of high school!" Arms rise into the air, holding cans of beer and red cups, and a chorus of hoots and whistles carries across the beach.

Music thumps from a stereo balanced on one of the logs near the bonfire. Rose takes the beer from me and shoves a larger bottle into my hand. Whiskey—it's being passed through the crowd. "It's awful," she confesses, her face still puckered. But then she smiles, wagging an eyebrow at me. I chug back a quick slog of the dark booze, and it burns my throat, sending goose bumps down my arms. I hand it off to my right, to Gigi Kline. She grins, not at me—she doesn't even seem to notice me—but down at the bottle as she takes it from my hands, tips it to her mouth, swallows down way more than I could ever manage, and then wipes at her perfect coral lips before passing the bottle to the girl on her right.

"Two hours until midnight," a boy across the bonfire announces, and another wave of whoops and hollers rolls through the group. And those next two hours pass in a fog of bonfire smoke and more beers and swigs of whiskey that burn less and less with each sip. I hadn't planned on drinking—or getting drunk—but the warmth radiating throughout my entire body makes me feel loose and floaty. Rose and I find ourselves swaying happily with people who we might normally never talk to. Who might normally never talk to us.

But when it's less than thirty minutes to midnight, the group begins to stagger down the beach to the water's edge. A few people, either too drunk or deep in conversation to leave the bonfire, stay behind, but the rest of us gather together as if forming a procession.

"Who's brave enough to go in first?" Davis McArthurs asks aloud so everyone can hear, his spiky blond hair pushed up from his forehead and his eyelids sagging lazily like he's about to take a nap.

A rumble of low furtive voices passes through the mob, and a few of the girls are pushed playfully forward, their feet splashing into the water only ankle deep before they scurry back out. As if a few inches of water were enough for the Swan sisters to steal their human bodies.

"I'll do it," a singsong, slurring voice announces. Everyone cranes their head to see who it is, and Olivia Greene steps forward, twirling in a circle so that her pastel yellow dress fans out around her like a parasol. She's obviously drunk, but the group cheers her on, and she bows forward as if greeting her adoring fans before turning to face the black, motionless harbor. Without any coaxing, she begins to wade out into the salty sea, arms outstretched. When she's waist deep, she does a very ungraceful dive forward, which looks more like a belly flop. She disappears from view for half a second before reappearing at the surface, laughing wildly with her tragic-black hair draped over her face like seaweed.

The crowd cheers and Lola steps into the water up to her knees, urging Olivia back to the shallows. Davis McArthurs calls again for volunteers, and this time there is only a half beat before a voice shouts, "I'll go in!"

I snap my gaze to the left where Rose has stepped out of the crowd, moving toward the water.

"Rose," I bark, reaching out and grabbing her arm. "What are you doing?"

"Going for a swim."

"No. You can't."

"I've never really believed in the Swan sisters anyway," she says with a wink. And the crowd pulls her from my grasp, ushering her toward the cold ocean. She smiles widely as she wades out into the water, past Olivia. She's barely up to her waist when she dives forward and slips beneath the surface. A ripple shudders out behind her, and everyone on the beach falls silent. The air constricts in my lungs. The water flattens again at the surface, and even Olivia—who's still calf deep in the shallows—turns to watch. But Rose doesn't reappear.

Fifteen seconds pass. Thirty. My hearts starts to clap against my chest—a painful certainty that something isn't right. I push out from the crowd, suddenly sober, watching for Rose's red hair to break through the surface. But there's not even a breeze. Not even a ripple.

I take a single step into the water—I have to go in after her. I don't have a choice. When beneath the bloodless half-moon, shattering the calm, she suddenly bursts above the waterline, reemerging several yards farther out into the harbor from where she went in, I let out a trembling sigh of relief and the crowd erupts in a collective cheer, raising their cups as if they just witnessed some impossible feat.

Rose flips onto her back and lifts her arms overhead in a fluid pinwheel, swimming toward shore—casual, as if she were doing laps in a pool. I expect Davis McArthurs to ask who else wants to go in, but the group has gotten rowdy and girls are now traipsing through the shallow ankle-deep water, but never actually going all the way in. People stretch out on the sand, some shotgun beers, and others do sloppy cartwheels into the water.

Rose finally reaches the beach, and I try to push over to her, but several senior guys have gathered around her, giving her high fives and offering her beers. I slink back from the group. She shouldn't have done that—gone into the water. Risked it. My cheeks blaze, watching her nonchalantly wipe the water from her arms as if she is pleased with herself, smiling up at the cluster of guys who've taken a sudden interest in her.

The moonlight makes a path up the beach, and I wander away from the noise of the party—not far, just enough to catch my breath. I drank too much, and the world is starting to buzz and crackle and tilt off axis. I think of my father vanishing on a night when there was no moon to see by, no stars to guide his way back from the dark. If there had been a moon, maybe he would have returned to us.

I consider heading back to the marina, ditching the party and returning to the island, when I hear the heavy breathing and staggered footsteps of someone stumbling up the sandy beach behind me. "Hey," a voice calls. I spin around and see Lon Whittamer—one of Sparrow High's notorious partiers—swaying toward me like I'm standing in his path.

"Hi," I answer softly, trying to step out of his way so he can continue his drunken walk up the beach.

"You're Pearl," he says. "No, Paisley." He laughs, tosses his head back, his brown eyes slipping closed briefly before focusing on me again. "Don't tell me," he says, holding up a finger in the air as if to stop me from giving away my name before he's had time to figure it out on his own. "Priscilla. Hmm, Pinstripe."

"You're just saying things that start with the letter *P*." I'm not in the mood for this; I just want to be left alone.

"Penny!" he shouts, cutting me off.

I take a step back as he leans forward, exhaling a boozy breath and almost falling into me. His dark brown hair is plastered to his forehead, and his narrow-set eyes seem unable to focus, blinking closed every couple seconds. He's wearing a neon orange shirt with palm trees and pink flamingos scattered across it. Lon likes to wear obnoxious Hawaiian shirts in all shades of bright tropical colors with exotic birds and pineapples and hula girls. I think it started as a joke or maybe a dare our sophomore year, and then it turned into his trademark style. It makes him look like an eighty-year-old man on permanent vacation in Palm Springs. And since I don't think he's ever been to Palm Springs, his mother must order them online. And tonight he's wearing one of his ugliest.

"I like you, Penny. I always have," he mumbles.

"Is that right?"

"Yup. You're my kind of girl."

"I doubt that. You didn't even know my name two seconds ago."

Lon Whittamer's parents own the only major grocery store in town: Lon's Grocery, which they named after him. And he's known for being a total narcissistic asshole. He considers himself a ladies' man—a self-proclaimed Casanova—only because he can offer his girlfriends discounts on makeup in the meager cosmetics aisle at his parents' store, and he uses this like a gold trophy he only hands out to girls who are worthy. But he's also known for cheating on his girlfriends and has been caught numerous times making out with other girls in his jacked-up, chrome-rimmed, mud flap–accessorized red truck parked in the school parking lot. Basically, he's a moron who doesn't even deserve the breath it takes to tell him to get lost.

"Why didn't you go into the water?" he asks slyly, inching closer to me again. "Like your friend did?" He brushes his hair back from his forehead and it sticks straight up, either from sweat or seawater.

"I didn't want to."

"You're afraid of the Swan sisters?"

"Yeah, I am," I answer honestly.

His eyes slide partway closed, and a stupid grin curls across his lips. "Maybe you should swim with me?"

"No thanks. I'm going back to the party."

"You didn't even wear a dress," he points out, and his eyes slide down my body like he's shocked by my appearance.

"Sorry to disappoint you." I start to take a step around him, but he grabs hold of my arm and digs his fingers into my skin.

"You can't just walk away." He hiccups, closes his eyes again, then snaps them open like he's trying to stay awake. "We haven't swum yet."

"I told you, I'm not getting in the water."

"Sure you are." He smiles playfully, like I must be enjoying this as much as he is, and begins dragging me with him into the shallows.

"Stop it." I use my other hand to push against his chest. But he continues to lurch backward, deeper into the harbor. "Stop!" I shout this time. "Let me go." I look up the shore to the mass of people, but they're all too loud and drunk and distracted to hear me.

"Just one swim," he coos, still smiling, slurring each word as they tumble from his lips.

We've staggered calf deep into the water, and I slam my fist against his chest. He winces briefly and then his expression changes, turns angry, and his eyes go wide.

"Now you're going all the way in," he announces more crisply, yanking against my arm so that I stumble several steps deeper, up to my knees. Not deep enough to risk being taken by a Swan sister, but still my heart begins to thump, fear pushing the blood out to my extremities and sending panic racing down my veins. I raise my arm again, ready to punch him directly in the face to keep him from dragging me in any farther, when someone appears to my left; someone I don't recognize.

It all happens in an instant: The stranger shoves a hand against Lon's chest; Lon's throat lets out a short wheezing sound. His grip on my arm releases at the same time he loses his balance, and suddenly he's careening backward, falling all the way into the water, arms flailing.

I take a staggering step back, sucking in air, and the person who pushed Lon off of me touches my arm to steady me. "You okay?" he asks.

I nod, my heart rate not yet receding.

Lon, a few feet away, stands up from the waist-deep water, gagging and coughing and wiping seawater from his face. His bright orange shirt is now sopping wet. "What the fuck?" he yells, looking directly at the stranger standing beside me. "Who do you think you are?" Lon demands, marching toward us. And for the first time I really look up at the face of the stranger, trying to place him—the rigid angle of his cheekbones and the straight slope of his nose. And then I know: It's him, the boy from the dock who was looking for work—the outsider. He's wearing the same black sweatshirt and dark jeans, but he's standing closer now, and I can clearly see the features of his face. The small scar by his left eye; the way his lips come together in a flat line; his short dark hair flecked with droplets of mist from the sea air. His gaze is still hard and unflinching, but in the moonlight he seems more exposed, like I might be able to read some clue in the rim of his eyes or the shiver of his throat when he swallows.

But I don't have time to ask him what he's doing out here because Lon is suddenly in his face, shouting about what an asshole he is and how he's going to get his face punched in for having the nerve to shove Lon into the water like that. But the boy doesn't even flinch. His gaze looks down at Lon—who is a good six inches shorter than him—and even though the muscles in his neck tense, he seems wholly unconcerned by Lon's threats of an ass-kicking.

When Lon finally takes a breath, the boy raises an eyebrow, like he wants to be sure Lon is done babbling before he responds. "Forcing a girl to do anything she doesn't want to is reason enough to kick your ass," he begins, his voice level. "So I suggest you apologize to her and save yourself a trip to the ER for stitches and a raging headache in the morning."

Lon blinks, opens his mouth to speak—to spew some rebuttal that would probably involve more cuss words than actual substance—but then thinks better of it and snaps his jaw shut. Standing beside the two of them, it's obvious Lon is outweighed, outmuscled, and probably outexperienced. And he must see it too, because he turns his head to face me, swallows his pride, and mutters, "I'm sorry." I can tell it pains him to say it, his expression twisting in disgust, the words sharp and foreign in his mouth. He's probably never apologized to a girl in his life . . . maybe never apologized to anyone ever.

Then, he turns and slogs up the beach back to the group, trailing seawater from his soaked clothes.

"Thank you," I say, wading out of the shallow water. My shoes and the lower half of my white jeans are drenched.

The boy's shoulders relax for the first time. "That guy wasn't your boyfriend, was he?"

"God, no," I snap, shaking my head. "Just some self-entitled prick from school. I've never even talked to him before."

He gives me a half nod and glances past me to the party in full swing. Music thumps; girls squeal and skip along the edge of the waterline; boys wrestle and crush empty beer cans between their palms.

"What are you doing here?" I ask, squinting up at him, tracing the arc of his eyebrows where they pinch together.

"I came down to sleep on the beach. I didn't realize there was a party."

"You're sleeping out here?"

"Planned to, up beside the rocks." His eyes flick up the shoreline to where the cliff rises, steep and jagged—an abrupt end to the beach.

I assume he checked the bed-and-breakfasts in town but there were no vacancies, or perhaps he couldn't afford to rent a room. "You can't sleep out here," I tell him.

"Why not?"

"High tide will be in at two a.m., and that whole stretch of beach by the cliff will be underwater."

His dark green eyes taper at the edges. But instead of asking where he should move his makeshift campsite to, he asks, "What's with the party? Something to do with June first?"

"It's the Swan party, for the Swan sisters."

"Who are they?"

"You've really never heard of them?" I ask. I think it's truly the first time I've met an outsider who came to Sparrow with no clue about what goes on here.

He shakes his head then looks down at my waterlogged shoes, my toes swimming in seawater. "You should get dry by the fire," he says.

"You're soaked too," I point out. He went into the water just as far as I did.

"I'm fine."

"If you're sleeping outside tonight, you should probably get dry so you don't freeze to death."

He glances up the beach to the dark cliff wall, where he'd planned to sleep, then nods.

Together, we walk to the bonfire.

It's late.

Everyone is drunk.

The stars sway and slip out of alignment overhead, reconfiguring themselves. My head thrums; my skin itches from the salt water.

We find a place to sit on an open log, and I untie my shoes, leaning them against the ring of rocks encircling the bonfire. My cheeks already feel flushed, and my toes tingle as the blood circulates back through my feet. The fire licks at the sky, licks at my palms.

"Thank you again," I say, looking at him from the corner of my eye. "For the rescue."

"Right place at the right time, I guess."

"Most guys aren't so chivalrous around here." I rub my palms together, trying to warm them, my fingers cold to the bone. "The town might be required to give you a parade."

He smiles full and big for the first time, a softness in his eyes. "The hero requirements in this town must be pretty low."

"We just really like parades."

Again he smiles.

And it means something. I don't know what, only that I'm intrigued by him. This outsider. This boy who glances at me from the corner of his eye, who feels both familiar and new all at the same time.

Down near the water's edge, I can see Rose still talking to three boys who've taken a sudden interest in her after her swim, but at least she's safe and out of the water. Half of the crowd has wandered back up to the bonfire, and beers are handed around. My head still feels swimmy from all the whiskey, so I set the beer in the sand at my feet.

"What's your name?" I ask the boy as he takes a long sip of his beer.

"Bo." He holds the can loosely in his right hand, casual, noncommittal. He doesn't seem uneasy in this foreign social setting, in a new town surrounded by strangers. And no one seems to think he looks out of place.

"I'm Penny," I say, glancing at him, his eyes so green it's hard to look away. Then, twisting my hair over my shoulder to ring out the small amount of seawater from the ends, I ask, "How old are you?"

"Eighteen."

I press my hands together between my knees. Smoke from the fire swirls over us, and the music continues to blare. Olivia and Lola stumble up to the edge of the bonfire, hugging each other around the waist and looking completely trashed.

"Are those the Swan sisters?" Bo asks. Olivia and Lola do look alike, with their jet-black hair and matching piercings, so I can see why he might think they're related.

But I let out a short laugh. "No, just friends." I dig the toes of my right foot into the sand. "The Swan sisters are dead."

Bo turns back to me.

"Not recently," I amend. "They died two centuries ago— drowned in the harbor."

"Drowned on accident or by intention?"

Olivia, who is standing on the other side of Bo, laughs hard and sharp. She must have overheard his question. "It was murder," she answers for me, peering down at him. Her coral lips arch into a smile. She thinks Bo is cute—who wouldn't?

"It wasn't murder," Lola counters, swaying left then right. "It was an execution."

Olivia nods in agreement then looks across the bonfire. "Davis!" she calls. "Tell the legend."

Davis McArthurs, who has his arm around a girl with pixie-cut dark hair, grins and walks closer to the fire. It's tradition to recount the story of the Swan sisters, and Davis seems rather pleased with himself to be the one to do it. He finds an open stump and stands on top, peering down at everyone around the bonfire. "Two hundred years ago—" he begins, voice booming, far louder than is necessary.

"Start at the beginning," Lola interrupts.

"I am!" he shouts back. He takes a drink of his beer then licks his lips. "The Swan sisters"—he continues, glancing around the group to be sure everyone is watching, everyone is listening—"arrived in Sparrow on a ship named . . . something I can't remember." He raises an eyebrow and grins. "But that's not important. What's important is this one thing: They lied about who they were."

"They did not," Gigi Kline yells up at him.

Davis scowls at this second interruption. "All girls lie," he says with a wink.

Several guys around the fire laugh. But the girls boo. One even tosses an empty beer can at his head, which he just barely dodges by ducking.

Gigi snorts, her head shaking in disgust. "They were beautiful," she points out. "It wasn't their fault that all the men in this town couldn't resist them, couldn't help but fall in love, even the married ones."

They weren't just beautiful, I want to say. *They were elegant and charming and winsome. Unlike anything anyone in this town had ever seen before.* We grew up knowing the stories, the legend of the sisters. How the locals in Sparrow accused the three sisters of being witches, of possessing the minds of their husbands and brothers and boyfriends, even if the sisters didn't intentionally set out to make the men fall for them.

"It wasn't love," Davis barks. "It was lust."

"Maybe," Gigi agrees. "But they didn't deserve what happened to them."

Davis laughs, his face turning red from the heat of the fire. "They were witches!"

Gigi rolls her eyes. "Maybe this town just hated them because they were different. Because it was easier to kill them than to accept that the men in this place are thick-skulled, misogynistic assholes."

Two girls standing near me break out into laughter, spilling their drinks.

Bo looks at me, eyes piercing, then speaks low so only I can hear. "They were killed for being witches?"

"Drowned in the harbor with rocks tied to their ankles," I answer softly. "They didn't need a lot of evidence back then to find someone guilty of witchcraft; most of the townspeople already hated the Swan sisters, so it was a pretty swift verdict."

He stares at me intently, probably because he thinks we're making the whole thing up.

"If they weren't witches," Davis counters, staring down at Gigi, "why the hell did they return the following summer? And every summer since?"

Gigi shrugs like she doesn't want to have this argument with him anymore, and she tosses her beer can onto the flames, ignoring him. She staggers away from the bonfire down to the shore.

"Maybe you'll be taken by a Swan sister tonight!" Davis shouts after her. "Then we'll see if you still think they weren't witches."

Davis pounds the rest of his beer and crushes the can in his grip. He's apparently completely over the idea of retelling the story of the Swan sisters as he clumsily steps down from the stump and slings his arm back over the pixie-haircut girl.

"What did he mean 'return the following summer'?" Bo asks.

"On the first of June the summer after the sisters were drowned," I begin, staring at the flames working their way through the dry beach wood, "locals heard singing from the harbor. People thought they were imagining it, that it was only the horns of passing ships echoing off the ocean's surface, or the seagulls crying, or a trick of the wind. But over the next few days, three girls were lured into the water, wading out into the sea until they sank all the way under. The Swan sisters needed bodies to inhabit. And one by one, Marguerite, Aurora, and Hazel Swan slipped back into human form, disguised as local girls who emerged from the harbor, but not as themselves."

Abigail Kerns staggers up to the bonfire completely drenched, her usually frizzy, dark hair slicked back with seawater. She crouches down as close to the fire as she can get without tumbling into it.

"That explains all the soaking-wet girls," Bo says, looking from Abigail back to me.

"It's become a yearly tradition, to see who is brave enough to go out into the harbor and risk being stolen by one of the Swan sisters."

"Have you ever done it—gone into the water?"

I shake my head. "No."

"So you believe it could really happen—that you could be taken over by one of them?" He takes another drink of his beer, his face lit by the sudden burst of flames as someone tosses another log onto the coals.

41

"Yeah, I do. Because it happens every year."

"You've *seen* it happen?"

"Not exactly. It's not like the girls come out of the water and announce that they're Marguerite or Aurora or Hazel—they need to blend in, act normal."

"Why?"

"Because they don't inhabit bodies just to be alive again; they do it for revenge."

"Revenge on who?"

"The town."

He squints at me, the scar beneath his left eye tightening, then he asks the obvious question. "What kind of revenge?"

My stomach swirls a little. My head pulses at my temples. I wish I hadn't drunk so much. "The Swan sisters are collectors of boys," I say, pressing a finger to my right temple briefly. "Seducers. Once they have each taken a girl's body . . . the drowning begins." I pause for effect, but Bo doesn't even blink. His face is hardened suddenly, like he's stilled on a thought he can't shake. Maybe he wasn't expecting the story to involve actual death. "For the next three weeks, until midnight on the summer solstice, the sisters—disguised as three local girls—will lure boys out into the water and drown them in the harbor. They're collecting their souls, stealing them. Taking them from the town as revenge."

Someone to my right hiccups then drops their beer onto the sand near my feet, the brown liquid spilling out.

"Every year, boys drown in the harbor," I add, staring straight ahead into the flames. Even if you don't believe in the legend of the Swan sisters, you can't ignore the death that plagues Sparrow for nearly one month every summer. I've seen the boys' bodies being pulled from the harbor. I've watched my mom console grieving mothers who've come to have their fortunes read, pleading for a way to bring back their sons—my mom patting their hands and offering little more than the promise that their hurt would eventually dull. There is no way to bring back the boys who've been taken by the sisters. There is only acceptance.

And it's not just local boys; tourists are persuaded into the water as well. Some of the boys standing around the bonfire, whose faces are flushed from the heat and the alcohol in their bloodstreams, will be discovered floating facedown, having swallowed too much of the sea. But right now, they aren't thinking about that. Everyone believes they're immune. Until they're not.

It makes me nauseous, knowing some of these boys, who I've known most of my life, won't make it through the summer.

"Someone must see who drowns them," Bo says, his curiosity evident now. It's hard not to feel drawn in by a legend that repeats itself without falter or fail each season.

"No one has ever seen the moment when they're taken into the harbor—their bodies are always discovered after it's too late."

"Maybe they drown themselves?"

"That's what the police think. That it's some sort of suicide pact devised by high school students. That the boys sacrifice themselves for the sake of the legend—to keep it alive."

"But you don't believe that?"

"It's pretty severe, don't you think—kill yourself for the sake of a myth?" I feel my heart beat faster remembering summers past: bodies bloated with seawater, eyes and mouths caught open like gutted fish, as they were pulled onto the docks in the marina. A chill sweeps through my veins. "Once a Swan sister has whispered into your ear, promised the touch of her skin, you can't resist her. She will lure you into the water then pull you under until the life spills out of you."

Bo shakes his head and then finishes his beer in one gulp. "And people actually come to watch this happen?"

"Morbid tourism, we call it. And it usually turns into a witch hunt, locals and tourists all trying to figure out which three girls in town are inhabited by a Swan sister—trying to determine who is responsible for the killing."

"Isn't it dangerous to speculate about something you can't prove?"

"Exactly," I agree. "The first few years after the sisters were drowned, many local girls were hanged because they were suspected of being taken over by one of the sisters. But obviously they never hanged the right girls, because year after year the sisters kept returning."

"But if you were inhabited by one of these sisters, wouldn't you know it, remember it? Once it was all over?" He rubs his palms together and turns them toward the bonfire—worn hands, rough in places. I blink and look away.

"Some girls claim they have a cloudy recollection of summer, of kissing too many boys and swimming in the harbor, staying out past curfew. But that could be from too much booze and not because a Swan sister was inside them. People think that when a sister takes over a body, she absorbs all the girl's memories so the girl can resume her normal life, behave naturally, and no one will suspect she's not herself. And when the sister leaves the body, the sister blots out all the memories she doesn't want her host to recall. They need to blend in because if they were ever found out, the town might do something awful just to end the curse."

"Like kill them?" Bo asks.

"It would be the only way to keep them from returning to the sea." I press all my toes down into the warm sand, burying them. "Kill the girl whose body they inhabit."

Bo leans forward, staring into the flames like he's recalling some memory or place that I can't see. "And yet you celebrate it each year," he finally says, sitting up straight. "You get drunk and swim in the harbor, even when you know what's coming? Even though you know people are going to die? You've just accepted it?"

I understand why it seems odd to him, an outsider, but this is what we know. It's how it's always been. "It's our town's penance," I say. "We drowned three girls in the ocean two centuries ago, and we've suffered for it every summer since. We can't change it."

"But why don't people just move away?"

"Some have, but the families who've been here the longest choose to stay. Like it's an obligation they must endure."

A soft breeze rolls suddenly through the crowd, and the bonfire snaps and flickers, sending sparks up into the sky like angry fireflies.

"It's starting," someone calls from the waterline, and those clustered around the fire begin moving down to the beach.

I stand up, still in my bare feet.

"What's starting?" Bo asks.

"The singing."

FOUR

The moonlight makes an eerie path down to the water's edge.

Bo hesitates beside the bonfire, resting his hands on his knees, his mouth an even, unbreakable line. He doesn't believe any of this. But then he stands up, leaving his empty beer can in the sand, and follows me down to the shore where people are huddled together. Several girls are totally soaked, shivering, hair dripping down their backs.

"Shhh," a girl whispers, and the group falls totally silent. Totally still.

Several seconds pass, a cool wind slides across the water, and I find myself holding my breath. Each summer it's the same, yet I listen and wait like I'm about to hear it for the first time. The start of an orchestra, the seconds of anticipation before the curtain lifts.

And then it comes, soft and languid like a summer day, the murmuring of a song whose words are indistinguishable. Some say it's French, others Portuguese, but no one has ever translated it because it's not a real language. It's something else. It curls up off the ocean and slips into our ears. It's gentle and alluring, like a mother whispering a bedtime riddle to a child. And as if on cue, the two girls standing closest to the waterline take several staggering steps into the sea, unable to resist.

But a group of boys go in after them and drag them back out. The time for dares has passed. There will be no more coaxing girls into the harbor, no more taunts to swim all the way out then back again. The danger is suddenly stark and real.

The lulling melody coils around me, fingers sliding across my skin and down my throat, tugging at me. Begging me to respond. I close my eyes and take a step forward before I even realize what I've done. But a hand—solid and warm—grabs ahold of mine. "Where you going?" Bo asks in a hush as he pulls me back to his side.

I shake my head. I don't know.

He doesn't release my hand, but squeezes it tighter, like he's afraid to let me go. "Is it really coming from the water?" he asks, his voice low, still facing the dark, dangerous sea, like he doesn't believe his own ears.

I nod, drowsy suddenly. The alcohol in my body has made me weak, more susceptible to the call of their song. "Now you know why the tourists come: to hear the sisters' song, to see if it's real," I say. The warmth of his palm pulses against mine, and I feel myself leaning into him, his firm shoulder an anchor keeping me from toppling over.

"How long will it last?"

"Until each of the three sisters has lured a girl into the water and taken her body." I clench my jaw. "Day and night the ocean will sing. Sometimes it takes weeks, sometimes only a few days. All three sisters could find bodies tonight if girls keep wading out into the bay."

"Does it scare you?" I realize we're the last two people standing at the water's edge—everyone else has gone back up to the safety of the bonfire, away from the tempting harbor—but his hand is still in mine, keeping me rooted to shore.

"Yes," I admit, the word sending a shiver down to my tailbone. "I usually don't come to the Swan party. I stay home and lock myself in my room." When my dad was still alive, he would stay up all night sitting in a chair beside the front door to be sure I didn't get drawn from my room—in case the urge to swim out into the sea was too great for me to resist. And now that he's gone, I sleep with headphones on and a pillow over my head each night until the singing finally stops.

I believe that I'm stronger than most girls—that I'm not so easily fooled by the sisters' ethereal voices. My mother used to say that we are like the Swan sisters—she and I. Misunderstood. Different. Outcasts living alone on the island, reading fortunes in the cosmos of tea leaves. But I wonder if it's even possible to be normal in a place like Sparrow. Perhaps we all have some oddity, some strangeness we keep hidden along our edges, things we see that we can't explain, things we wish for, things we run from.

"Some girls want to be taken," I say in a near whisper, because it's hard for me to imagine wanting something like that. "Like it's a badge of honor. Others claim that they've been taken in summers past, but there's no way to prove it. Most likely they just want the attention."

The Swan sisters have always stolen the bodies of girls my age— the same age the sisters were when they died. As if they desire to relive that moment in time, even if just briefly.

Bo blows out a breath then turns and looks back up at the

48

bonfire, where the party has resumed in full upheaval. The goal of tonight is to stay awake until sunrise, to mark the start of summer, and for all the girls to survive without being inhabited by a Swan sister. But I sense Bo's hesitation—that maybe he's had enough.

"I think I'll head back to my camp and find a new place to sleep." He releases my hand, and I rub my palms together, feeling the residual warmth. A spire of unnerving heat coils up the center of my chest into my rib cage.

"Are you still looking for work?" I ask.

His lips press flat, as if he's contemplating the next few words, sifting them around in his mouth. "You were right about no one wanting to hire an outsider."

"Well, maybe I was wrong about not needing any help." I let out a breath of air. Maybe it's because he's an outsider like my dad, because I know this town can be cruel and unaccepting. Maybe I know he won't last long without someone to keep him safely away from the harbor once all three sisters have found bodies and begin their revenge on the town. Or maybe it's because it would also be a relief to have some help with the lighthouse. I know almost nothing about him, but it feels as if he's always been here. And it might be nice having someone else on the island, someone who I can talk to—someone who isn't fading into a slow, numbing madness. Living with my mom is like living with a shadow. "We can't pay you much, but it's a free place to stay and free meals."

Dad has never officially been declared deceased, so there's never been a life insurance check waiting for us in the mailbox. And shortly after he vanished, Mom stopped reading tea leaves, so the money stopped coming in. Thankfully, Dad had some savings. Enough that we've been able to survive on it these last three years—and it will probably get us through another two before we'll need to find an alternative source of income.

Bo scratches at the back of his neck, turning his head slightly away. I know he doesn't have any other options, but still he's considering it.

"All right. No guarantees on how long I'll stay."

"Deal."

I grab my shoes from beside the fire and find Rose talking to Heath Belzer. "I'm going home," I tell her, and she reaches out for my arm.

"No," she says in an exaggerated slur. "You can't."

"If you want to come with me, I'll walk you home," I say. She lives only four blocks from here, but far enough in the dark that I don't want her doing it alone. And drunk.

"I can walk her," Heath offers, and I look up at the soft, agreeable features of his face. Loose grin, dark eyes, reddish-brown hair that's always spilling across his forehead so he's constantly brushing it back out of the way. He's cute, likable, even if the curves of his face have that mildly dopey look. Heath Belzer is one of the good ones. He has four older sisters who've all graduated and moved away from Sparrow, but his whole life he's been known as Baby Heath, the kid who was beaten up by girls his entire childhood. And I once saw him save a blue jay that got trapped in the science lab at school by spending his entire lunch period trying to catch it then finally setting it free through an open window.

"You won't ditch her?" I ask Heath.

"I'll make sure she gets home," he says, looking me square in the eyes. "I promise."

"If anything happens to her—" I warn.

"Nothing's going to happen to me," Rose mumbles, squeezing my hand and pulling me into a hug. "I'll call you tomorrow," she whispers with whiskey-stained breath into my ear.

"All right. And no swimming."

"No swimming!" she repeats loudly, lifting her beer into the air, and a chorus of echoes pass through the crowd as everyone begins shouting in unison, "*No swimming!*" I can hear the chant all the way down the beach as Bo and I walk toward the bluff to retrieve his backpack, intermixing with the singing of distant voices blowing in with the rising tide.

Otis and Olga are waiting on the dock when I steer the skiff slowly up alongside it and kill the engine. We motored across the harbor in the dark, without even a flashlight to mark our path through the wreckage, the inviting whispers of the Swan sisters sliding languidly over the water so that it felt like we were being swallowed by their song.

I secure the ropes to the dock then bend down to stroke each cat's slender back, both of them slightly damp and probably unhappy that I'm returning so late. "Did you wait all night?" I whisper down to them then lift my head to see Bo stepping onto the dock, carrying his backpack in one hand. He cranes his head up, looking across the island to the lighthouse. The beacon of light illuminates us briefly before continuing its clockwise cycle out over the Pacific.

In the dark, Lumiere Island feels eerie and macabre. A place of ghosts and mossy hollows, where long-dead sailors surely haunt the reeds and wind-scoured trees. But it's not the island you should fear— it's the waters surrounding it.

"It's not as creepy in daylight," I assure Bo, passing my father's old sailboat, the *Windsong*, bobbing on the other side of the wood dock, sails down, unmoved for the last three years. My father didn't name the boat. It was called the *Windsong* when he purchased it ten years ago from a man who moored it south of Sparrow in a small seaside harbor. But the name *Windsong* had always seemed fitting, considering the voices that rise up from the sea each summer.

Otis and Olga trot after me, and Bo falls into step behind them.

The island is shaped like a half-moon with the flat side facing inland and the opposite side curved by the endless waves crashing against its banks. A two-story, robin's-egg-blue house—where my mom and I live—stands near the lighthouse, and a collection of smaller buildings are scattered across the island, built and torn down and added on to over the years. There is a wood shed and a toolshed and a greenhouse long since abandoned, and there are two cottages that serve as living quarters—Old Fisherman's Cottage and Anchor Cottage—and I lead Bo to the newer of the two, a place where staff was once housed, cooks and maintenance men, when such people were required to keep this place up and running.

"Have you always lived on the island?" he asks from the darkness as we follow the winding, sometimes broken wood-slated path up through the interior of the island, the air foggy and cool.

"I was born here."

"On the island?" he asks.

"My mom would have preferred to have had me at the hospital in Newport an hour away or at least at the clinic in Sparrow, but out here fate is determined by the sea, and a winter storm blew in, covering the island with a foot of snow and making the harbor a complete whiteout. So she delivered me at the house." The dizzying swirl of alcohol still thumps through me, and my head feels roomy and unfocused. "My dad said I was meant for this place," I explain. "That the island didn't want to let me go."

I may belong here on the island, but my father never did. The town always hated that an outsider purchased the island and the lighthouse—even if my mom was a local.

Dad was a freelance architect. He designed summer homes along the coast, and even a new library up in Pacific Cove. Before that, he worked at an architectural firm in Portland after he and Mom got married. But Mom always missed Sparrow—her hometown—and she wanted desperately to move back. Even though she had no family here, her parents were long dead and she was an only child, it had always felt like home to her. So when they saw the listing for Lumiere Island for sale, including the lighthouse, which was going to be decommissioned by the state—no longer of use since Sparrow was not a large shipping harbor anymore—they both knew it was exactly what they wanted. The lighthouse was a historic structure—one of the first buildings in town—and local fishermen still needed it to navigate into the harbor. It was perfect. Dad had even planned to renovate the old farmhouse someday—fix it up when he had the time, make it ours—but he never got the chance.

When he disappeared, the police came out to the island, filed a report, and then did nothing. The townspeople didn't rally together, didn't organize search parties, didn't climb aboard their fishing boats to scan the harbor. To them, he had never belonged here in the first place. For this, a part of me hates this town, this place, and these people for being so callous. They fear anyone and anything that isn't them. Just like they feared the Swan sisters two hundred years ago . . . and they killed them for being different.

We turn right, away from the glowing lights of the main house, and walk deeper into the unlit center of the island, until we reach the small stone cottage.

ANCHOR COTTAGE is written in letters formed out of frayed fishing rope then nailed to the wood door. It isn't locked, and thankfully when I flick on the light switch just inside the front door, a floor lamp across the room blinks on.

Otis and Olga zip past my feet into the cottage, curious about the building, which they've rarely had the opportunity to explore. It's cold and dank and there is a mustiness that can't be cleaned away.

In the kitchen I flip on the switch beside the sink and a light shivers on overhead. I kneel down and grab the power cord for the refrigerator and plug it into an outlet in the wall. Instantly it begins to hum. A small bedroom is situated just off the living room; a peeling wood dresser is against one wall and a metal bed frame sits beneath a window. There is a mattress, but no pillows or blankets. "I'll bring you sheets and bedding tomorrow," I tell him.

"I have a sleeping bag." He drops his backpack on the floor just inside the bedroom doorway. "I'll be fine."

"There's wood inside the shed just up the path if you want to start a fire. There's no food in the kitchen, but we have plenty up at the main house. You can come up in the morning for breakfast."

"Thanks."

"I wish it weren't so . . ." I'm not sure what I want to say, how to apologize for it being so dark and mildewed.

"It's better than sleeping on the beach," he says before I can locate the right words, and I smile, feeling suddenly exhausted and light-headed and in need of sleep.

"See you in the morning," I say.

He doesn't say anything else, even though I stand mute for a moment too long, thinking he might. And then I turn, my head swaying, and slip out the door.

Otis and Olga follow me out, and we trudge up the slope to the main house, where I left the back porch light on.

THE ISLAND

The wind is constant.

It howls and tears at siding and rips shingles from roofs. It brings rain and salt air, and in the winter sometimes it brings snow. But for a time each spring, it carries in the lurid and seductive voices of three sisters held captive by the sea, aching to draw out the girls of Sparrow.

From the black waters of the harbor, their song sinks into dreams, permeates the brittle grass that grows along steep cliffs and rotting homes. It settles into the stones that hold up the lighthouse; it floats and swirls in the air until it's all you can taste and breathe.

This is what cajoles the weak-hearted from sleep, pulls them out of bed and beckons them down to the shore. Like fingers wrapped around their throats, it drags them into the deepest part of the bay among the wreckage of ships long abandoned, pulling them under until the air spills from their lungs and a new thing can slip inside.

This is how they do it—how the sisters are freed from their brackish grave. They steal three bodies and make them their own. And this season, they do it swiftly.

FIVE

I wake with the choking sense of seawater in my throat. I sit upright, fisting my white sheet in both hands. The feeling of drowning claws at my lungs, but it was only a nightmare.

My head throbs, temples pulse, the lingering taste of whiskey still on my tongue.

It takes a moment to orient myself, last night still whirling through my head. I push back the sheet and stretch my toes over the hardwood floor, feeling stiff and achy and like a hammer is cracking against my skull from the inside. Sunlight peeks through the daffodil-yellow curtains, reflecting off the white walls and the white dresser and the high white ceiling—blinding me.

I press my fingers to my eyes and yawn. In the full-length mirror mounted to the closet door, I catch my reflection. Dark circles rim both eyes, and my ponytail has slid partway free so that strands of coffee-brown hair drift across my face. I look horrible.

The floor is cold, but I plod to one of the massive windows overlooking the choppy sea and slide the window upward in its frame.

In the wind I can still hear it: the faint cry of a song.

* * *

The scent of powdered sugar and maple syrup hangs in the air like a soft winter snowfall. I find her in the kitchen standing at the stove—Mom—her dark hair tied in a braid down her back, a serpent of brown, folded and coiled. And I feel like I'm still caught in a dream, my head swirling, my body rocking side to side like it's being pushed inland by an invisible tide.

"Are you hungry?" she asks without turning around. I absorb her movements, the sedated way she slides the spatula under a doughy pancake and flips it in the pan. She doesn't normally make breakfast—not anymore—so this is a rare occurrence. Something's up. For a moment I let a memory materialize in my mind: her making waffles with homemade blackberry jam, her cheeks flushed from the heat of the stove, her eyes and lips smiling, the morning sun on her face. She was happy once.

I touch my stomach, clenched and queasy. "Not really," I answer. There's no way I could eat right now. And keep it down. I move past her to the counter, where a row of identical silver tins sit perfectly spaced. They are unmarked, but I know the contents of each one: Lavender Chamomile, Rose Earl Grey, Cardamom Chai, Moroccan Mint, and Jasmine Dragon Pearl. I boil water then set my tea to steep—Rose Earl Grey—and lean against the counter breathing in the rustic, sweet scent.

"We have guests," she says suddenly, sliding the lightly browned pancakes onto a white plate.

I glance around the kitchen then back at her. The house is silent. "Who?"

She looks over at me, examining the creases around my eyes from lack of sleep; the queasiness that comes in waves when I pinch my lips tightly together to keep from vomiting. She stares for a moment, eyes pinched like she doesn't quite recognize me. Then she drops her gaze. "That boy you brought to the island last night," she says. The memory pours back through me: the beach, Bo, and my offering him a job on the island. Again I press my palms to my eyes.

"Is he a local boy?" she asks.

"No." I recall the moment on the dock when he said he was looking for work. "He came into town yesterday."

"For the Swan season?" she asks, setting the skillet back on the stove and turning off the burner.

"No. He's not a tourist."

"Can we trust him?"

"I don't know," I answer honestly—I don't actually know anything about him.

"Well," she says, turning around to face me and sliding her hands down into the pockets of her thick black robe, "he's just waking up. Take him some breakfast. I don't want a stranger inside the house." This is one of her gifts: She knows when people are near, when they're coming to the island—she senses their arrival like a nagging in the pit of her stomach. And this explains why she decided to cook breakfast—what drove her from bed just after the sun rose, compelled her into the kitchen to turn on the stove and pull out her good skillet. She might not want a stranger in the house, she might not trust him, but she won't allow him to starve. It's just her nature. Even her grief can't keep her from kindness.

She pours maple syrup over the stack of warm pancakes then

hands me the plate. "And take him some blankets," she adds. "Or he'll freeze out there." She doesn't ask why he's here, why I brought him to the island—for what purpose. Maybe she just doesn't care.

I tug on the green rubber boots beside the front door and a black raincoat, then grab a set of sheets and a thick wool blanket from the hall closet. Holding a palm over the plate of pancakes to keep the rain from turning them into a soggy heap of sugar and flour, I step outside.

Pools of water collect in divots and holes beside the walkway, and sometimes the rain seems to rise up from the ground instead of from overhead—a snow globe effect, but with water. A swift wind crashes against my face as I make my way down to the cottage.

The sturdy wood door rattles when I knock, and Bo opens it almost instantly, as if he had been just about to step outside.

"Morning," I say. He's standing in jeans and a charcoal-gray raincoat. A fire crackles in the fireplace behind him. And he looks rested, showered, and new. Nothing like how I feel. "How'd you sleep?"

"Fine." Yet his voice is weathered and deep, betraying perhaps a lack of sleep after all. His eyes stare unblinking, soaking me in, and my skin prickles with the intensity of it. He is not someone who looks through you, past you, like you're not even there. His gaze is sharp, incisive, and an itch settles behind my eyes, making me want to look away.

He shuts the door behind me, and I set the plate of pancakes on the small square wood table in the kitchen then brush my palm down my jeans even though there is nothing to wipe off. The cottage feels different with him inside it, and the glow from the fireplace smooths over all the hard, rough edges so that everything feels muted and soft.

I place the sheets and wool blanket on the musty gray couch facing the fireplace, and he sits at the table. "Can you show me the lighthouse today?" he asks, taking a bite of the pancakes. In this light, in the scarlet hue of the fire, he reminds me of the boys who come into town aboard fishing boats, green and wild looking, like they've been cast off by the winds, set adrift.

He reminds me of someone who has left his past behind.

"Sure." I bite the inside of my bottom lip. My eyes scan the cottage. The tall wood bookshelves beside the fireplace are crowded with books and old almanacs and tide-chart periodicals, all covered in a decade of dust. Lumps of aqua-blue sea glass, collected over the years from the island's rocky shores, are piled into a small porcelain dish. On the top shelf sits a large wood clock that probably once lived on the deck of a ship. This cottage has served as the living quarters for a variety of staff and hired laborers, men who stayed a week and others years, but almost all left something behind. Trinkets and mementos, hints about their lives, but never the full story.

When Bo finishes breakfast—so quickly that I know he must have been starving—we leave the warmth of the cottage and are submerged by the drizzling rain. The ash-gray sky presses down against us—a weight that is tangible. Water trickles through my hair.

We pass the small greenhouse where herbs and tomato plants and leafy greens were once tended and grown, the glass walls now tarnished and smudged so that you can no longer see inside. The island has taken back most of the structures, decaying walls and rot seeping up from below. Moss covers every surface: a weed that feeds off the constant moisture and cannot be contained. Rust and mildew. Slop and mud. Death has found its way into everything.

"The singing hasn't stopped," Bo says when we're halfway to the lighthouse, our feet making hollow clomping sounds that echo against the wood walkway. But in the wind, the voices are still there, sliding lazily in with the sea air. It's so familiar that I hardly discern it from the other sounds of the island.

"Not yet," I agree. I don't glance back at him. I don't let his eyes find mine again.

We reach the lighthouse, and I pull open the metal door, corroded at the hinges. Once inside the entryway, it takes a moment for our eyes to adjust to the dim. The air is stark and smells of moisture-soaked wood and stone. A rounded staircase serpents its way up the interior of the lighthouse, and I point out to Bo where not to step as we ascend—many steps have rotted away or broken—and at times I pause to catch my breath.

"Have you ever been taken?" Bo asks when we're almost to the top of the stairway.

"I wouldn't know if I had," I say between gasps for breath.

"Do you really believe that? If your body was inhabited by something else, you don't think you'd know?"

I stop on a solid step and look back at him. "I think it's easier for the mind to forget. To sink into the background." He doesn't seem satisfied, his jaw shifting to the left. "If it makes you feel better," I say with a partial grin, "if a Swan sister is ever inside me, I'll let you know if I can tell."

He raises an eyebrow and his eyes smile back at me. I turn and continue up the stairway.

The wind rattles the walls the higher we climb, and when we

finally reach the upper lantern room, a howling gust screams through cracks in the exterior.

"The first lighthouse keeper was a Frenchman," I explain. "He named the island Lumiere. It was a lot more work to keep the lighthouse running back then—maintaining the lanterns and the prisms. Now it's mostly automated."

"How did you learn all this?"

"My dad," I answer automatically. "He studied lighthouses after my parents bought the island." I swallow hard then continue. "We need to check the glass and the bulb each day. And everything needs to be cleaned a couple times a week to keep the salty air from building up. It's not hard. But during a storm or a thick fog, this lighthouse can save the lives of fishermen out at sea. So we have to keep it running."

He nods, walking to the windows to look out over the island.

I eye him, tracing the outline of his shoulders, the curve of his assured stance. Arms at his sides. *Who is he? What brought him here?* Fog has rolled in over the island, creating a sheer veil of gray so that we can't make out any features of the terrain below. After a few minutes of staring through the glass, he follows me back through the doorway and down the winding staircase.

Otis is sitting on the wood walkway outside, waiting with eyes blinking against the rain, and I pull the lighthouse door closed. Olga is several yards up the path, licking her orange-striped tail. They're both used to the relentless downpour, their cat instincts to escape wet weather have gone dormant.

We walk up the path to the high center of the island, through the old orchard, where rows of Braeburn apple and spindly Anjou pear trees grow in wild, unruly directions. People used to say that fruit trees couldn't grow in the sea air, but they've always thrived on Lumiere Island. An anomaly.

"What about the orchard?" Bo asks, pausing at the end of a row.

"What about it?"

"These trees haven't been trimmed in years." I squint at him and he reaches up to touch one of the bony, leafless branches, as if he can sense the tree's history just by touching it. "They need to be limbed and the dead ones cut down."

"How do you know?" I ask, shoving my hands into the pockets of my raincoat. They've started to go numb.

"I grew up on a farm," he answers vaguely.

"My mom doesn't really care about the trees," I say.

"Someone cared about them once." He releases the spindly branch from his fingers and it springs back into place. He's right; someone did care about this orchard once. And there used to be more rows and a variety of hardy apples and pears. But not anymore. The trees are overgrown and windswept, only producing small, often bitter fruit. "They could live another hundred years if someone maintains them," he says.

"You could really bring them back to life?"

"Sure, it will just take some work."

I smile a little, scanning the rows of trees. I've always loved the orchard, but it's been years since it's seen a real bloom. Just like the rest of the island, it's fallen into decay. But if the trees could be saved, maybe the whole island could too. "Okay," I say. "Let's do it."

He smiles faintly, and our eyes meet for an instant.

I show Bo the other buildings on the island, and we circle around the perimeter. He's careful not to walk too close to me, keeping his arm from brushing mine when we walk side by side, his steps deliberate and measured over the stony landscape. But his eyes flick over to me when he thinks I'm not looking. I swallow. I tighten my jaw. I look away.

When we reach the cliffs facing west, the ocean slamming against the shoreline in violent waves that spray water and foam against the rocks, he stops.

This close to the sea, the song of the sisters feels like a whisper in our ears. As if they were standing beside us, breath against our necks.

"How many people have died?" he asks.

"Excuse me?"

"During the months when the Swan sisters return?"

I cross my arms, the wind brushing the hair over my eyes. "They each drown one boy . . . usually."

"Usually?"

"More or less. It depends."

"On?"

I shrug, thinking about the summers when five or six boys were found tumbling with the waves against the shore. Sand in their hair. Salt water in their lungs. "How vengeful they're feeling . . . I suppose."

"How do they choose?"

"Choose what?"

"Who they're going to kill?"

A breath sticks in my throat, trapped like a hook in a fish's mouth. "Probably the same way they chose lovers when they were alive."

"So they love the boys they drown?" I think maybe he's being

67

sarcastic, but when I tilt my gaze to look at him, his dark eyes and punctuated full lips have stiffened.

"No. I don't know. I doubt it. It's not about love."

"Revenge, then?" he asks, echoing my words from last night.

"Revenge."

"The perfect justification for murder," he adds, his stare slipping away from mine to look out over the hazy brume rising up from the sea like smoke.

"It's not . . ." But I stop myself. *Murder.* That's precisely what it is. Calling it a curse does not unmake the truth of what happens here each year: murder. Premeditated. Violent, cruel, barbaric. Monstrous even. Two hundred years' worth of killing. A town reliving a past it can't change, paying the price year after year. An eye for an eye. I swallow, feeling a pain in my chest, in my gut.

It's as predictable as the tide and the moon. It ebbs and flows. Death comes and it goes.

Bo doesn't press me to finish my thought. And I don't offer to. My mind is now twisting like a snake into a deep dark hole. I lift my shoulders and shiver, the cold seething through me.

We peer out at the churning sea, and then I ask, "Why are you really here?"

"It was the last stop on the bus line," he repeats. "I needed work."

"And you've never heard of Sparrow before?"

His eyes slide to mine and the rain catches on his lashes, lingers on his chin, and spills from his dark hair. "No."

Then something changes on the wind.

An abrupt hush breaks over the island and sends a quick chill across the nape of my neck.

The singing has stopped.

Bo takes a step closer to the edge of the cliff, like he's straining to hear what is no longer there. "It's gone," he says.

"The sisters have all found bodies." The words seem pulled from my throat. The quiet settles between each of my ribs, it expands my lungs, it reminds me of what's to come. "They've all returned." I close my eyes, focusing on the silence. It's the fastest it's ever happened before.

Now the drowning will begin.

A WARNING

We wait for death. We hold our breath.
We know it's coming, and still we flinch when it claws at our throats
and pulls us under.

—Plaque located on the stone bench on Ocean Avenue,
facing the harbor (commissioned in 1925)

SIX

The soil squishes away beneath my rain boots. A steady, uninterrupted drizzle collects on the waterproof sleeves of my raincoat as I move back down the rows of the orchard.

Bo is back in his cottage. We parted ways an hour ago. And even though I thought about going back to bed—my head still pounding, my skin rattling against my bones—I decided I wanted to be outside, alone.

I find the familiar old oak tree that grows at the center of the orchard, where Bo and I passed by not long ago. But we didn't stop here.

This is my favorite place on the island—where I feel protected and hidden among the old, rotted fruit trees. Where I let memories slide over me like a cool stream. This oak tree stands alone among the rest, ancient and weathered from the sea air—its growth stunted. But it's been here since the beginning, nearly two hundred years, back when the Swan sisters first stepped onto land, when they were still alive.

I run my fingers along the crude heart etched into the wood, cut there by lovers long ago dead. But the heart remains, the bark fallen away, permanent.

I slide down against the trunk of the tree and sit at its base, leaning my head back to look up at the sky, speckled with dark clouds caught in the fickle ocean winds.

The Swan season has begun. And this little town tucked along the shore will not come out unharmed.

A storm is blowing in from the ocean.

The clock beside my bed reads eleven p.m. Then midnight. I can't sleep.

I walk from my bedroom into the bathroom across the hall, my thoughts straying to Bo. He's not safe, even on the island.

I can hear Mom's fan blowing in her room two doors down while she sleeps. She likes to feel a breeze, even in winter; she says she has nightmares without it. I flick on the bathroom light and look at myself in the mirror. My lips are pale, hair lying flat across my shoulders. I look like I haven't slept in days.

And then a sliver of light blinks through the bathroom window and reflects back at me in the mirror. I lift a hand to block it. It's not the beam of light from the lighthouse. It's something else.

I squint through the rain-streaked window. A boat is pulling up to the dock down on the lower bank.

Someone is here.

I shrug into my raincoat and boots and slip out the front door quietly. The wind howls over the rocky outcroppings on the island, blowing the hardy sea grass sideways and swirling my hair across my face.

As I get closer, I see a light pass over the dock—a large flashlight—the kind used to see into the fog when you're trying to pick your way through the wreckage of the harbor back to port. There is a low exchange of voices and the stomping of feet on the wood dock. Whoever it is, they aren't trying to be quiet or covert.

I lift a hand over my face to block the wind. And then I hear my name. "Penny?"

In the dark, I make out Rose's wild hair caught up in a gust. "Rose—what are you doing out here?"

"We brought wine," says Heath Belzer—the boy who walked Rose home from the Swan party last night, and who is now standing beside her, holding up a bottle for me to see.

The boat behind him has been secured sloppily to the dock, ropes hanging down into the water, and I assume it must be Heath's parents' boat.

"The singing stopped," Rose says in a hush, like she doesn't want the island to hear.

"I know."

She takes several steps toward me, swaying a bit, obviously already a little intoxicated. Heath looks back at the harbor, the sea lapping against the dock. Out there, in the darkness, is where at least three boys' lives will be taken.

"Can we go up in the lighthouse?" Rose asks, changing the subject. "I want to show Heath." Her eyebrows lift, and she bites the side of her cheek—looking like a cherub all rosy-cheeked and saucer-eyed. I can't help but love her—the way she always brightens the air around her as if she were a light bulb. Like she were a summer day and a cool breeze all in one.

"Okay," I say, and she smiles big and dopey, tugging me up the boardwalk with Heath following.

"I seem to recall a boy with you last night," she whispers in my ear, her breath hot and sharp with alcohol.

"Bo," I answer. "I gave him a job on the island. He's staying in Anchor Cottage."

"You did what?" Her mouth drops open.

"He needed work."

"You must have been drunk if you were willing to take in an outsider. You realize he's probably just a tourist."

"I don't think so."

"Then why's he here?"

"I'm not sure."

"Penny," she says, slowing her pace up the path. "He's living on the island with you. . . . He could murder you in your sleep."

"I think he has more to fear than I do."

"True," she agrees, pulling down the sleeves of her white sweater so her fingers are tucked in out of the cold wind. "He couldn't have shown up at a worse time. We'll see if he makes it until summer solstice."

A chill shuttles down my spine.

Once we reach the lighthouse, Rose giggles as she sways unsteadily up the spiral staircase, and Heath keeps grabbing on to her to prevent her from tumbling backward.

At the top of the stairs, I push through the door into the lantern room. But it's not dark like I was expecting. The lamp resting on the white desk on the right-side wall has been switched on, and a silhouette is standing at the glass, one shoulder leaning against it.

"Bo?" I ask.

"Hey." He turns around, and I notice a book held in his right hand. "I came up to watch the storm."

"Us too," Rose squeaks. She steps forward to introduce herself. "I'm Rose."

"Bo."

Rose grins and looks back at me, mouthing *he's cute* so no one else will see.

Bo and Heath shake hands, then Heath holds up the bottle. "Looks like we have a small party."

"I should probably head down," Bo offers, tucking the book under his arm.

"No way," Rose says, grinning. "You're staying. Three isn't a party, but four is perfect."

Bo glances at me, as if looking for permission, but I stare back at him blankly, unsure what to think about him up here all alone, reading or watching the storm. Whatever the truth might be.

"All right," he agrees, a hint of reluctance in his eyes.

Heath produces an opener from his coat pocket and begins uncorking the bottle.

"Heath stole two bottles from his parents' B and B," Rose says. "We drank one on the way over." Which explains why she's already so tipsy.

There aren't any glasses, so Heath takes a swig, but before he passes it around, he says, "Should we take bets?"

"On what?" Rose asks.

"How long until the first body turns up in the harbor."

"That's morbid," Rose says with a grimace.

"Maybe. But it's going to happen whether we want it to or not."

Bo and I exchange a look.

Rose exhales a breath through her nose. "Three days," she says meekly, grabbing the bottle from Heath's hands and taking a drink.

"Three and a half," Heath guesses, eyeing her. But I think he only says it to be cute, playing off her number.

Rose hands the bottle to Bo and he holds it low, looking down at it like the answer is somewhere inside. "I hope it doesn't happen at all," he finally says.

"That's not really a guess," Rose points out, lifting an eyebrow.

"Sure it is," Heath defends. "He's guessing no days. Which has never happened, but I suppose it's possible. Maybe no one will drown this summer."

"Unlikely," Rose adds, looking a little disgusted with this whole game.

Bo takes a quick slug of the red wine then holds it out for me. I take it carefully, sliding my thumb down the neck of the bottle, then look up at the group. "Tonight," I say, tipping the bottle to my lips and taking a full swig.

Rose shivers slightly and Heath wraps an arm around her. "Let's talk about something else," she suggests.

"Whatever you want." And he smiles down at her.

"I want to count ghosts!" she chirps, her mood returned.

Heath releases her and frowns, confused. "You want to do what?"

"It's a game Penny and I used to play when we were kids, remember Penny?" She looks to me and I nod. "We'd look for ghosts in the beam of light from the lighthouse as it circled around the island. You get points for every one that you see. One point if you see it on the island and two points if you see one out on the water."

"And you actually see these ghosts?" Heath asks, one eyebrow scrunching up into his forehead.

"Yes. They're everywhere," Rose answers with an artful smirk. "You just have to know where to look."

"Show me," Heath says. And even though he's obviously skeptical, he smiles as she drags him to the window. It's a childish game, but they press their palms against the glass, laughing already.

I hand the bottle back to Bo, and he takes another drink.

"What are you reading?" I ask.

"A book I found in the cottage."

"About what?"

He slides it out from under his arm and sets it on the white desk. *The History and Legend of Sparrow, Oregon.* The front cover is an old photograph of the harbor taken from Ocean Avenue. A cobblestone sidewalk is in the foreground, and the harbor is crowded with old fishing boats and massive steamships. It's more of a pamphlet than a real book, and you can find it at just about every coffee shop and restaurant, and in the lobby of each bed-and-breakfast in town. It's a tourist's guide to everything that happened in Sparrow two centuries ago and everything that has occurred since. It was written by Anderson Fotts, an artist and poet who used to live in Sparrow until his son drowned seven years ago and then he moved away.

"Brushing up on our town's history, huh?"

"Not much else to do in the evening around here." He has a point.

I stare down at the book, knowing its contents all too well. On page thirty-seven is a portrait of the three Swan sisters sketched by Thomas Renshaw, a man who claimed to have met the sisters before they were drowned. Marguerite stands on the left, the tallest of the three, with long auburn hair, full lips, and a sharp jaw, her eyes staring straight ahead. Aurora is in the middle with soft waves of hair and bright full-moon eyes. Hazel, on the right, has plain, smaller features and a braid twisted across her shoulder. Her eyes are focused away, like she's looking at something in the distance. They are all beautiful—captivating, as if they were shifting slightly on the page.

"So you believe in the sisters now?" I ask.

"I haven't decided."

The beam of light slides across his face, and I follow it out to sea, where it cuts through the storm and the impending rain, warning sailors and fishermen that an island lies in their path. "You shouldn't go into town if you don't have to from now on," I tell him.

Both his eyebrows lift. "Why not?"

"It's safer if you stay here on the island. You can't trust anyone in town. . . . Any girl you meet could be one of them."

His eyelids lower, partly concealing the dark tint of his green eyes. Verdant and rueful. He is familiar in a way I can't pin down. Like seeing someone you knew a long time ago, but they've changed in the passing years, become someone different and new. "Even you?" he asks, like I'm joking.

"Even me." I want him to understand how serious I am.

"So no talking to girls?" he clarifies.

"Precisely."

The right side of his mouth turns up into a grin, a fractional parting of lips, and he looks like he might laugh, but then he takes a sip from the bottle instead. I know it sounds absurd, maybe even a little irrational, to warn him against speaking to any girls. But I wouldn't say it if I didn't mean it. Most local boys—if they truly believe in the legend—will steer clear of all girls until the summer solstice. Better to minimize the risk. But Bo, like most outsiders, won't take it seriously. He's in danger just by being in this town.

"That's three!" Rose bellows from the window, and Heath shakes his head. Apparently, Rose is winning the ghost-hunting game. As usual.

"Where are you from?" I ask Bo, after the beam of light passes around the lighthouse a full three times.

"Washington."

I arch an eyebrow at him, expecting him to narrow it down to a city or county or nearest proximity to a Starbucks. But he doesn't. "That's extremely vague," I say. "Can you be more specific?"

His cheekbones tighten, a rivulet of tension. "Near the middle" is all he offers up.

"I can see this won't be easy." I rub my tongue along the roof of my mouth.

"What?"

"Figuring out who you really are."

He taps his fingers against the side of the bottle, a rhythm to a song, I think. "What do you want to know?" he asks.

"Did you go to high school in this fictional, *near-the-middle* town?"

Again I think he's going to smile, but he stifles it before it escapes his lips. "Yeah. I graduated this year."

"So you graduated then promptly escaped your make-believe town?"

"Basically."

"Why'd you leave?"

He ceases the tapping against the bottle. "My brother died."

A blast of wind and sideways rain sprays the windows, and I flinch. "I'm . . . sorry." Bo shakes his head and tips the bottle to his lips. The minutes pass, and the question resting inside my throat starts to feel strangled, cutting off the air to my lungs. "How did he die?"

"It was an accident." He swirls the bottle, and the carmine wine spins up the sides. A mini cyclone.

He looks away from me, like he's considering heading for the door and leaving. Saying good night and vanishing into the storm.

And although I'm curious exactly what kind of accident, I don't press it any further. I can tell he doesn't want to talk about it. And I don't want him to leave, even though our conversation feels tightened along the edges, tugged and constrained because he's holding things in. I'm also not quite ready for this night to be over. There are things I like about him—*no*, that's not right. It's not him exactly. It's me. I like how I feel standing beside him. Eased by his presence. The steady buzz along my thoughts, the ache in my chest tamped down. Softened.

So I take the bottle from him and sit cross-legged on the cold floor, staring out at the storm. I know what it is to lose the people around you. And I take a long, slow drink of the wine, warming my stomach and making my head swim, wiping away the hangover. Bo sits beside me, forearms resting on his bent knees.

"Have you been in a lot of fights before?" I ask after a stretch of silence.

"What?"

"On the beach last night, with Lon, you seemed like you weren't afraid to fight him."

"I don't like fighting, if that's what you mean. But yeah, I've been in a few. Although not because I wanted to." He exhales slowly, and I think he's going to change the subject. His lips stall partway open. "My brother was always getting himself into trouble," he continues. "He liked taking risks—jumping into rivers in the middle of winter, climbing bridges to watch the sunrise, driving his truck too fast down the centerline just for the rush. Things like that. And sometimes he'd say things he shouldn't, or hit on girls he shouldn't, and find himself in a fistfight." Bo shakes his head. "He thought it was funny, but I was always the one who had to step in and save him, keep him from getting his ass kicked. He was my older brother, but my parents were always asking me to keep an eye on him. But since he died . . ." His gaze dips to the floor, voice trailing, memories sliding through him. "I haven't had to defend him." I hand him the bottle of wine, and he takes a long drink. Holding it between his knees with both hands, he asks, "Do you ever think about leaving this town?"

I lift my chin. "Of course."

"But?"

"It's complicated."

His thumb taps the neck of the bottle. "Isn't that what people say when they just don't want to admit the truth?"

"Probably . . . but the truth is complicated. My life is complicated."

"So after you graduate, you're not going to leave Sparrow—you're not going to college somewhere?"

I shrug. "Maybe. It's not something I think about." I shift uneasily on the floor, wishing we could change the subject back to him.

"What's keeping you here?"

I almost laugh but don't, because the answer isn't funny. Nothing about the reasons why I'm stuck here is funny. "My family," I finally say, because I have to say something. "My mom."

"She doesn't want you to leave?"

"It's not that. She's just . . . she's not well." I look away from him, shaking my head. The truth slips between the edges of the lies.

"You don't want to talk about it?" he asks.

"Just like you don't want to talk about where you're from," I say softly. "Or what happened to . . ." I almost bring up his brother again but stop myself.

He makes a low exhaling sound then hands the bottle back to me. We're swapping sips of wine instead of sharing the truth. Like a drinking game we just invented: If you don't want to talk about something, take a drink.

"There're always reasons to stay," he says. "You just need to find one reason to leave." His eyes hold mine, and something familiar stirs inside me—something I want to pretend isn't there. A flicker that illuminates the darkest part of my insides. And I absorb it like sunlight.

"I guess I haven't found that reason yet," I say. I know my cheeks are blazing pink, I can feel the heat against my skin, but I don't look away from him.

The storm blows against the windows, rattling the glass in the casings.

Bo looks out at the rain, and I watch his gaze, wishing I could pluck more thoughts from his head. Pain rests behind his eyes, and I feel myself suddenly wanting to touch his face, his skin, his fingertips.

Then, like a machine being switched off, the wind outside stops, the rain scatters and turns to mist, and the moody black clouds begin to push farther south, revealing a backdrop of black sky with pinhole pricks for stars.

Rose hops up from the floor and twirls herself in a circle. "We need to go make wishes," she announces. "Tonight."

"The shipwreck?" Heath asks from his place still sprawled out on the floor.

"The shipwreck!" she repeats.

"What's the shipwreck?" Bo asks, flinching his gaze away from mine for the first time.

"You'll see," Rose answers.

We tromp through the darkness and down the wood path to the dock. Heath insists we take his boat, and we pile into the small, narrow dinghy. Bo takes my hand, even though I don't need it to keep my balance—I'm as steady on the water as I am on land—and he doesn't let go until I'm seated beside him on one of the benches.

The interior is sparse and tidy, a stack of orange life vests strapped to the gunwale. Heath pulls on the engine cord once, and the motor revs to life.

Maybe I shouldn't go with them. It's late, and my head rocks gently with the sloppiness of wine purring through my bloodstream. But the looseness is also addictive; it rounds out the rough edges of my mind, the worry that is constant there, that lives beneath my fingernails and at the base of my neck.

So I grip the edge of the bench seat, and slowly we chug across the eerily calm harbor. It's as if the water has died, surrendered after the storm. The ruins of sunken ships are like tombstones jutting up from the water ahead of us, jagged spikes of metal, rusted, turning to sand from the relentless tide.

"I wish we had more wine," Rose murmurs, but her voice is soft and unconcerned, so no one responds.

The green mast, covered in a layer of moss and algae, rises the tallest of all the wreckage in the harbor, the flag that once hung from its peak long ago disintegrated and blown away.

Heath slows the boat as we approach then kills the engine entirely so that we drift within only a few feet of the mast. Dark, murky outlines of the rest of the ship sit beneath us, close enough to tear apart the propeller on Heath's boat if he didn't shut off the motor when he did. It's dangerous to be this close to wreckage, but it's also why kids come out here, to test their nerve. If it weren't dangerous, it wouldn't be fun.

"Did anyone bring coins?" Rose asks.

Bo looks from Rose to me. "For what?"

"To make a wish," I tell him.

"This was a pirate ship," Heath explains. "The legend says that if you drop a coin down to the dead pirates who still haunt the ship, they will grant you a wish."

"There's probably hundreds—no, thousands of dollars in quarters down there," Rose says, waving a hand in the air as if she were a magician.

"Or just a pile of pennies," I say.

Heath checks his pockets and produces a dime and a quarter. Bo pulls out three quarters and several pennies. "The higher denomination the coin, the greater the chance that they'll grant your wish.

Pirates are greedy, obviously," Rose says as she snatches the quarter from Heath's palm.

Bo and I each take a penny, and Heath holds the dime. Apparently, Bo and I aren't very optimistic about our wishes actually coming true.

But still, I know what my wish will be—the same wish I've always had.

We each extend our arms over the side of the boat, fists clenched, and Rose counts us down from three. "Two . . . one," she says, and we all open our palms and let our coins plop into the water. They flit down quickly, reflective at first as they sink among the serrated, cavernous angles of wreckage, and then they're gone.

We are still for a moment, holding our breath . . . waiting for something immediate to happen. But when nothing does, Bo lets out a breath of air, and I cross my arms, feeling chilled. Anxious even.

We shouldn't be here, I think suddenly. Out on the water so soon after the sisters have returned. It's dangerous, risky for Heath and Bo. And something doesn't feel right. "We should head back to the island," I suggest, trying not to sound panicked, looking up at Heath, hoping he'll start the engine.

The ocean seems too calm. The singing now gone, the storm passed. Only a ripple laps up against the side of the boat.

I sense it even before I see it: The temperature drops; the sky yawns open so huge that the stars could swallow us like a whale drinking down a school of fish. The sea vibrates.

My eyes lock on something dark swaying with the current. A body is drifting faceup only a couple yards from the boat, eyes open but lost of all color. The first dead boy.

* * *

"Oh my God," Rose screeches, eyes bursting to globes, finger pointing at the corpse.

The arms are spread wide, the legs half-sunk beneath the water, and a navy-blue sweatshirt hangs from the torso like it's two sizes too big.

"Shit," Heath mutters under his breath, like he's afraid to speak too loudly or he might wake the dead.

The moon breaks through the clouds, shining over the water. But it's not a milky white, it's a pale red. Blood on the moon—a bad omen. We shouldn't have come out here.

"Who is it?" Rose asks, her voice trembling, fingers reaching for something to grab on to. Like she's reaching for the body.

The face comes into view: ashen, hollow cheeks. Short blond hair swaying outward from a pale scalp. "Gregory Dunn," Heath answers, wiping a palm over his face. "He graduated this year. Was going to college out east in the fall. Boston, I think."

Bo and I are completely silent. He touches the side of the boat, blinks, but doesn't speak.

"We have to do something!" Rose says, standing up suddenly. "We can't leave him in the water." She takes a step forward, toward the starboard side of the dinghy, which has now drifted closer to the body. But her movements shift the boat off center, and it rocks toward the water.

"Rose," I bark, reaching out for her. Heath makes an attempt to grab for her too, but the momentum has tipped the boat too far and she stumbles, her legs unbalanced, hands scrambling to brace herself on something. She pitches headfirst into the icy water.

Bo, for the first time, reacts. He's at the side of the boat before I've even had time to process what's happened. Ripples cascade outward toward the corpse of Gregory Dunn. Thankfully, Rose didn't land *on* him when she went over.

Bo leans over the starboard side of the boat, plunges his arms down into the frigid water, wrapping his hands beneath Rose's arms, and hoists her in one swift motion back into the boat. She collapses instantly, knees pulled up, shaking and convulsing uncontrollably. Health grabs a blanket from under one of the seats and wraps it around her. "We need to get her to shore," Bo says in a rush, and Heath starts the motor again. I crouch down next to Rose, an arm wrapped around her, and we race toward the marina, leaving the body of Gregory Dunn behind.

When we reach the shore, I walk quickly up the docks to the metal bell that hangs from a wood archway facing the harbor. The Death Bell, everyone calls it. Whenever a body is discovered, someone will ring the bell to alert the town that a body has been found. It was installed twenty years ago. And during the month of June, up until the summer solstice, the bell becomes the tolling sound of death.

Each time it rings, locals wince and the tourists grab their cameras.

I reach for the rough fiber of the rope and clank it twice against the inside of the bell. A hollow tolling sound echoes up through town, bouncing among the damp walls of shops and homes, waking everyone from sleep.

It takes an hour for the police and local fisherman to finally head back into port, having retrieved the body of Gregory Dunn from the water. They took their time collecting any evidence, of which there will be none. No blood, no marks, no sign of a struggle. There never is.

Rose is shivering beside me, sipping numbly on a cup of hot chocolate that Heath retrieved from the Chowder, which opened early—three a.m.—to serve the townspeople who awoke to come see the first body pulled from the sea.

We all wait on the docks, watching the parade of boats slice through the water. People stand in their pajamas and wool caps and rain boots. Even children have been pulled from bed, stumbling down with blankets slung over their shoulders to see this annual, gruesome event.

But the local police have learned to minimize the spectacle. And when they move the body onto a stretcher on the dock, they make sure it's completely covered. But people still snap photos, kids still begin to cry, and people gasp then cover their mouths with gloved hands.

"You were right," Bo whispers against my ear when the ambulance whirls away with Gregory Dunn's body strapped onto a cold metal stretcher in the back. "You said it would happen tonight, and it did."

I shake my head. It's not a contest I wanted to win.

The crowd around us slowly dissolves, and people begin tromping back to their beds or to the Chowder to discuss this first drowning. Heath approaches, eyebrows cut sharply into a grave frown. "I'm going to take Rose home," he says. "She's pretty shook up."

"Okay." I glance to Rose, who has already slipped away from my side and is walking up the dock, the striped red-and-gray blanket from Heath's boat falling from her shoulders. She looks stunned, and I know I should probably go with her, but she seems to only want Heath right now, so I let him take her.

"I'll come back to take you guys over to the island," Heath says before walking after Rose.

I nod. Then Bo and I follow the drowsy stream of people to Shipley Pier, where a waitress at the Chowder is wearing blue polka-dot pajamas and fuzzy Ugg boots. "Coffee?" she asks us. I scan her face, settling on her eyes, but she looks normal. Human.

"Sure," Bo answers.

"Black tea, please," I tell her.

She frowns briefly and makes a snort sound, like my request for tea will require more effort than she's willing to give at this hour, but she shuffles away in her boots, and Bo and I stand at the end of the pier, leaning against the railing and facing out to sea, waiting for the sunrise.

Voices murmur all around us, and speculation begins to circulate almost immediately. Over the next couple weeks, we will be in the middle of an all-out witch hunt.

Several girls from school have gathered on the outdoor deck, sipping coffee and popping bits of blueberry muffin and biscotti into their mouths, chatting loudly even though it's the middle of the night and they can't possibly be fully awake. I examine their features, the hue of their eyes, the chalky porcelain of their skin. I am look-ing for something unnatural, a gossamer creature suspended behind human flesh. But I don't see it.

The waitress brings us our drinks without even a smile. "How could Gregory Dunn have been led into the harbor without anyone seeing?" Bo asks, keeping his voice low, holding his coffee between his hands but not yet taking a drink.

I lift my shoulders, biting my lower lip. "The Swan sisters don't *want* to be seen," I say. "They've been doing this for two hundred years; they're good at it. They're good at not getting caught." I circle a finger around the rim of my white cup.

"You say it like you don't want them to get caught, like the town deserves it."

"Maybe it does." The anger I feel for this town, these people, burns inside me—it beats against my skull. So many injustices—so much death. They've always treated outsiders cruelly, cast them off because they didn't belong. "The sisters were killed by the people of this town," I say, my voice weighted with something that doesn't sound quite like me. "Drowned unfairly because they fell in love with the wrong men. Maybe they have a right to their revenge."

"To kill innocent people?"

"How do you know Gregory Dunn didn't deserve it?" I can hardly believe my own words.

"I don't," he says sharply. "But I doubt every person who's been drowned did deserve it."

I know he's right, yet I feel inclined to argue the point. I just want him to understand *why* it happens. Why the sisters return every year. It's not without cause. "It's their retribution," I say.

Bo stands up straight and takes a sip of his coffee.

"Look, I'm not saying it's right," I add. "But you can't start thinking that you can prevent it or change what happens here. Gregory Dunn was just the first. There will be more. Trying to stop it has only ever made things worse."

"What do you mean?"

"The town has killed innocent girls because they thought they were inhabited by one of the sisters. It's just better to leave it alone. There's nothing you can do."

The sun starts to edge up from the east, dull and pink at first. At the marina, fishermen begin slogging down the docks to their boats. And then I spot Heath, walking down Ocean Avenue, returned to give us a ride back to the island.

Bo doesn't speak, his mind likely wheeling over thoughts that don't line up: trying to resolve what he's seen tonight. A dead body. A two centuries–long curse. A town that has accepted its fate.

It's a lot to take in. And he only just got here. It's going to get worse.

We start down the pier, the light changing, turning pale orange as it streaks over the town. Two girls are walking toward us, headed to the Chowder. My gaze slides over them briefly.

It's Olivia and Lola—the best friends who danced around the bonfire at the Swan party shortly after the singing started. They are both fully dressed, no pj's or messy hair, as if the death of Gregory Dunn were a social event they wouldn't dare miss. One they were expecting. Lola's dyed-black hair is woven back in a French braid. Olivia's is loose across her shoulders, long and wavy. Her nose ring glints against the encroaching sun.

And when my eyes meet hers, I know: Marguerite Swan is occupying her body.

The white, spectral image of Marguerite hovers beneath Olivia's soft skin. Like looking through a thin pane of glass, or beneath the surface of a lake all the way down to the sandy bottom. It isn't a clear, crisp outline of Marguerite, but like a memory of her, wavy and unsettled, drifting inside this poor girl's body.

I've found her.

A part of me had dared to hope I wouldn't see them this year, that I could avoid the sisters, avoid the ritual of death that befalls this town. But I won't be so lucky after all.

I wish I weren't staring through Olivia's snow-white skin at Marguerite hidden beneath. But I am. And I'm the only one standing on Shipley Pier who can. This is the secret I can't tell Bo—the reason why I know the Swan sisters are real.

Her lurid gaze settles on me, not Olivia's—Olivia is gone—but Marguerite's, and then she smiles faintly at me as they stride past.

I feel briefly paralyzed. My upper lip twitches. They continue down the pier, Lola chatting about something that my ears can't seem to focus on, oblivious that her best friend is no longer her best friend. Just before they reach the Chowder, I glance over my shoulder at them. Olivia's hair swings effortlessly over her shoulders and down her back. "You all right?" Bo asks, turning to look at Olivia and Lola.

"We need to get back to the island," I say, spinning back around. "It's not safe here."

Marguerite has found a host in the body of Olivia Greene. And Marguerite is always the first to make a kill. Gregory Dunn was hers. The drowning season has started.

PERFUMERY

The Swan sisters might have dabbled in witchcraft in the years before they arrived in Sparrow—an occasional hex or potion to detour jealous wives or bad spirits—but they certainly wouldn't call themselves witches, as the people of Sparrow had accused.

They were businesswomen, shop owners, and when they arrived in Sparrow two centuries ago, they brought with them an array of exotic scents to be crafted into delicate perfumes and fragrant balms. At first the women in town gathered together inside the Swan Perfumery, swooning over scents that reminded them of the civilized world. They purchased small glass bottles of rose water and honey, lemongrass and gardenia. All perfectly blended, subtle and intricate.

It wasn't until Marguerite, the oldest of the sisters at nineteen, was caught in bed with a ship's captain, that everything began to crumble. The sisters couldn't be blamed. It wasn't witchcraft that seduced the men of Sparrow—it was something much simpler. The Swan sisters had a charm that was born into their blood, like their mother: Men could not resist the softness of their skin or the gleam of their aquamarine eyes.

Love came easily and often for them. While Marguerite liked

older men with money and power, Aurora fell for boys who others said couldn't be seduced—she liked a challenge, typically falling for more than one boy at a time. Hazel was more particular. Precise. She didn't delight in the affection of numerous men, like her sisters, yet they adored her anyway, a trail of heartbroken boys often left in her wake.

The sisters brought about their fate like someone stumbling into a poison ivy bush in the dark, unaware of the consequences that would befall them by morning.

SEVEN

For three awful weeks, tourists and locals will accuse nearly every girl of being a Swan sister. Any offense, any deviation in behavior—a sudden interest in boys they used to despise, spending too many nights out late, a twitch or flick of an eye that seems out of place—will make you a suspect.

But I know who the sisters really are.

Heath gives us a ride across the harbor, and when we reach the island, we all say a swift good-bye, and then Heath chugs back to town.

Bo and I don't speak as we walk up the path, until we reach the place where the walkway splits. A mound of old buoys and crab pots that have washed ashore over the years sit just to the left of the walkway. A decomposing heap. A reminder that this place has more death than life.

"I'm sorry," I say. "We never should have gone out there." I'm used to the gruesome shock of death, but Bo isn't. And I'm sure he's starting to consider leaving this place as soon as possible. And I wouldn't blame him if he did.

"It wasn't your fault." His eyelashes lower, and he kicks a pebble from the walkway. It lands in a patch of yellow grass and vanishes.

"You should get some sleep." We've both been awake all night, and the delirium of exhaustion is starting to feel like a freight train clamoring back and forth between my ears.

He nods, removes his hands from his coat pockets, and heads up the path to Anchor Cottage. He doesn't even say good-bye.

I won't be surprised if he starts packing as soon as he gets back to the cottage.

Mom is already awake and listening to the radio in the kitchen when I walk through the back door. It's a local station that announces storm warnings and tide reports, and today the host, Buddy Kogens, is talking about the body that authorities pulled from the water early this morning.

"This town is black with death," she says morosely, facing the kitchen sink, her hands gripping the white tile edge. "It's saturated with it." I don't answer her. I'm too tired. So I slip out into the hall and upstairs to my bedroom. From the window, I see Bo moving up the path, almost to Anchor Cottage near the center of the island. His gait is slow and deliberate. He looks back once, as if he feels me watching him, and I duck back from the window.

Something nags at me. I just can't put my finger on it.

The afternoon sky shatters apart, revealing a swath of milky blue.

Last night we found Gregory Dunn's body in the harbor.

This morning we watched the sunrise from the pier as his body was brought ashore.

Day one of the Swan season: one boy dead.

I slip from bed, rubbing my eyes, still groggy even though the sun has been up for hours, and dress in an old pair of faded jeans and a navy-blue sweater. I take my time. I stand at the dresser, not meeting my own gaze in the mirror on the wall, running my fingers over a meager collection of things. A bottle of old perfume—Mom's—which I bring to my nose. The vanilla scent has turned sharp and musty, taken on the tinge of alcohol. There's a silver dish filled with pebbles gathered from the shore: aqua and coral and emerald green. Two candles sit at one corner of the dresser, the wicks hardly burned down. And hanging by a length of yellow ribbon from the top of the mirror is a triangle piece of glass with flowers pressed between it. I can't dredge up the memory of where it came from. A birthday gift, maybe? Something Rose gave me? I stare at it, the small pink flowers flattened and dried, preserved for eternity.

I turn and lean against the dresser, taking stock of the room. Sparse and tidy. White walls. White everything. Clean. No bright colors anywhere. My room says little about me. Or maybe it says it all. A room easily abandoned. Left behind with hardly a hint that a girl ever lived here at all.

Mom is not in the house. The floorboards groan as I walk down the stairs into the kitchen. A plate of freshly baked orange muffins sits on the table. That's two mornings in a row she's made breakfast. The two mornings that Bo's been on the island. She can't help herself, she won't let a stranger starve, even though she'd easily let herself or me go hungry. Old habits. The social decorum of a small town— feed anyone who comes to visit.

I grab two muffins then head out onto the front porch.

The air is warm. Calm and placated. Seagulls spin in dizzying circles overhead, swooping down to the steep shoreline and snatching up fish caught in the tide pools. I catch the silhouette of Mom inside the greenhouse, walking among the decomposing plants.

I peer across the island to Anchor Cottage. Is Bo still inside? Or did he pack his bag and find a way off the island while I slept? A knot tightens in my stomach. If I find the cottage empty, cold, and dark, how will I feel? Despair? Like my gut has been ripped out?

But at least I'll know he's safe, escaped this town before he wound up like Gregory Dunn.

A noise draws my focus away from the cottage. A low sawing sound—the cutting of wood. It echoes over the island. And it's coming from the orchard.

I follow the wood-slat path deeper into the island, but before I've even stepped into the rows of perfectly spaced trees, I can tell that things are different. The wood ladder that normally rests at the farthest row against a half-dead Anjou tree, protected from the wind, has been moved closer to the center of the grove and has been positioned beside one of the Braeburn trees. And standing on the highest rung, leaning into the thicket of branches, is Bo.

He didn't leave after all. He didn't do the smart thing and flee when he had the opportunity. Relief swells inside my chest.

"Hey," he says down to me, holding on to one of the low branches. The sun makes long shadows through the trees. "Is everything okay?"

He takes several steps down the ladder, his hat turned backward on his head.

"Fine," I answer. "I just thought maybe you'd . . ." My voice dissipates.

"What?"

"Nothing. I'm just glad you're still here."

He squints and wipes at his forehead. "You thought I would leave?"

"Maybe."

The sunlight catches his eyes, making the dark green seem like pieces of emerald glass, an entire world contained within them. His gray T-shirt sticks to his chest and arms. His cheeks are flushed. I watch him a moment too long.

"Have you slept?" I ask.

"Not yet." He smiles from one side of his mouth—his mood seems to have lifted slightly since this morning. While I was curled up in bed, sheets pulled over my head to block out the sun, he's been out here working. Sleep probably seemed like an impossibility after last night, after what he saw. "I wanted to get started on the orchard." He hooks a wide-toothed handsaw over a low, crooked limb then climbs down the ladder, brushing his hands across his jeans.

I hand him one of the freshly baked orange muffins. "What are you doing exactly?"

He cranes his head up to the tangled limbs above us, squinting. The scar beneath his left eye pinches together. "Cutting out any new growth. We only want the oldest limbs to stay because those are the ones that produce fruit. And see how some of the branches grow straight up or down? Those also need to go." He blinks away from the sun then looks at me.

"Can I help?"

He sets the muffin on a rung of the ladder then lifts the hat from his head and scrubs a hand through his short hair. "If you want to."

101

"I do."

He drags out a second ladder from the old woodshed and finds another, smaller handsaw. He places the ladder against the tree next to the one he had been pruning and I climb carefully to the top, a little unsteady at first as it wobbles beneath me. Once I feel settled, I realize I'm shrouded by a veil of limbs, hidden in a world of branches, and then Bo climbs up behind me, standing one rung down. He extends the handsaw up to me and then wraps his arms around my waist, gripping the ladder to keep me from falling.

"What do you see?" he asks, his voice at my neck, my ear, and I shiver slightly at the feeling of his breath against my skin.

"I'm not sure," I say truthfully.

"The trees haven't bloomed yet," he explains. "But they will soon, so we have to take out all the branches that are crowding the older limbs—the *old wood*, it's called."

"This small one," I say, tapping it with my finger. "It's growing straight up from a thicker branch, and it still looks a little green."

"Exactly," he praises. And I lift the saw, holding it to the limb. On my first stroke across the branch, the saw slips out, and I lurch forward to keep from dropping it. Bo tightens his arms around me, and the ladder teeters beneath us. My heartbeat spikes upward. "The saw takes some getting used to," Bo adds.

I nod, gripping the top of the ladder. And then I feel the sharp stinging in my left index finger. I turn my palm up so I can examine it, and blood beads to the surface along the outer edge of my finger. When the blade slipped, it must have cut into my skin where my hand was holding the branch. Bo notices it at the same time, and he leans closer into me, reaching around to grab my finger.

"You're cut," he says. The blood drips down the tip of my finger and plummets all the way to the ground, six feet below. I notice Otis and Olga sitting in the swath of sun between rows, orange-and-white heads titled upward, watching us.

"It's okay," I say. But he yanks out a white handkerchief from his back pocket and presses it to the cut, staunching the bleeding. "It's not that deep," I add, even though it stings pretty good. The white fabric turns red almost instantly.

"We should clean it out," he says.

"No. Really, I'm fine."

This close, with his face directly beside mine, I can feel each breath as it rises in his chest, see his lips move as he exhales. His heart is racing faster than it should. Like he was worried I might have just cut my entire hand off, and it would have been his fault for allowing me to wield a saw.

He lifts the handkerchief away to inspect the cut, leaning into me.

"Do we need to amputate?" I ask lightheartedly.

"Most likely." His eyes slide to mine, the corner of his mouth lifting. He tears off a small strip of the handkerchief, holding my hand in his, then ties the narrow piece of fabric around my finger like a makeshift tourniquet. "This should keep the finger from falling off until we operate."

"Thanks," I say, smiling even though it still burns. My lips so close to his I can almost taste the saltiness of his skin.

He slides what's left of his handkerchief into his back pocket and straightens up behind me so that his chest is no longer against my back. "It's probably safer with just one person on the ladder," he amends.

I nod, agreeing, and he climbs down, jumping the last couple feet to the ground and leaving me weightless atop the ladder without him.

He scales back up his ladder, and we work side by side, sawing away the unwanted limbs on each tree. I'm careful to keep my fingers out of the way, and soon I feel confident with the saw. It's a tedious, slow process, but gradually we work our way down the first row.

This becomes our routine.

Each morning we meet in the orchard, moving our ladders to a new row. Bringing the fruit trees back to life. I don't mind the work. It feels purposeful. And by the end of the week my hands have a roughness like I've never felt before. My skin has browned, and my eyes taper away from the midday sun. It hasn't rained once all week, and the summer air feels light and buoyant and sweet.

On Saturday we collect all the sawn limbs and pile them at the north end of the orchard. And just after sunset we set them ablaze.

The sooty night sky sparks and shivers, the stars dulled by the inferno we've created on land.

"Tomorrow we'll cut down the dead trees," Bo says, arms crossed and staring into the fire.

"How?" I ask.

"We'll saw them down to stumps then burn them out from the ground."

"How long will that take?"

"A couple days."

I feel like I've been suspended in time this last week, protected from a season that comes each year like a violent squall. In moments, I've even forgotten entirely about the world outside this little island. But I know it will find a way in. It always does.

* * *

It takes three days to trim the two dead apple trees and one pear tree down to only stumps. And by the end of the third day, my arms can barely move. They ache just lifting them through my T-shirt in the morning.

We walk through the orchard, examining our hard work—today we will torch the three tree stumps—when Bo stops beside the single oak tree at the center of the grove, the one with the heart cut into the trunk. It looks like a ghost tree, white moss dripping from the limbs, two hundred years of history hidden in its trunk. "Maybe we should burn this one down too," he comments, surveying the limbs. "It's pretty old and not that healthy. We could plant an apple tree in its place."

I press my palm against the trunk, over the etched heart. "No. I want to leave it."

He lifts a hand to block the sun.

"It feels wrong to cut it down," I add. "This tree meant something to someone." A gentle wind blows my ponytail across my shoulder.

"I doubt whoever carved that heart is still alive to care," he points out.

"Maybe not, but I still want to keep it."

He pats the trunk of the tree. "All right. It's your orchard."

Bo is careful and precise before he lights the three dead trees on fire, making sure we have several buckets of water and a shovel at each tree in case we need to dampen the flames. He strikes a match and instantly the first stump ignites. He does the same to the next two trees, and we watch the flames slowly work their way through the wood.

The sun fades, and the flames lick upward from the tall stumps like arms reaching for the stars.

I make two mugs of hot black tea with cardamom then carry them down to the orchard, and we stay up to watch the fires burn through the night. The air is smoky and sweet with apples that will never bloom because these trees have reached their end.

We sit on a stack of cut logs watching the fires burn for nearly an hour.

"I heard your mom used to read tea leaves," Bo says, blowing on his tea to cool it.

"Where did you hear that?"

"In town, when I was looking for work and found the flyer. I had asked someone how to get to the island, and they thought I was looking to have my fortune read."

"She doesn't do it anymore, not since my dad left." I lean forward and pull up a clump of brittle beach grass at my feet then roll it between my palms to crush it, feeling the broken fibers before I scatter the fragments back across the ground. I have a memory of my dad walking across the island, kneeling down occasionally to pull up a gathering of dandelions or clover or moss, then rubbing them between his worn hands. He liked the way the world felt. Loam and green. The earth giving up things we often ignored. I wipe the memory away with a quick closing of my eyes. It hurts to think of him. Pain skipping through my chest.

"Do you read tea leaves?" He asks with a quirk of an eyebrow.

"Not really." A short laugh escapes my throat. "So don't get your hopes up. I won't be revealing your future any time soon."

"But you *can* do it?"

"Used to. But I'm out of practice."

He holds out his mug for me to take.

"You don't fully believe in the Swan sisters, but you believe that fortunes can be seen in tea leaves?" I ask, not accepting his mug.

"I'm unpredictable."

I smile and raise both eyebrows at him. "I can't read the leaves with liquid still in the cup. You have to finish it and then the pattern of leaves left inside is where your fortune lives."

He looks down into his mug like he might be able to read his own future. "Spoken like a true witch."

I shake my head and smile. It's hardly witchcraft. It doesn't involve spells or potions or anything quite so intriguing. But I don't correct him.

He takes a long drink of his tea and finishes it in one gulp, then extends it out to me.

I hesitate. I really don't want to do this. But he's looking at me with such anticipation that I take the cup and hold it between both palms. I tilt it to one side, then the other, examining the whirl of leaves around the edges. "Hmm," I say, as if I were considering something important, then peek at him from the corner of my eye. He looks like he's moved closer to the edge of the log, about to fall off if I don't tell him immediately what I see. I lift my head and look at him fully. "Long life, true love, piles of gold," I say, then set the mug on the log between us.

One of his eyebrows lifts. He glances at the mug then at me. I try to keep a straight face, but my lips start to tug upward. "Very astute reading," he says, smiling back then laughing. "Perhaps you shouldn't make a career of reading tea leaves," he says. "But I do hope you're right about my future on all accounts."

"Oh, I'm right," I say, still grinning. "The leaves don't lie."

He laughs again, and I take a sip of my own tea.

Sparks dance and writhe up into the sky. And I realize how at ease I am sitting here with Bo. How normal it feels. As if this were something we do each evening: set trees on fire and laugh together in the dark.

I don't feel the gnawing at the base of my skull that usually plagues me each summer—a ticking clock counting down the days until the summer solstice and the end of the Swan season. Bo has distracted me from all the awful things lurking in this town, in the harbor, and in my mind.

"People used to say that the apples and pears that grew on the island had magical healing properties," I tell him, tilting my head back to watch the waves of smoke spiral upward like mini tornados. "They thought they could heal ailments like a bee sting or hay fever or even a broken heart. They would sell for twice the normal price in town."

"Did your family used to sell them?" he asks.

"No. This was long before my family lived here. But if the orchards could produce edible fruit again, maybe we could sell it."

"By next summer, you should be able to harvest ten to twenty pounds from each tree. It'll be a lot of work, so you'll probably need to hire more help."

He says "you," like he won't be around to see it.

"Thank you for doing this," I say, "for bringing them back to life."

He nods and I touch my index finger, now wrapped with a

Band-Aid. The stinging is gone, the cut almost healed. But it will probably leave a tiny scar. My gaze slides to Bo, to the scar beneath his left eye, and I have to ask, "How did you get that?" I nod to the smooth, waxy line of skin.

He blinks, the scar puckering together, as if he feels the pain of it again. "I jumped out of a tree when I was nine. A branch cut me open."

"Did you get stitches?"

"Five. I remember it hurting like hell."

"Why'd you jump out of a tree?"

"My brother dared me. For a week he had been trying to convince me that I could fly if I had enough speed." His eyes smile at the memory. "I believed him. And I also probably just wanted to impress him since he was my older brother. So I jumped."

He tilts his head back to look up at the sky, sewn together with stars.

"Maybe you didn't have enough speed," I suggest, smiling and craning my head back to look up at the same stars.

"Probably not. But I don't think I'll test the theory again." His smile fades. "My brother felt terrible," he goes on. "He carried me all the way back to our house while I sobbed. And after I got stitches, he sat beside my bed and read me comics for a week. You'd think I lost a leg, he felt so guilty."

"He sounds like a good brother," I say.

"Yeah. He was."

A breath of silence weaves between us.

Sparks swirl up from the charred tree trunk into the dark. Bo clears his throat, still staring into the flames. "How long has that sailboat been sitting down by the dock?"

The question surprises me. I wasn't expecting it. "A few years, I guess."

"Who does it belong to?" His tone is careful, as though he's unsure if he should be asking. The focus has quickly shifted from him to me. From one loss to another.

I let the words tumble around inside my skull before I answer, conjuring up a past that lies dormant in my mind. "My father."

He waits before he speaks again, sensing that he's venturing into delicate territory. "Does it still sail?"

"I think so."

I stare down into the mug held between my palms, absorbing its warmth.

"I'd like to take it out sometime," Bo says cautiously, "see if it still sails."

"You know how to sail?"

His lips part open—a gentle smile—and he looks down at his feet like he's about to reveal a secret. "I spent almost every summer sailing on Lake Washington growing up."

"Did you live in Seattle?" I ask, hoping to narrow down the city where he's from.

"Near there." His answer is just as vague as the last time I asked. "But a much smaller town."

"You realize I have more questions about you than answers." He was built to conceal secrets, his face revealing not even a hint of what's buried inside. It's both intriguing and infuriating.

"I can say the same about you."

I draw my lips to one side and squeeze the mug tighter between my hands. He's right. We're deadlocked in a strange battle of secrecy.

Neither of us is willing to tell the truth. Neither of us is willing to let the other one in. "You can take the sailboat out if you want," I say, standing up and tucking a loose strand of hair back behind my ear. "It's late. I think I'll head up to the house." The flames burning in each stump have been reduced to hot embers, slowly chewing through the last of the wood.

"I'll stay up and make sure the fires are out completely."

"Good night," I say, pausing to look back at him.

"Night."

EIGHT

The orchard looks different. Pruned and tidy, like a manicured English garden. It reminds me of how it used to be in summers past, when ripe fruit would hang bright and vibrant beneath the sun, beckoning the birds to pick at the ones that had fallen to the ground. The air always smelled of sweet and salt. Fruit and sea.

In the early morning I walk down the rows. The three burned stumps send out thin strands of smoke even though they are now nothing but piles of ash.

I wonder how late Bo stayed up, watching the last of the embers turn black. I wonder if he slept at all. I walk to his cottage and stand facing the door. I lift my fist, about to knock, when the door swings open, and I suck in a startled breath.

"Hey," he says reflexively.

"Hi . . . sorry. I was just about to knock," I stammer. "I came to say . . . good morning." A dumb explanation. I'm not even sure why I've come.

His eyebrows screw into a confused line, but his lips form an easy half grin. He's wearing a plain white shirt and jeans that sag low over his hips, and his hair is pressed to one side like he's just woken up. "I was coming out to check on the trees," he says. "Make sure they didn't reignite in the last couple hours."

"They're only smoldering," I tell him. "I was just up there."

He nods then extends his arm to open the door wider. "You want to come inside? I can make coffee."

I step past him, feeling the warmth of the cottage fold over me.

Otis and Olga are already inside, curled up on the couch as if this was their new home. As if they now belonged to Bo. There is no fire, but the windows are all open, a warm breeze purring through the cottage. The weather has shifted, turned mild and buoyant—the air blowing in from the sea stirs up the dust motes and scares away the ghosts. Every day that he's here on the island, in the cottage, I can feel the space changing, becoming brighter.

Bo stands in the kitchen, his back to me, and turns on the faucet in the sink, filling the coffeepot with water. He's tan after a week outside under the sun. And the muscles in his shoulders flex beneath the thin cotton of his shirt.

"How do you like your coffee?" he asks, turning around to face me, and I quickly flick my eyes away so he doesn't catch me staring.

"Black is fine."

"Good . . . because I don't have anything else." I wonder if he bought coffee grounds in town before I invited him out to the island. Brought it with him in his backpack? Since I doubt there was coffee here when he moved in.

A stack of books sits on the low table in front of the couch and more books are lined up on the floor, all pulled from the shelves. I pick up a book resting on the arm of the couch. *Encyclopedia: Celtic Myths and Fables Vol. 2.*

"What are all these?" I ask.

Bo dries his hands on a kitchen towel then walks into the living room. Otis wakes up and begins rubbing a paw over one ear.

"All the books in here are about legends and folklore," he answers.

I run a finger over a row of books on the bookshelf beside the fireplace. The spines are printed with titles like *Native American Legends of the Northwest, How to Break an Unwanted Curse*, and *Witches and Warlocks: A Guide to Understanding*. They are all like this—a library of books on topics of the unnatural, the mystical, similar to what's happening in Sparrow. Collected by someone and stored in the cottage . . . *but who*?

"You didn't know?" Bo asks. Coffee begins streaming into the glass pot behind him, the warm roasted scent filling the room.

I shake my head. *No, I didn't know these were in here. I had no idea.* I sink down onto the couch, touching the page of a book left open on one of the cushions. "Why are you reading them?" I ask, closing the book with a *thud* then setting it on the coffee table.

"I don't know. Because they're here, I guess."

Olga hops down from the couch and coils herself around Bo's leg, purring up at him, and he bends down to scratch gently behind her ear. "And what about the Swan sisters—do you believe in them now?" I ask.

"Not exactly. But I also don't believe people drown themselves for no reason."

"Then why are they drowning?"

"I'm not sure."

My foot taps against the floor, my heart thuds inside my rib cage—a scratching at my thoughts. *So many books. All these books.*

Placed here—hidden in here. "And what about the singing from the harbor—how do you explain that?"

"I can't," he answers. "But it doesn't mean it won't eventually be explained. Have you seen those rocks in Death Valley that move across the desert floor on their own? For years people didn't understand how it happened. Some of the rocks weighed over six hundred pounds, and they left trails in the sand as if they were being pushed. People thought it might be UFOs or some other bizarre cosmic event. But researchers finally discovered it's just ice. The desert floor freezes, and then strong winds slide these massive boulders across the sand. Maybe the Swan sisters' legend is like this. The singing and the drownings just haven't been explained yet. But there's some perfectly logical reason why it happens."

The coffeepot has stopped sputtering behind him, but he makes no move to walk back into the small kitchen.

"Ice?" I repeat, looking at him like I've never heard anything so absurd in my life.

"I'm just saying that maybe someday they'll discover that none of this has anything to do with three sisters who were killed two hundred years ago."

"But you've seen firsthand what happens here; you saw Gregory Dunn's body in the harbor."

"I saw a body. A boy who drowned. That's it."

I tighten my lips together. My fingernails dig into the fabric edge of the couch. "Did you really come to Sparrow by accident?" I ask—the question piercing the air between us. Splitting it apart. It's been nagging me since he showed up, a needle at the very base of my neck, a question I've wanted to ask but felt I shouldn't. Like the answer didn't matter. But maybe it does. Maybe it matters more than anything else. There's something he's not telling me. A part of his past or maybe his present, a thing that rests between the ribs, a purpose—a reason why he's here. I sense it. And although I don't want to push him away, I need to know.

The sunlight through the window spills over half of his face: light and dark. "I already told you," he says, his voice sounding a little hurt.

But I shake my head, not believing. "You didn't just come here by accident, because it was the last stop on the bus. There's another reason. You're . . . you're hiding something." I try to see into his eyes, into his thoughts, but he is carved by stone and brick. Solid as the rocks bordering the island.

His lips part, his jaw tenses. "So are you." He says it quickly, like it's been on his mind for a while, and I shift uncomfortably on the couch.

I can't meet his eyes. He sees the same thing in me: a chasm of secrets so deep and wide and unending that it bleeds from me like sweat. We both carry it. A mark on our skin, a brand burned into flesh from the weight of our past. Perhaps only those with similar scars can recognize it in others. The fear rimming our eyes.

But if he knew the truth—what I see what I peer through Olivia Greene, the creature hidden inside. If he knew the things that haunt my waking dreams. If he saw what I saw. If he *saw*. He'd leave this island and never come back. He'd leave this town. And I don't want to be alone on the island again. There have only ever been ghosts here, shadows of people that once were, until he arrived. I can't lose him. So I don't tell him.

I stand up before our words tear apart the fragile air between us. Before he demands truths I can't give. I never should have asked him why he came to Sparrow, unless I was willing to give up something of myself. Otis blinks at me from the gray cushion, stirred by my movement. I walk past Bo to the door, and for a moment I think he's going to reach out for me, to stop me, but he never actually touches me, and my heart wrenches. Spills onto the floor, seeps into the cracks between the wood boards.

A burst of bright morning sun pours into the cottage when I open the door. Otis and Olga don't even attempt to follow me. But before I can pull the door closed behind me, I hear something in the distance, beyond the edges of the island. There is no wind to carry it across the water, but the stillness makes it audible.

The bell at the marina in Sparrow is ringing.

A second body has been found.

TAVERN

The Swan sisters were never ordinary, even at birth.

All three were born on June first, exactly one year apart. First Marguerite, then came Aurora a year later, and Hazel the year after that. They did not share the same father, yet fate would bring them into this world on precisely the same day. Their mother had said they were destined for one another, bound by the stars to be sisters.

And so upon their birthday, during their first year in Sparrow, they closed up their shop early and strode down to the White Horse Inn and Tavern. They ordered pints and a bottle of brandy wine. The liquid was dark and red and bittersweet, and they passed it among them, drinking straight from the bottle. The men in the tavern shook their heads and whispered of the sisters' boldness—women rarely entered the tavern, but the sisters were not like other women in town. They laughed and spilled wine onto the damp wood floor. They sang songs they had heard the fishermen bellow when heading out to sea, enticing the winds to be calm and kind. They tipped in their chairs. They toasted their mother, who they hardly remembered now, for bringing them into this world, one year apart from each other, but on precisely the same day.

The moon shone bright over the harbor, and the whale-oil lamps flickered from atop each table inside the tavern. Marguerite stood from her chair, scanning the musty room filled with fishermen and farmers and seamen who would be here for only a week or two before they set out again. She grinned, eyeing them with the heat of booze in her cheeks. "They all think we're witches," she hissed down to her sisters, waving the bottle of brandy wine around the room. The rumors had been seething through town for months, suspicion rooting itself in the framework of homes along the seaport, passing from lips to ears until each tale became more vile than the last. The people of Sparrow had begun to hate the sisters.

"Yes, witches." Aurora laughed. She tilted her head back and nearly toppled from her chair.

"No, they don't," Hazel protested, frowning.

But Aurora and Marguerite laughed even harder, for they knew what their youngest sister didn't want to believe: that the entire town had already decided they were witches. A coven of three sisters, come to Sparrow to unleash treachery and ill deeds.

"You all think we are witches, yes?" Marguerite shouted.

The men seated at the bar turned to look. The barkeep set down the bottle of whiskey in his hand. But no one answered her.

"Then I hex you all," she announced, still smiling, lips ruddy from the wine. She circled a finger in the air then pointed it at a man seated at a nearby table. "You will grow a beard made of sea snakes." She roared with laughter then swayed her finger to a man leaning against the wall. "You will trip and fall on your way home tonight, hit your head, and see your future death." Her eyes, it would be said later, seemed alight with fire, like she was casting spells from an inferno that would burn alive anyone caught in her stare. "You will marry a mermaid," she told another man. "You will taste fish, no matter what you eat, for the rest of your life," she said to a man hunched over the bar. And as Marguerite's finger waved around the room, calling out imaginary spells, the men began to flee, certain her hexes would come true. Aurora laughed from deep within her belly, watching her sister frighten even the toughest men in Sparrow. But Hazel, horrified by the looks on the men's faces, grabbed her sisters and dragged them from the tavern as Marguerite continued to shout nonsense into the salty night air.

Once outside, the three sisters locked arms and even Hazel laughed as they staggered up Ocean Avenue, past the docks, to the small living space they shared behind the perfumery. "You can't do that," Hazel said through her laughter. "They'll think us real witches."

"They already do, my sweet sister," Aurora told her.

"They just don't understand us," Hazel offered, and Marguerite kissed her on the cheek.

"Believe what you want," Marguerite murmured, tilting her head to the starry sky, to the moon, which seemed to await her command. "But one day they will come for us." They all fell silent, the wind brushing through their hair, making it weightless. "But until then, we drink." She still had the bottle of wine and they passed it among them, letting the constellations guide them home.

Later, when Arthur Helm hit his head, he swore he saw his death as Marguerite predicted. Even though he didn't actually fall on his way home from the tavern—he was struck in the jaw by his plow horse a week later—the town still believed Marguerite had caused it. And when Murrey Coats married a woman with long ribbons of hair the color of wheat, people said she was once a mermaid he had caught in his fishing net—proof of Marguerite's spell coming true.

Four weeks later, on the summer solstice of 1823—a day chosen by the townspeople because a solstice was said to guarantee a witch's death—the three sisters were drowned for their accused witchery. Marguerite was the oldest at nineteen on the day of her death, Aurora eighteen, Hazel seventeen.

Born on the same day. Died on the same day.

NINE

B o appears behind me in the doorway just as the tolling bell from across the harbor begins to fade. "Another one?" he asks, hand lifted as if he could see out over the water all the way to the docks.

"Another one."

He sidesteps around me, his shoulder grazing mine, then starts down the path.

"Where are you going?"

"Town," he answers.

"You're safer here," I call after him, but he doesn't stop. I have no choice but to follow—I can't let him go alone. Marguerite is in the body of Olivia Greene. And this latest kill is likely Aurora's. But I haven't seen her yet—don't yet know whose body she has stolen. So when Bo reaches the skiff, I climb in after him and start the motor.

A cluster of boats have gathered in the harbor just offshore from Coppers Beach.

I can't see the body from this distance, but I know there must be one, newly discovered, floating, being pulled aboard one of the boats—so we motor over to the marina, Bo's face hardened against the blustery wind.

We dock the skiff, and see that a crowd has already assembled on Ocean Avenue awaiting the return of the harbor police boats, cameras ready. There are signs at the top of the marina that read: DOCK MEMBERS ONLY, NO TOURISTS ALLOWED. But there are always people who ignore the signs and tromp down to the docks anyway, especially after the bell has been rung.

I push through the clot of tourists, past the stone bench facing the harbor, when someone grabs my arm. It's Rose. Heath is standing beside her.

"There's two of them," she says with shaking breath, her blue eyes magnified. She still looks pale and weak, like she hasn't yet shaken off the chill of falling into the water over a week ago, only inches from Gregory Dunn's corpse.

"Two bodies?" Bo asks, stepping in beside me so the four of us form a tight circle on the sidewalk, our breath coming out in bursts of steamy white.

Rose nods her head.

Aurora, I think. She's greedy and impulsive, can never decide, and so she will take two boys at once.

"That's not all," Heath says. "They saw one of the Swan sisters."

"Who did?" I ask.

Heath and Rose exchange a look. "Lon Whittamer was out on his dad's boat this morning, patrolling the harbor. He and Davis decided to take shifts, like vigilantes; they thought they could catch one of the sisters in the act. Apparently, Lon was the first to spot the two bodies in the harbor. Then he saw something else: a girl swimming, her head just above the waterline. She was kicking frantically back to Coppers Beach." Heath pauses and it feels like time stops, all of us holding our breath.

"Who did Lon see?" I press, my heartbeat rising into my throat, about to burst.

"Gigi Kline," he answers in one swift exhale.

I blink, a cold spire of ice slipping down the length of my spine.

"Who's Gigi Kline?" Bo asks.

"A girl from my school," I answer, my voice a near hush. "She was at the Swan party on the beach."

"Did she go in the water?"

"I'm not sure."

I glance up Ocean Avenue, where the mass of people has grown larger, tourists pressed together, trying to get a better view of the docks where the bodies will be brought ashore. *This* is what they came for—to glimpse death, proof that the legend of the Swan sisters is real.

"Who knows about Gigi?" I ask, looking back at Heath.

"I don't know. I saw Lon when he reached the docks, and he told me what he saw. Now he and Davis are searching for her."

"Shit," I mutter. If they find her, who knows what they'll do.

"Do you think it's true?" Rose asks. "Could Gigi be one of them?" Her expression seems tight and anxious. She's never fully believed in the Swan sisters before—it scares her, I think, the idea that they could be real, that she could be taken and not even know it. It's a survival mechanism for her, and I understand why she does it. But now the waver in her voice makes me think she's not so sure what she believes anymore.

"I don't know," I answer. *I won't know for sure until I see her.*

"They already found her," Heath interrupts, his cell phone in his hand, the screen lit a vibrant blue.

"What?" I ask.

125

"Davis and Lon, they have her." His throat catches. "And they're taking her to the old boathouse past Coppers Beach. Everyone's headed over there." Word is traveling fast, at least among the inner circle of Sparrow High students. "I'm going down there," Heath adds, clicking off his phone.

Bo nods and Rose twines her fingers through Heath's. We're all going, apparently. Everyone will want to see if Gigi Kline—last year's homecoming princess and star cheerleader—has been inhabited by a Swan sister. But I'm the only one who will know for sure.

The harbor police boats are just starting to motor into port, carrying two bodies whose identities we don't yet know, when the four of us push through the crowds toward the edge of town. We pass Coppers Beach then turn down a dirt road almost completely overgrown by blackberry bushes and a tangle of wind-beaten shrubs.

The air smells green here, damp and sodden, even with the sunlight glaring down. No cars pass down this road. The property is abandoned. And when we emerge from the dense thicket of green, the boathouse comes into view at the edge of the waterline. The old stone walls of the structure are slowly turning brownish green from the algae inching its way up the sides, and the wood-shingled roof is covered in a slimy layer of moss. A sheer cliff stands to the right of the boathouse and a rocky embankment to the left. You can't see the town or the beach from here; it's completely secluded. Which is why kids come here to smoke or make out or ditch classes. But it's not exactly a pleasant place to spend longer than an afternoon.

As we get closer, I notice that the small door into the boathouse is ajar several inches, and voices echo out from inside.

Heath is the first to step into the dark interior, and several faces turn to look at us as we shuffle in behind him. It smells worse inside. The room has a rectangle cut out of the floor near the far doors where a boat once sat protected from the weather, and seawater laps up into the interior, making reflective patterns across the walls. The stench of fuel, fish guts, and seaweed permeates the space.

Davis McArthurs and Lon Whittamer are standing against the right side wall on the narrow three-foot-wide walkway that stretches down either side of the boathouse. Three other girls who I recognize from school—but whose names I can't recall—are crowded just inside the door, as if they're afraid to get too close to the water splashing up from the floor with each wave that rolls in. And sitting in a plastic lawn chair between Davis and Lon, zip ties around her wrists and a red-and-white-checkered bandanna tied over her mouth, is Gigi Kline.

We seem to have walked into the middle of a discussion already unfolding, because one of the girls, wearing a bright pink parka, says, "You don't know for sure. She looks fine to me."

"That's the point," Davis says, jutting out his square jaw. Davis reminds me of a slab of meat, broad and thick. With a nose like a bull. There is nothing delicate about him. Or especially kind, for that matter. He's a bully. And he gets away with it because of his size. "They look like everyone else," he continues, firming his glare on the pink-parka girl. "She killed those two guys in the harbor. Lon saw her."

"You can't keep her tied up," another girl interjects, her smooth dark hair pulled up into a ponytail, and she points to Gigi with one long, sharp finger.

"We sure fucking can," Lon snaps back, while Davis scowls at the girl. Lon is wearing one of his standard Hawaiian shirts—light blue with neon yellow anchors and parrots. I feel Bo shift closer to me, like he wants to protect me from whatever is unfolding in front of us. And I wonder if he recognizes Lon from the night at the Swan party, when he was wasted and Bo pushed him into the sea.

"There's no way to prove she did anything," ponytail girl points out.

"Look at her fucking clothes and hair," Lon says sharply. "She's soaking wet."

"Maybe she . . ." But ponytail girl's voice trails off.

"Maybe she fell in," pink-parka girl offers. But everyone knows that's a weak excuse, and unlikely considering the circumstances. Two boys are being hauled from the harbor as we speak, and Gigi Kline is found completely drenched—it's not hard to put the pieces together.

Davis uncrosses his arms and takes a step toward the group. "She's one of them," he says coldly, his deep-set eyes unblinking. "And you all know it's true." He says it with such finality that everyone falls silent.

My eyes slide over Gigi Kline, her cropped blond hair dripping water onto the wood-plank floor. Eyes bloodshot like she's been crying, lips parted to accommodate the bandanna stretched across her mouth and tied at the back of her head. She looks cold, miserable, terrified. But while everyone speculates as to whether she might no longer be Gigi Kline, I know the truth. I can see right through the delicate features of her face, through her tear-streaked skin, right down into her center.

A pearlescent, threadlike creature resides just beneath the surface—

silky, atmospheric, shifting behind her human eyes. The ghost of a girl long dead.

Gigi Kline is now Aurora Swan.

Her gaze circles around the room, like she's looking for someone to help her, to untie her, to speak up, but when her eyes settle on mine, I look quickly away.

"And now," Davis says, rolling his tongue along the inside of his lower lip, "we're going to find the other two." I think of Olivia Greene, now inhabited by Marguerite Swan. But she will be harder to catch—Marguerite is careful, precise, and she won't allow these boys to discover what she really is.

And no sooner have I thought her name than Olivia and Lola step into the boathouse through the little door behind us. Hardly anyone takes notice of their arrival.

"How are we going to find them?" the third girl asks, chomping on a piece of gum and speaking up for the first time. If she only knew—if all of them only knew—how close they really are.

"We set a trap," Lon says, grinning like he's about to crush an insect beneath the sole of his shoe. "We have one of them now. The other two sisters will come for her. Gigi is our bait."

A short laugh at the back of the group breaks apart Lon's words. "You think the Swan sisters would be stupid enough to fall for that?" It's Marguerite who's spoken, and she rolls her eyes when everyone turns to look at her.

"They're not just going to leave her here," Davis points out.

"Maybe they'll think she deserves to be tied up for being dumb enough to get caught. Maybe they'll want her to learn her lesson." Marguerite stares directly at Gigi when she says it, her gaze penetrating deeply so that Aurora knows she's speaking to her: one Swan sister to another. It's a threat. Marguerite is upset that Aurora allowed herself to be captured.

"I guess we'll find out," Davis says. "And until then, we don't let any girls near the boathouse."

"That's not fair," pink-parka girl asserts. "Gigi's my friend and—"

"And maybe you're one of them," Davis snaps, cutting her off.

"That's insane." She snorts. "I didn't even get in the water at the Swan party."

"Then we should question everyone who did."

The girl with the perfect ponytail drops her gaze to the floor. "Almost everyone swam that night."

"Not everyone," Lon adds, "but you did." His eyes are harpooned on her. "And so did Rose." He nods to Rose, who is standing a half step behind me, next to Heath.

"This is ridiculous," Heath pipes up. "You idiots can't start blaming every girl who was at the party that night. It might not have even happened at the party—the sisters might have stolen bodies later, after everyone was too wasted to remember anything. Or even the next morning."

Lon and Davis exchange a look, but they're obviously undeterred, because Davis says, "Everyone is a suspect. And Gigi is staying in here until we find the other two."

"She can't stay in here until the summer solstice; it's over a week away," parka girl says, her voice pitched.

"Well, we sure as shit can't let her go," Davis rebukes. "She'll just kill someone else. Probably *us*, for tying her up." Davis slaps Lon against the shoulder, and Lon cringes a little, like he hadn't considered this—that he and Davis might be next on the drowning kill list for capturing a Swan sister.

Gigi tries to shake her head, to make a sound, but only muffled, garbled noises manage to make it through. The bandanna is tied too tightly.

Gigi's parents will certainly get suspicious when she doesn't come home; the police will be called, a search party sent to look for her. But the boys did get one thing right: Gigi Kline *is* a Swan sister—the only problem is that they can't prove it. And I'm not about to tell them the truth.

Still, this is bad. Aurora has been captured. Marguerite knows it. And the summer solstice will be here soon—things are getting complicated. Aurora's capture has made it complicated. And I just want to stay as far away from them and this mess as I can.

Heath has had enough, and I see him grab Rose's hand. "Come on," he whispers to her, then leads her out of the boathouse.

A new group of three guys—one I recognize as Thor Grantson, whose father owns the *Catch* newspaper—and one girl shuffle in through the doorway, coming to see Gigi Kline and determine for themselves if they think she's been infected by a Swan sister.

The room suddenly feels claustrophobic.

"Hell no!" Davis says loudly, pointing a finger at Thor. "You'd better not write about this in your shitty paper, Thor, or tell your father."

Thor lifts both hands in the air in a gesture of innocence. "I just came to see her," he says amiably. "That's it."

"You're a fucking snitch and everyone knows it," Lon chimes in.

Pink-parka girl starts arguing with Davis in Thor's defense, and soon the room is a cacophony of voices, all the while Gigi Kline sits tied to a chair and Olivia Greene stands calmly at the back of the group, leaning against the wall.

I can't stay in here anymore, so I slip through the new group of people and stumble back out into the daylight, opening my mouth to breathe in the warm, salty air.

Rose and Heath are standing a couple yards away, but Rose's arms are crossed. "They're bullies," I hear her say. "They can't do this. It's not right."

"There's nothing we can do," Heath says. "It's going to be a witch hunt. And they could just as easily lock you up in there."

"He's right," I say, and they both look up. "None of us are safe."

"So we just let them keep her locked up and accuse whoever they want?"

"For now," I say, "yeah, we do."

The door to the boathouse swings open and Bo steps out behind me, blinking away the sunlight.

"Maybe they're right," Heath offers, reaching out to touch Rose's arm. "Maybe Gigi did drown those two boys. Maybe she's one of them. It's better if she's in there, where she can't kill anyone else."

"You don't really believe that girl could be dangerous?" Bo asks, crossing his arms. I glance over my shoulder at him and a stillness settles over the four of us—each of us considering how dangerous she could really be, picturing her hands around a boy's throat, her eyes wicked with revenge as she forced him below the waterline, waiting for bubbles to escape his nostrils and break at the surface.

Then Rose says, "Penny?" as if she's hoping I might have an answer. As if I might know how to fix everything and make it all okay. And suddenly I feel the urge to tell her the truth: that Gigi is indeed occupied by Aurora Swan, and that the town is safer with her tied up inside the old boathouse. That setting a trap to catch the remaining two Swan sisters might be a smart move.

But instead I tell her, "We need to be careful. Act normal. Don't give them any reason to suspect we could be one of them."

"But we aren't one of them!" Rose says sharply.

My eyes feel dry, unable to blink. Rose sounds so certain, she's so sure that she understands the world around her, that she'd be able to see something as villainous as a Swan sister if it were tucked inside of Gigi Kline. She trusts her eyes to tell her the truth. But she can't see a thing. "They don't know that," I say. "We shouldn't even be here; we shouldn't be anywhere near Gigi."

I have a flash of a memory, of Rose talking with Gigi in C hall last year. They were laughing about something, I can't seem to recall what exactly. It doesn't matter. But it reminds me that they were friends once, in grade school, and perhaps Rose is more upset by what's happened because it's happening to Gigi. Someone who she was once so close with. And if it can happen to Gigi, it can happen to her, or to me, even.

The boathouse door opens again and several people spill out, all chatting in low voices. Lola walks out by herself, staring down at her cell phone, probably sending out more text messages about Gigi's current incarceration inside the boathouse.

"I want to get out of here," Rose murmurs, and Heath twines his fingers through hers and starts leading her back up the road.

"You're really okay just leaving that girl gagged and tied to a chair in there?" Bo asks me.

"We don't have a choice right now."

"It's kidnapping and wrongful imprisonment. We could call the cops."

"But what if they're right?" I pose. "What if she's a Swan sister and just killed those two boys?"

"Then the cops will arrest her."

From the corner of my eye, I see Olivia Greene finally exit the boathouse, her onyx hair shimmering in the light, her skin papery and transparent so that I can see the inhuman thing resting inside. A watery, grayish-white image that flickers and shifts, similar to an old black-and-white film. Never solidifying or taking shape, always liquid—drifting elegantly but cruelly beneath the features of Olivia's face. The dark, inky eyes of Marguerite flicker out from behind Olivia's skull and settle on me.

"Let's go," I say to Bo, touching his forearm to urge him to follow me. We start back up the road, Rose and Heath a good distance ahead of us, already pushing through the bramble and overgrown brush.

"What's wrong?" Bo asks, sensing my unease.

But before I can answer, I hear Olivia's voice cut through the crashing waves and the cawing of seagulls circling over the tide pools on the rocky shore. "Penny Talbot!" she calls.

I try to keep walking, but Bo stops and turns around.

Olivia has already broken away from the group gathered outside the boathouse and is walking toward us.

"Don't stop," I hiss to Bo, but he looks at me like I'm not making any sense. He doesn't realize he's in danger just by being close to her.

"Leaving already?" Olivia asks, coming to a stop in front of us with a hand planted smugly on her hip, nails still painted a shiny, morbid black. Marguerite has fully embraced this body. It suits her, fits her already vain, indignant personality.

"We've seen enough," I answer, willing Bo not to speak, not to make eye contact with Olivia or allow her to touch him.

"But I haven't met your new friend," she says with a vampish grin, her pale blue eyes sliding over Bo like she could devour him. "I'm Olivia Greene," she lies, holding out her hand. She smells like black licorice.

Bo lifts his arm to shake her hand, but I grab onto his wrist just before they touch and pull it back down. He frowns at me, but I ignore it. "We really have to go," I say, more to him than to Olivia. And I take a couple steps up the road, hoping he'll follow.

"Oh, Penny," Olivia says blithely, moving forward so she's only a few inches from Bo, her eyes pouring through him. "You can't keep him all to yourself on that island." Before I can stop her, she slides her fingers up to his collarbone, holding his gaze steady on hers. And I know he has no choice, he can't look away. He's captured in her stare. She leans in close so her face is next to his, her lips hovering against his ear. I can't make out what she's saying, but she's whispering something to him, serpentine words that can't be undone. Promises and vows, her voice twining around his heart, drawing it forth from his chest, making him want her—crave her. A *need* that will be planted deep inside him, that won't be satiated until he sees her again, can feel her skin against his. Her fingertips trail up his neck to his cheekbone, and a fury of emotions spark straight down into my gut. Not just fear but something else: jealousy.

"Bo," I say sharply, grabbing his arm again, and Olivia releases him from her snare. He blinks, still watching her like she were a goddess formed of silks and sunsets and gold. Like he has never seen anything so perfect or mesmerizing in his entire life. "Bo," I say again, still holding on to him and trying to snap him from his reverie.

"When you get bored on that island," Olivia says, winking at him, "when you get bored with her . . . come find me." Then she spins around, sauntering back to the group.

She touched him. She wove words together against his ear, enticing him. She wants to make him hers for eternity, pull him into the sea and drown him. She is collecting boys, and now she's dug her delicate, bewitching claws into Bo.

TEN

I start a fire in Bo's cottage.

I know I shouldn't trust this feeling, this unraveling in my heart. It will only end up in a tangled heap. But I need to protect him. Watching Olivia run her fingers up his throat, touching the hard line of his jaw, a sickening lump of dread wretched up from my stomach. *Don't let yourself care*, I recite in my mind. Boys die all too often in this town. But maybe Marguerite's words didn't work, didn't stick. Maybe he resisted. I just need to keep him safe until the summer solstice, keep him from wandering out into the sea in search of her, and then he will leave the island and this town, and we'll never see each other again. Simple. Uncomplicated.

I stand up once the flames have ignited over the logs, sending sparks in a cyclone up the chimney. Bo is sitting on the couch, elbows on his knees, forehead pressed into his palms.

"What did Olivia whisper to you?" I ask, sitting down beside him.

He drops his hands, forehead lined with confusion. "I don't know."

"Do you remember anything?"

His thumb taps against the side of his knee. "I remember her."

His eyes lift, staring into the fire. I don't think I want to hear what he remembers about her, but he tells me anyway. "She was so close, it was like her voice was inside my head. And she was . . . beautiful." He swallows immediately after he says it, like he can't believe his own words.

I push up from the couch and cross my arms beside the fire.

"I can't stop thinking about her," he adds, shaking his head, squinting like he could squeeze her from his mind. But it's not that easy.

"That's how it works," I say, bending down to put another log on the growing flames.

He stares up at me. "You think she's one of them?"

"I know you don't believe any of this, but how can you explain that you can't remember what she said to you? And that you can't stop thinking about her; that you're suddenly so captivated by her?"

"I'm not—" But his words break off. He knows I'm right: He knows his mind keeps slipping back to thoughts of Olivia Greene. Her fingertips against his skin, her eyes sinking so deeply into his, it was like she was looking at the exact center of his soul. A part of him craves her now, wants her as much as she wants him. And it tears at him. He won't be able to stop thinking about her until they're together again. "I don't know anymore. I don't trust my own thoughts."

I pace across the room. *How do I undo this? How do I rid Olivia from his mind?* I don't think it's ever been done before—I don't think it's even possible. He belongs to her now.

I run my tongue along the inside of my teeth. "You have to get away from here. You have to leave town."

Bo stands up from the couch, and the movement makes me

flinch. He walks to the fireplace, stepping in front of me, willing me to look up at him, but I can't. He unsettles me, cracks apart my insides, and I bite down on the feeling, willing it away.

From beneath my eyelashes, I see his lips flatten together, and our breathing seems to settle into the same rhythm. I want him to speak, to cut through the silence, and all at once I feel light-headed, like I might reach out for him to steady myself. But then his lips open and he says, almost like a confession: "My brother was drowned in Sparrow." His eyes cease to blink, his body a stone outline in front of me.

"What?" I lift my gaze.

"That's why I'm here. Why I can't leave . . . not yet. I told you he died, but I didn't tell you how. He drowned here in the harbor."

"When?" My fingertips begin to tingle; the hairs on the back of my neck rise on end as if a cool breeze were gliding across my skin.

"Last summer."

"That's why you came to Sparrow?"

"I didn't know about the Swan sisters. I didn't know about any of it. The police told us that he'd committed suicide, that he'd drowned himself. But I never believed it."

I shake my head a fraction of an inch, trying to understand.

"His name was Kyle," he starts. It's the first time he's said his name out loud to me. "After he graduated high school last year, he and two of his friends took a road trip down the coast. It was supposed to be a surf trip; they planned to drive all the way to Southern California, but they never made it that far." He chokes back something, an emotion threatening to spill past his bulletproof veneer. "They stopped in Sparrow for a night. I don't think they had any idea about the town, about the drownings. They were staying at the

139

SHEA ERNSHAW

Whaler Bed-and-Breakfast. Kyle left his room sometime just after sunset . . . and he never came back. His body was found the next morning tangled in a fishing net not far from shore."

"I'm . . . sorry," I manage, barely above a whisper. A ripple of something shudders through me. A pain that I crush back down.

"He had a scholarship to Montana State in the fall. He had a girlfriend who he wanted to marry. It didn't make any sense. I know he didn't commit suicide. And he was a good swimmer. He surfed every summer; it's not like he would have accidentally drowned."

He takes a step back, unmooring me, and I let out a swift breath I didn't even realize I had been holding in. "None of them committed suicide," I say, thinking of all the boys who've waded out into the harbor, lured to their death.

We look at each other, the seconds stretching out between us.

"Maybe you're wrong about the Swan sisters," he says, extending an arm to touch the mantel over the fireplace, index finger brushing over a scratch in the wood. The heat from the fire has made his cheeks flushed, his lips pink. "Maybe it's just a story that locals tell to explain why so many people have drowned. Maybe someone really is killing them; maybe that girl in the boathouse, Gigi Kline, did do it. Not because she has some ancient witch inside her who's seeking revenge, but because she's just a murderer. And maybe she's not the only one; maybe there are other girls who are killing too . . . who killed my brother."

"But that doesn't explain why boys have drowned in Sparrow for the last two centuries." I need him to believe—to know the Swan sisters exist.

"Maybe it's like a cult," he answers, refusing to accept the truth,

140

"and every generation, its members drown people for some unexplained sacrifice or something."

"A cult?"

"Look, I don't know how cults work. I'm just trying to figure this all out as I go."

"So if you really believe it's just some cult . . . then what?"

"Then I have to stop them from killing anyone else."

"I thought you wanted to go to the police and tell them about Gigi Kline locked in the boathouse? Let them handle it?"

"Maybe that's not enough. Maybe that's not justice—for my brother, for everyone else who's been killed."

"Then what? What would justice be?"

"Putting an end to whatever is happening in this town."

"Killing a Swan sister, you mean? Killing Gigi?"

"Maybe there's no other way," he says.

I shake my head. "There is another way—you can leave Sparrow," I say. "You can go and never come back, and maybe someday you'll even start to forget this place, as if you were never here at all." I don't mean the words I say. I don't want him to leave. Not really. Except I need him to leave so he doesn't get hurt, so he doesn't end up like his brother.

A storm builds in the features of his face, a coldness in his eyes I haven't seen before. "You don't know what it feels like—this pain that won't go away," he says. "I know my brother would do this for me; he wouldn't stop until he found out who was responsible for my death. And he would get revenge."

"This town was built on revenge," I say. "And it's never made anything better or right."

"I'm not leaving," he says with such finality that I feel my throat tighten.

I look up at him like I'm seeing him for the first time, the resoluteness in his eyes, the anger in his jaw. He's searching for a way to rid himself of the pain of losing his brother, and he's willing to sacrifice everything, do whatever it takes, pay any price. Even end someone else's life. "It wasn't those girls," I tell him, pleading with him to understand. "It was the thing inside them."

"Maybe," he answers, lifting his gaze. "But maybe there's no difference between the girl and whatever evil makes them commit murder."

The fire crackles, spitting out sparks onto the wood floor that darken and turn to ash. I walk to the bookshelf beside the fireplace, examining the spines of each book, looking for a way to make him understand without telling him what I know—what I can see.

"Why are you so certain it's real?" he asks, reading my thoughts, and I let my hand fall away from one of the books. I shift onto my heels and turn to face him. He's stepped closer to me, so close I could reach out and touch his chest with the tips of my fingers. I could take one swift step forward and tell him everything, tell him all my secrets, or I could press my lips to his and silence the turmoil rattling around inside my head. But instead I ignore every urge snapping through my veins.

I draw in my lips before I speak, careful to control each word. "I want to tell you," I say, a thousand tons of stones sinking into my stomach. "But I can't."

His eyes flatten on me at the same moment the fire ignites over a dry log and floods the room with a sudden burst of glowing orange light. I was right about Bo, and I was also wrong: He didn't end up in Sparrow by accident. But he's also not a tourist. He came for his brother—to find out what happened to him. And what he found here is far worse than anything he could have imagined.

The pressure in my head expands, the cottage walls start to rotate off axis like a carnival ride out of control, and I feel like I might be sick. I can't stay in here with him. I don't trust myself. I don't trust my heart, thumping wildly like I might do something reckless that I can't take back. I don't know what I'm supposed to feel, supposed to say. *I shouldn't allow myself to feel anything.* It's dangerous, these emotions, the fear pumping through my chest, cracking along each rib. My head isn't thinking straight; it's tangled up with my heart, and I can't trust it.

So I walk to the door and touch the knob, running my fingers around the smooth metal. I close my eyes for a half second and listen to the sounds of the fireplace behind me—warmth and fury, the same exploding conflict happening inside my head—then I open the door and steal out into the evening light.

Bo doesn't try to stop me.

THE OUTSIDER

A year earlier, five days into the start of Swan season, Kyle Carter left the Whaler Bed-and-Breakfast just as the rain lifted. The sidewalks were slick and dark, the sky muted by a cloak of soft white clouds. He had no destination. But the allure of the marina drew him closer.

He reached the metal gangway that led to the marina, rows of boats lined up like sardines in a tin can, and he spotted a girl walking down one of the docks, ebony brown hair loose and sweeping across her back. She looked over her shoulder at him, settled her deep, ocean-blue eyes on his, and then he found himself stumbling after her.

She was the most stunning thing he had ever seen—graceful and enticing. A rare species of girl. And when he reached her, she stroked a hand through his dark hair and pulled him close into a kiss. She wanted him, desired him. And he couldn't resist. So he let her spool her fingers between his and pull him out into the sea. Their bodies entwined, languid and insatiable. He didn't even feel the water when it entered his lungs. All he could think about was her: warm fingers against his skin, lips so soft they melted his flesh, eyes seeing into his thoughts, unraveling his mind.

And then the ocean drew him under and never let go.

ELEVEN

My mind stirs and rattles with all the secrets held captive inside it. I won't be able to sleep. Not now that I know the truth about Bo, about his brother's death.

And I need to keep him safe.

I make a cup of lavender tea, turn on the radio, and sit at the kitchen table. The announcer repeats the same information every twenty minutes: The identity of the two drowned boys has not yet been released, but the police don't believe them to be locals—they're tourists. Eventually, the drone of the announcer's voice bleeds into a slow, drowsy song—a piano melody. Guilt slithers through me, a thousand regrets, and I wish for things I can't have: a way to undo all the deaths, to save the people who've been lost. Boys die all around me. And I do nothing.

I don't realize I've dozed off until I hear the ringing of the telephone mounted to the kitchen wall.

I jerk upright in the stiff wood chair and look to the window over the sink. The sun is barely up—it's morning—the sky still a subdued, pastel gray. I stand and fumble for the phone. "Hello?"

"Did I wake you?" It's Rose's voice on the other end.

"No," I lie.

"I stayed up all night," she says. "Mom kept feeding me cakes, hoping it would help me forget everything that's happened in the last week, but I was so jittery from all the sugar that it made it worse."

I feel distracted, and Rose's words slip ineffectually through my mind. I keep thinking of Bo and his brother.

"Anyway," Rose continues after I don't respond, "I wanted to tell you not to come into town today."

"Why?"

"Davis and Lon are on some kind of crusade. They're questioning everyone; they even cornered Ella Garcia in the girls' bathroom at the Chowder, wouldn't let her leave until she proved she wasn't a Swan sister."

"How'd she prove it?"

"Who knows. But Heath heard that she just started bawling, and Davis didn't think a Swan sister would cry so hysterically."

"Isn't anyone stopping them?"

"You know how it is," Rose says, her voice drifting away from the phone briefly like she's reaching for something. "As long as they don't break any laws, everyone would be relieved if Davis and Lon actually figured out who the sisters were—then maybe they could put an end to all of this."

"There's no ending it, Rose," I reply, thinking back to my conversation with Bo last night in his cottage. He wants to end this too—an eye for an eye. One death for another. But he's never taken a life before—it isn't who he is. It will change him. I hear a *ding* pass through Rose's phone.

"Heath is texting me," she says. "I'm supposed to meet him at his house."

"Maybe you shouldn't leave your house either," I warn.

"My mom doesn't know about Heath yet, so I can't invite him over here. She thinks I'm meeting you for coffee."

"Just be careful."

"I will."

"I mean be careful with Heath."

"Why?"

"You never know what will happen. We still have a week to go."

"He might drown, you mean?" she asks.

"I don't want you to lose someone you care about."

"And what about Bo? Aren't you worried you're going to lose him?"

"No," I say too quickly. "He's not my boyfriend, so I don't . . ." But I feel the lie churning inside my chest and it takes the weight out of my words. I am worried—and I wish I weren't.

Another text chimes through her phone. "I gotta go," she says. "But I'm serious about not coming into town."

"Rose, wait," I say, as if I have something else I need to tell her: some warning, some advice to keep her and Heath safe from the Swan sisters. But she hangs up before I can.

I pick up my mug of cold tea from the table and walk to the sink. I'm about to pour it out when I hear the creaking of floorboards.

"Were you practicing reading the leaves?" she asks from the doorway.

I turn on the faucet. "No."

"You should practice every day." She's chewing on the side of her lip, wearing the black robe that hangs loose across her frame. Soon she'll be so tiny that the wind will carry her away when she stands on the cliff's edge. Maybe that's what she wants.

When I meet her eyes, she's looking at me like I'm a stranger, a girl she no longer recognizes. Not her daughter, but merely a memory.

"Why don't you read the leaves anymore?" I ask, rinsing out the mug and watching the amber tea spiral down the sink. I know this question might stir up bad memories for her . . . but I also wonder if talking about the past might bring her back, shake her loose from her misery.

"Fate has abandoned me," she answers. A shiver passes through her, and her head tilts to the side like she's listening for voices that aren't really there. "I don't trust the leaves anymore. They didn't warn me."

The old silver radio sitting on the kitchen counter is still on—I never shut it off before I fell asleep last night at the table—and music quietly crackles through the speakers. But then the song ends and the announcer promptly returns. "*She has been identified as Gigi Kline,*" he is saying. "*She left her home on Woodlawn Street on Tuesday morning and hasn't been seen since. There is some speculation that her disappearance may have something to do with the Swan season, but local police are asking anyone who may have seen her to contact the Sparrow Police Department.*"

"Do you know Gigi?" Her voice shakes as she asks it, her eyes penetrating the radio. The announcer repeats the same information again then fades to a commercial.

"Not really." I think of Gigi spending the night inside the boathouse, probably hungry and cold. But it's not Gigi who will remember being tied to a chair; only Aurora—the thing inside her—will recall these frigid, shivering nights for years to come. And she will probably seek her revenge on Davis and Lon—if not in the body of Gigi Kline, then next year, inside the body of another girl. Assuming they let Gigi go eventually, and Aurora is able to return to the sea before the Swan season ends.

"When your father disappeared, they announced it on the radio too," she adds, walking to the sink and staring out the window, pushing her hands down into the deep pockets of her robe. "They asked for volunteers to search the harbor and the banks for any sign of him. But no one came out to help. The people in this town never accepted him—their hearts are cold, just like that ocean." Her voice wavers then finds strength again. "It didn't matter, though; I knew he wasn't in the harbor. He was farther out at sea—he was gone, and they'd never find him." This is the first I've heard her speak of him as if he was dead, as if he wasn't ever coming back.

I clear my throat, trying not to lose myself in a wave of emotion. "Let me make you some breakfast," I offer, walking past her. The sunlight is spilling across her face, turning it an unnatural ashen white. I open a cupboard and set one of the white bowls on the counter. "Do you want oatmeal?" I ask, thinking that she needs something warm to shake off the chill in the house.

But her eyes sweep over me and she grabs on to my wrist with her right hand, her fingers coiling around my skin. "I knew," she says coldly. "I knew the truth about what happened to him. I always have." I want to look away from her, but I can't. She's looking through me, into the past, to a time we'd both like to forget.

"What truth?" I ask.

Her dark hair is tangled and knotted, and she looks like she hasn't slept. Then her eyes slide away from mine, like a patient slipping back into a coma, unable to recall what had stirred them from unconsciousness in the first place.

Gently, I pull my arm away from her, and I can see that she's already forgotten what she said.

"Maybe you should go back to bed," I suggest. She nods, and without any protest, she turns and shuffles across the white tile kitchen floor, out into the hall. I can hear her slow, almost weightless footsteps as she makes her way up the staircase and down to her room, where she will likely sleep for the rest of the day.

I lean against the edge of the counter, pinching my eyes shut then opening them again. Against the butter-yellow wallpaper on the far wall of the kitchen is a distorted, stretched-out shadow of me, formed by the morning sunlight spilling in through the window over the sink. I stare at it for a moment, trying to match up elbows and legs and feet. But the more I look at the gray outline against the sun-bleached daffodil wallpaper, the more unnatural it seems. Like an artist's abstract sketch.

I push away from the counter and head for the front door. I can't get out of the house fast enough.

The skiff floats perfectly still against the dock. Not a ripple of water or gust of wind blows across the harbor. The sun is hot overhead, and a fish jumps from the surface of the water then splashes back into the deep.

I've just begun untying the boat and tossing the lines over the side when I sense someone watching me. I whip around and Bo is standing on the starboard side of the sailboat—the *Windsong*—one arm raised, holding on to the mast.

"How long have you been out here?" I ask, startled.

"Since sunrise. I couldn't sleep—my mind wouldn't turn off. I needed to do something."

I imagine him out here, climbing aboard the sailboat, the sun not fully risen, checking the sails and the rigging and the hull to see what's still intact after all these years and what will need to be repaired. His mind working over the problems—anything to keep him from thinking about yesterday at the boathouse, about last night in his cottage. *I have to stop them from killing anyone else*, he had said to me. A promise—a threat—that he would find his brother's killer.

"Are you going into town?" he asks, his jade eyes shivering against the early sunlight.

"Yeah. I have to go do something."

"I'm coming with you," he says.

I shake my head, tossing the last rope into the bow of the boat. "I need to do this by myself."

He drops his arm from the mast and steps over the side rail of the sailboat then hops down onto the dock in one fluid motion. "I need to talk to that girl in the boathouse—Gigi," he says. "I need to ask her about my brother, see if she remembers him."

"That's not a good idea."

"Why not?"

"Olivia might be waiting for you."

"I'm not worried about Olivia."

"You should be," I say.

"I think I can resist whatever powers of seduction you think she has over me."

I let out a short laugh. "Have you been able to stop thinking about her since she touched you yesterday?"

His silence is the only answer I need. But I also feel a sharp stab in the core of my heart, knowing he's been thinking about her all night, all morning, unable to shake the image of her. Only her.

"You're safer here," I tell him, stepping onto the skiff as it begins to drift away from the dock.

"I didn't come here to be trapped on an island," he says.

"Sorry." I start the engine with a swift pull on the cord.

"Wait," he calls, but I shift the boat into gear and pull away from the dock, out of reach.

I can't risk bringing him with me. I need to do this alone. And if Marguerite sees him in town, she might try to take him into the harbor, and I don't know if I can stop her.

Today is the annual Swan Festival in town.

Balloons bounce and swerve across the skyline. Children squeal for shaved ice and saltwater taffy. A red-and-yellow banner stretches across Ocean Avenue announcing the festival, with cartoon cobwebs and full moons and owls printed at the corners.

It's the busiest day of the year—when people drive in from neighboring towns up and down the coast or board buses that shuttle them into Sparrow early in the morning, then haul them back out in the evening. Each year attendance grows, and this year the town feels close to bursting.

Ocean Avenue has been closed off to traffic and is lined with booths and stands selling all manner of both witchy and unwitchy items: wind chimes and wind socks and local boysenberry jam. There is a beer garden selling old-style craft beers in large steins, a woman dressed as a Swan sister reading palms, and even a booth selling perfumes claiming to be some of the original fragrances the sisters once sold at their perfumery—although everyone in Sparrow knows they aren't authentic. Much of the crowd is dressed for the period in high-waisted gowns with ruffles at the sleeves and low necklines. Later tonight, at the stage set up near the pier, there will be a reenactment of the day the sisters were found guilty and drowned—an event I avoid each year. I can't bear to watch it. I can't stand the spectacle it's become.

I push through the crowds, winding my way up Ocean Avenue. I keep my head down. I don't want to be seen by Davis or Lon—I don't need an interrogation from them right now. I leave town and the bustle of the festival, reaching the road that winds through the brambles to the boathouse. There's no way to access it except from this road; I don't have a choice but to walk straight down it.

Seagulls turn and spiral overhead like vultures waiting for death, sensing it.

When the road widens and the ocean comes into view, flat and glittery, the boathouse seems small and plain, more sunken into the earth than it did yesterday. Lon is sitting on a stump against the right side of the boathouse. At first I think he's staring up at the sky, soaking up the sun, but as I inch closer I realize he's asleep, his head canted back against the outer wall. He's probably been out here all night guarding Gigi, one leg stretched out in front of him, arms hanging limp at his sides, jaw hung slightly open. He's wearing one of his stupid floral-print shirts, teal with purple flowers, and if it weren't for the dreary backdrop he'd almost look like he was on a tropical beach somewhere, working on his nonexistent tan.

I move quietly, careful not to step on a twig or dried leaf that might give me away, and when I reach the boathouse, I pause to look down at Lon. For a brief moment, I think maybe he's not breathing, but then I see his chest rise and his throat swallow.

The wood door isn't locked, and I push it easily inward.

Gigi is still sitting in the white plastic chair, arms tied, chin to chest like she's sleeping. But her eyes are open, and she slides them up to meet mine as soon as I step inside.

I walk toward her and pull the gag out of her mouth then take a swift step back.

"What are you doing here?" she asks, lifting her chin, her cropped blond hair falling back from her face. She stares at me through her lashes, and her tone is not sweet, but low, almost guttural. The waspy, flickering outline of Aurora shifts lazily beneath her skin. But her emerald-green eyes, the same inherited color of each Swan sister, blink serpent-like out at me.

"I'm not here to save you, if that's what you think," I tell her, keeping my distance back from the white chair that has become her cage.

"Then what do you want?"

"You killed those two boys they pulled from the harbor, didn't you?" She eyes me like she's trying to understand the real motivation behind my question. What purpose I have for asking it.

"Maybe." Her lips tug at the edges. She's holding back a smile—she finds this amusing.

"I doubt it was Marguerite." At this her eyes broaden to perfect orbs. "Only you would drown two boys at once."

She shifts her jawbone side to side then wriggles her fingers like she's trying to stretch them, her wrists confined by zip ties. The lime-green polish on her fingernails is starting to chip, and her hands look waterlogged and pale. "You came here just to accuse me of killing those boys?" she asks.

I stare through her sheer exterior, beyond Gigi, finding the monster inside her—meeting Aurora's gaze. And she knows it. Knows I'm looking at the real her.

Her expression changes. She grins, revealing Gigi's bleached white and perfectly aligned teeth. "You want something," she says pointedly.

I take a deep breath. *What do I want?* I want her to stop. Stop killing. Stop seeking revenge. Stop this vicious game she's been playing for too long. I'm a fool to believe she would listen to me. Hear my words. But I try anyway. For Bo. For me. "Stop this," I finally say.

"Stop?" Her tongue pushes against the inside of her cheek, and she examines me through lowered eyelashes.

"Stop drowning boys."

"I can't do much drowning tied up in here, can I?" She sucks in a long breath through her nostrils, and I'm surprised when she doesn't grimace—the boathouse smells fouler than I remember. Her eyes narrow. "If you untie me, then perhaps we can discuss this little idea of yours."

I examine the zip ties around her wrists and ankles. A quick yank, and I might be able to break them free. If I had a knife, I could easily slice through the plastic. But I won't do that. I won't set her loose on Sparrow again.

I shake my head. "I can't."

"You don't trust me?" She doesn't even try to hide the wicked curl of her upper lip or the playful arch of her left eyebrow. She knows I don't trust her—why would I? "'Trust' is an irrelevant word anyway," she sneers when I don't respond. "Merely a lie we tell each other. I've learned not to trust anyone—a symptom of two centuries of existence. You have the time to consider such things." She tilts her head, looking at me from the side. "I wonder who you trust? Who you would trust with your life?"

I stare at the thing beneath Gigi's skin, eyes milky white and watching me.

"Who would you trust with yours?" I counter.

This forces a laugh from deep within her gut, eyes watering. I take a step back. Then her laughter stops, blond hair sliding forward to cover part of her face. Her arms stiffen against her restraints and her real eyes cut through me. Her mouth twists into a snarl. "No one."

The door behind me suddenly bangs open and Lon bursts into the room. "What the fuck are you doing in here?" His eyes are huge.

I glance from Gigi back to him. "Just asking her a couple questions."

"No one's allowed in here. She'll trick you into letting her go."

"That only works on the weak-minded male specimen," I tell him.

His lips stiffen together, and he takes a quick step toward me. "Get the hell out of here. Unless you want to confess to being one of them, then I'll gladly lock you up too."

I glance at Gigi, who sits defiantly blinking back at me, the side of her lip turned upward. She looks like she might even dare to laugh—she finds his threat amusing—but she holds it in. Then I step back out the door into the daylight.

"You realize the police are looking for Gigi," I tell Lon when he follows me out, closing the door behind him with a loud clatter.

"The police in this town are idiots."

"Maybe. But it's only a matter of time before they check the boathouse."

He waves a hand in the air dismissively, his floral shirtsleeve flapping with the motion, and returns to his post on the stump, leaning back against the wall and closing his eyes, obviously not concerned about Gigi escaping. "And tell your friend Rose not to come back either."

I stop midstride. "What?"

"Rose . . . your friend," he says mockingly, as if I don't know who she is. "She was here twenty minutes ago, caught her sneaking through the brush."

"Did she talk to Gigi?"

"My job is to keep people out, so no, I didn't let her talk to Gigi."

"What did she want?" I ask, although I'm certain whatever she told him was a lie.

"Hell if I know. Said she felt bad for Gigi or some crap, that it was cruel to keep her locked up. But you both had better stay away unless you want to be suspects." His voice lowers a bit like he's telling me a secret, like he's trying to help me. "We're going to find all the Swan sisters one way or another."

I turn and hurry up the road.

* * *

Alba's Forgetful Cakes smells like vanilla bean frosting and lemon cake when I step through the door. A dozen people crowd the small store—some wearing festival costumes, kids with faces painted in glitter and gold—picking out tiny cakes from the glass cases to be boxed up and tied with bubblegum-pink ribbon. Mrs. Alba stands behind one of the deli cases helping a customer, carefully placing petit fours into white boxes. Two other employees are also moving quickly around the shop, ringing people up and answering questions about the effectiveness of the cakes at wiping away old, stagnant memories.

But Rose is not in the store, and I wait several minutes before Mrs. Alba is free.

I press my fingertips against a glass case, hoping to get her attention. "Penny," Mrs. Alba chirps when she sees me, her grin stretching wide across the soft features of her face. "How are you?"

"I'm looking for Rose," I say quickly.

Her expression sags and then her eyes pinch flat. "I thought she was with you." On the phone, Rose told me that she had lied to her mother, saying that she was meeting me for coffee when she was really meeting Heath. But since she obviously wasn't meeting Heath, either, unless they went to the boathouse together to see Gigi, I thought Mrs. Alba might actually have seen her.

"I think I just got the time wrong, or where we were supposed to meet," I say with an easy smile—I don't want to get Rose into trouble. "I thought maybe she'd be here."

"You can check the apartment," she says, turning her gaze as several more customers enter the shop.

"Thank you," I answer, but she's already shuffled away to help the new patrons.

Back outside, I turn right and climb the covered stairs up to the second floor. The gray-shingled walls of the building are protected from the rain under a narrow roof, and at the top of the stairs there is a red door under a white archway. I press my finger against the doorbell, and the ring echoes through the spacious apartment. Their dog, Marco, begins yapping furiously, and I can hear the clatter of his paws as he races to the door, barking from the other side. I wait, but no one comes. And there's no way Rose could be inside and not know someone was at the door.

I head back down the stairs and push through the crowds across Ocean Avenue. I start down Shipley Pier toward the Chowder, when I spot Davis McArthurs. He's standing halfway down the pier among the throngs of people, talking to a girl I recognize from the boathouse when they first caught Gigi. She had argued with Davis about keeping Gigi locked up. His arms are crossed, his eyes surveying the outdoor tables like he's looking for any girl he's missed—who he hasn't yet interrogated for being a Swan sister.

A burning fury rises inside me at seeing Davis. But there's nothing I can do.

Rose wouldn't be on the pier anyway, not with Davis strutting around. She's probably back at Heath's house, but I don't know where he lives—and I'm not about to ask around and make myself known. So I hurry back to the marina before Davis sees me, and I motor across the harbor to the island.

FORETELLING

A woman stepped through the door of the Swan Perfumery early one morning on a Thursday, a week after the sisters' night at the tavern.

Aurora was sweeping the shop floor, Marguerite was leaning against the counter daydreaming about a boy she had seen working the rigging on a ship in the harbor the day before, and Hazel was scribbling notes on a piece of paper for a new scent she had been imagining: myrrh, tansy, and rose hips. A fragrance to ease sadness and clear away mistrust in others.

When the woman entered, Marguerite straightened and smiled pleasingly as she did whenever a new customer visited the shop. "Good morning," Marguerite spoke elegantly, as if she were raised by royals, when in fact all three sisters were raised by a woman who'd lewdly dabbed perfume between her thighs to entice her lovers.

The woman did not respond, but walked to a wall of bottled perfumes all containing hues of citrus and other fruit, meant for daytime wear, often cajoling memories of late summer winds and warm evenings. "A perfume shop seems a tad presumptuous in this town," the woman finally spoke. "Illicit even."

"Women in any town deserve the allure of a good scent,"

Marguerite responded, raising an eyebrow. Marguerite did not show it, but she recognized the woman—she was the wife of a man Marguerite had flirted with outside the Collins & Gray General Store three days earlier.

"*Allure*," the woman repeated. "An interesting choice of words. And this allure—" She paused. "It comes from the spells you cast in your scents?"

Marguerite's mouth quirked sharply upward on one side. "No spells, madam. Just perfectly arranged fragrances, I assure you."

The woman glared at Marguerite then swiftly moved toward the door. "Your devious work will not go unnoticed for long. We see what you really are." And in a whir of salty sea air, she opened the door and hurried back out to the street, leaving the three sisters staring after her.

"They really do think we're witches, don't they?" Hazel said aloud.

"Let them think it. It gives us power over them," Marguerite answered.

"Or gives them reason to hang us," Aurora added.

Marguerite sauntered to the center of the store, winking back at her sisters. "The boys all seem to like it," she replied with a sway of her hips.

Both Hazel and Aurora laughed. Marguerite had always been unabashed and they admired this quality in her, even if at times it got her into trouble. The three sisters were close, devoted to one another. Their lives interwoven as tightly as a sailor's knot.

They didn't yet know the things that would divide them.

For in a place like Sparrow, rumors spread quickly, like small pox or cholera, confusing the mind, rooting itself into the fabric of a town until there's no telling truth from speculation.

TWELVE

I dial Rose's cell when I get back to the house, but she doesn't answer, so I leave a message: "Call me when you get this."

I don't know why she went to see Gigi at the boathouse, but whatever the reason, I need to tell her to stay away.

Through the kitchen window, I see Mom standing out on the cliff, her black robe billowing around her legs with an updraft of wind. She didn't stay in bed all day after all.

I wait by the phone for most of the day, but Rose never calls. I dial her number three more times, but she doesn't answer. *Where is she?*

When the sun starts to settle over the ocean, I curl up in bed, knees to chest. I fall asleep with the wind rattling the glass in the windows, the sea air driving against the house.

Just after dawn it starts raining, gently pattering against the roof. The sky is painted in brushstroke ribbons of violet and coral pink. I stay in my room, but still no word from Rose. The rain keeps everyone inside. Mom locks herself in her bedroom, and I don't see Bo leave the cottage all day. There are things I should say to him—confessions buried inside me. The way my heart feels unmoored when I'm with him. My head loose with thoughts I can't explain. I should say I'm sorry. I should walk down through the rain and beat my fist against his door. I should touch his skin with my fingertips and tell him there are things I want, I crave. But how do you let yourself unravel in front of someone, knowing your armor is the only thing keeping you safe?

So I don't say anything. I keep my heart hidden deep and dark in my chest.

Evening eventually presses down and I slump in the chair beside my bedroom window, watching the sky peel apart and the rainclouds fade. Stars illuminate the dark. But I feel anxious, wishing Rose would just call, explain why she went to the boathouse. She's acting suspicious—making herself seem like one of them. Why?

And then I see something through the window.

Movement down on the path, a silhouette passing beneath the cascade of blue moonlight. It's Bo, and he's heading toward the dock.

And in my gut, I sense that something isn't right.

I pull on a long black sweater over my cotton shorts and tank top and hurry down the stairs to the front door. The air hits me as soon as I step outside, a blast of cold that cuts straight down to my marrow.

I lose sight of him for a moment, the darkness absorbing him, but when I reach the point in the path where it slopes down toward the water, I see him again. And he's almost to the dock.

The evening wind has stirred up from the west, and it pushes waves against the shore in intervals, spilling up over the rocks and leaving behind a layer of foam. Everything smells soggy from the rain. My bare feet are slapping against the wood walkway, but I still catch up to him just as he stops at the far end of the dock.

"Bo?" I ask. But he doesn't move, doesn't turn to look at me. Like he can't even hear me. And I already know. Under the dark sky and the pale, swollen moon, I can tell he's not himself.

I take two careful steps toward him. "Bo," I say again, trying to get his attention. But in one swift motion, he steps forward and falls straight off the edge of the dock and down into the water. "No!" I yell, scrambling forward.

The harbor heaves and churns. He's already gone under, sunk beneath the waves. I hold my breath, counting the seconds—how long does he have until there's no more air left in his lungs? I scan the water, afraid to blink. Then, ten yards out, he appears, sucking in a breath of air as he breaks through the surface. But he doesn't turn back for shore. He doesn't even look over his shoulder. He keeps going, swimming farther out into the harbor.

No, no, no. This is bad.

I strip out of my black sweater and drop it onto the dock. I draw in a deep breath, reach my arms over my head, and dive in after him.

The cold water cuts through my skin like needles, and when I gulp in the night air, it stings the inner walls of my lungs. But I start swimming.

He is already a good distance ahead of me, determined, being beckoned deeper into the bay. But my arms and legs find a fluid rhythm that is faster than his. His feet, still in his shoes, kick little explosions of water out behind him. When I'm finally within reach, I grab on to his T-shirt and pull hard. His arms stop circling overhead, and his legs pause their kicking. He lifts his head, hair slicked sideways over his forehead, lips parted, and looks at me.

"Bo," I say, meeting his stony eyes. His eyelashes drip with sea-water, his expression slack, unaware of where he is or what he's doing. "We need to go back," I yell over the wind.

He doesn't shake his head, doesn't protest, but he also doesn't seem to register anything I've said, because he drops his gaze and roughly pulls away, resuming his swim across the harbor. I suck in a few quick breaths. The beam of light from the lighthouse circles around, sweeping over the harbor and illuminating the masts of sunken ships. He's being summoned to the wreckage, by *her*.

"Shit." My skin is chilled and weighted from my clothes. But I push my legs out behind me and swim after him, through the dark, knowing that a boat passing through the harbor likely wouldn't see us in time. We'd be forced under by the bow, churned up by the prop, and might never come back up again. But if I let him go, I know what will happen. I will lose him for good.

I kick hard, my arms cutting through the water, the cold starting to slow my heartbeat and the blood pumping out to my extremities. But after several more rotations of the lighthouse—the only thing marking time—I manage to catch up to him again. I wrap my fist around the hem of his shirt and yank him back toward me. He turns to look at me, the same expression etched permanently on his face.

"You need to wake up," I scream at him. "You can't do this!"

His eyebrows pucker a fraction of an inch. He hears me, but he's also lost to Marguerite—her voice cycling through his mind, calling to him, begging him to find her somewhere out there.

"Bo," I say, harder this time, twisting my other fist around his shirt and pulling him closer to me. My legs kick quickly beneath me to keep from sinking under. "Wake up!"

He blinks. His lips are ghostly, lost of all color. He opens his mouth, squints slightly, and a word forms softly against his lips. "What?"

"She's in your head, making you do this. You need to get her out, ignore what she's telling you. It's not real."

Several yards ahead, toward the mouth of the harbor, the bell buoy rings against the force of the waves. An eerie sound that rolls across the water.

"I need to find her," he says, voice slurred. I know the image she has placed in his mind: of her, swimming in a pearl-white dress, fabric thin and transparent swirling around her body, hair long and silken, her beguiling voice slipping into his ears. Her words promise warmth, the velvet of her kiss and her body pressed to his. He is caught in her spell.

She will drown him like all the others.

"Please," I beg, staring into eyes that can't focus—that only see her. "Come back with me."

He shakes his head slowly. "I . . . can't."

I clench my jaw and wrap my hands around the back of his neck, forcing him so close that our bodies slide weightlessly together. I do it without thinking, without breathing. I crush my lips to his. Water spills between us, and I taste the sea on his skin. I dig my nails into the base of his neck, trying to spur him from his waking dream. My heartbeat drives against my chest, and I press my lips harder. I open my mouth to feel the warmth of his breath, but he doesn't move, doesn't react. Maybe this won't work—maybe it was a mistake.

But then one of his arms slides around me, bracing against my shoulder blades. His mouth parts open, and the heat from his body suddenly pours into me. His other hand finds my cheekbone and then weaves through my hair. He draws me in deeper, folding me in the circle of his arms. And with my lips, I wipe away the memory of Marguerite Swan from his mind. I take him from her, and he lets me. He kisses me like he wants me more than he's ever wanted anything. And for a second, none of it feels real. I am not swimming in the harbor, wrapped in Bo's arms, his mouth sweeping over mine, my heart pattering wildly against the cage of my chest. We are somewhere else, far away from here, coiled against each other under a warm sun with warm sand at our backs and warm breath on our lips. Two bodies bound together. Fearing nothing.

And then he pulls his mouth away, slowly, water dripping between us, and everything focuses into a single narrow pinprick. I expect him to release me, to resume his swim across the harbor, but he keeps a hand tangled at the back of my skull and the other against my back, our legs kicking rhythmically beneath us. "Why did you do that?" he asks, his voice raw and near breaking.

"To save you."

His eyes glance out at the dark forbidding sea, as if waking up from an all-too-real nightmare.

"We need to get back to shore," I tell him, and he nods understanding, his eyes still bleary and unfocused, like he's still not entirely sure where he is or why.

We swim side by side back to the dock. We've drifted farther away from it than I realized, the current drawing us out to sea, and after several minutes of swimming hard, we finally reach it. He wraps his hands around my waist and hoists me up to the edge of the dock, and then he pulls himself up after. We're too cold to speak, collapsing onto our backs on the dock, heaving in the chilled night air. I know we need to get inside and get warm before hypothermia sets in—a real possibility out here. So I touch his hand and we both rise, jogging up the wood path to his cottage.

We tug off our shoes and Bo kneels down beside the fireplace—a few embers are still alive beneath the charred logs—while I curl up on the couch with two wool blankets held tightly over my shoulders. Otis and Olga appear from the bedroom, stretching and looking sleepy. They've been spending all their time in here with Bo; they like him. Maybe more than they like me.

Bo adds more logs to the fire, and I crawl onto the floor beside him, stretching out my arms to warm my palms against the meager flames. My teeth chatter, and my fingertips are wrinkled. "You're freezing," he says, looking down at my trembling body beneath the blankets. "You need to get out of those clothes." He stands up and walks back into his bedroom, returning a moment later with a plain white T-shirt and a pair of green boxer shorts. "Here," he says. "You can wear these."

I consider telling him that I'm fine, but I'm not fine. My shorts and tank top are so drenched that they're starting to soak the blankets as well. So I stand up, thank him, and take the clothes into the bathroom.

The white tile floor is cold beneath my feet, and for a moment I stand scanning the tiny bathroom. A razor and a toothbrush sit beside the sink. A towel hangs from the rack. Hints that someone has been living in this cottage after so many years vacant. I slog out of my clothes then drop them heavily onto the floor in a pile. I don't even bother folding them.

Bo's shirt and boxers smell like him, minty and sweet, but also like a forest. I take in a deep breath and close my eyes before stepping back out into the living room. The fire now crackles and flames spark up the chimney, filling the cottage with warmth.

I sit on the floor beside Bo and pull the blankets around me. He doesn't turn to look at me; he is staring into the flames, biting his lower lip. While I was in the bathroom, he changed into dry jeans and a dark blue T-shirt. Both of us are now rid of our waterlogged clothes. "What happened out there?" he asks.

I tighten the blankets across my chest. The rain batters against the roof; the wind howls. "You were being led into the harbor."

"How?"

"You know how."

"Olivia," he says, as if the name has been trapped on his lips for days. "I could see her . . . out in the water."

"She was calling to you. Her voice infiltrated your mind."

"How?" he asks again.

"At the boathouse she whispered something in your ear. She claimed you as hers, making it impossible for you to think of anything or anyone else. It was only a matter of time until she beckoned you. Since you've remained on the island, hidden, she couldn't physically pull you out into the water, so she had to slip her voice into your mind and make you come in search of her."

He shakes his head, unable to rectify what has just happened to him.

"Olivia Greene," I tell him bluntly, "is Marguerite Swan. She was waiting for you out in the harbor; she would have pulled you to her, her lips on yours, and then she would have drowned you."

He leans forward against his knees, teeth clamped shut. I stare at the scar beside his left eye, his cheekbones are starting to blaze from the heat of the fire. My focus slides back to his lips, to the way they felt pressed to mine. "But how do you know that?" he asks. "How can you be so sure it's Marguerite Swan who's taken over Olivia's body? And not one of the other sisters?" He squints, like he can't believe his own question, that he's even asking it.

"You just need to trust me," I say. "Marguerite wants to kill you. And she won't stop until she finds a way to do it."

"Why me?" he asks.

"Because she saw you with me at the boathouse."

"What does that have to do with anything?"

My fingers tremble slightly; my heart pushes against my ribs, warning me not to tell him the truth. But the truth tastes like letting go, like the sharpness of sunlight on a spring day, and my head begins to pulse with every heartbeat. "I can see them," I confess, the words tumbling out before I can catch them.

"Them?"

"The sisters. I can see Aurora inside of Gigi Kline and Marguerite inside of Olivia Greene. I know whose bodies they've taken."

He straightens, lifting his elbows away from his knees. "How's that even possible?"

I shake my head, the air gone from my lungs, and a shiver races up my entire body.

"You can see them and you haven't said anything?"

"No one knows."

"But . . ." His mouth dips open, eyes narrowed on me. "You can see what they really are?"

"Yes."

I stand up, crossing my arms. I can tell he's trying to piece it all together, make everything fit. But his mind is fighting him. He doesn't want to believe what I'm telling him could be true. "How long have you been able to do this?"

"Always."

"But how?"

I lift my shoulders. "I don't know. I mean . . . it's just something I've always been able to do. . . . I . . ." I'm rambling, getting lost in the explanation. In the deception beneath the truth.

"Can your mom see them too?"

I shake my head.

He frowns and looks down into the fire, rubbing the back of his neck with his right hand. "Do they know . . . do the sisters know you can see them?"

"Yes."

Again his mouth parts open, searching for words, for the right question to make this all make sense. "What about the third one—the third sister?"

"Hazel," I answer for him.

"Where is she? Whose body has she stolen?"

"I don't know."

"You haven't seen her yet?"

"No."

"But she's out there somewhere?"

"Yes."

"And she hasn't killed anyone yet?"

I shake my head. "Not yet."

"So there's still time to find her and stop her."

"There's no stopping them," I answer.

"Have you tried?"

I can't meet his eyes. "No. It's pointless to try." I think about my encounter with Gigi in the boathouse. I had thought—foolishly—maybe I could talk to her, the *real* her. Aurora. Maybe some part of her was still human, still had a beating heart that would be tired of the killing. But Lon interrupted us. And I sense she's too far gone anyway. My words would never be enough.

Bo drops his palm from the back of his neck. And I can see in his eyes that he's starting to believe me. "Fuck, Penny," he says, standing up and taking a step toward me. "So Lon and Davis were right? They do have a Swan sister locked in that boathouse?"

I nod.

"And Olivia . . . or Marguerite—whatever her name is—is trying to kill me?"

"She's already slipped into your mind. She can make you see things that aren't there, feel things that aren't real."

"When I saw her," he says, "in the water . . . waiting for me. It felt like I needed her, like I'd die if I didn't get to her. Like . . ." He swallows back the words, choking on them.

"Like you loved her?" I finish for him.

"Yeah." His eyes find mine.

"She can convince you that you've never loved anyone quite so much or ever will again."

He clenches his fists together at his sides and I watch the motion, his forearms flexing, his temples pulsing.

"And then you were there," he says, recounting the moment

when I jumped into the ocean after him. "I could hear you but I couldn't focus on you. You seemed so far away. But then I felt your hands. You were right in front of me." He looks up, the darkest centers of his eyes like the darkest depths of the ocean. "And then you kissed me."

"I . . ." My voice feels strangled in my throat. "I had to stop you."

A beat of silence. My heart stumbles, catches, restarts again.

"After that," he says, "I didn't feel her calling me anymore. I still don't."

"Maybe we broke her hold on you," I say, my voice feeling small.

"*You* broke her hold on me."

Words tangle up on my tongue. All the things I want to say. "I needed to bring you back. I couldn't let you go; I couldn't lose you. I couldn't let . . ." The weight of my honesty rattles the very center of my ribs, my stomach, the place just behind my eyes. "I couldn't let her have you."

I don't allow myself to look away from him—I need him to speak, to wash over my words with his own. In his eyes, a storm waits at the edges. His hand lifts, and his fingers slide up the ridge of my cheekbone and behind my ear. The sensation of his fingertips against my skin unweaves the stone knitted together at the base of my heart. I close my eyes briefly then open them again, a craving rising up inside me, pure and uncorrupt. He pulls me forward, and I pause only a feather's width from his mouth. I look into his eyes, trying to root myself in the moment. And then he kisses me like he needs me to root him here too.

His lips are warm and his fingertips cold. All at once I am wrapped up in him: his heart battering just beneath his chest, his hands in my hair, his mouth searching my lower lip. He is every-where, filling my lungs and the space between each breath. And I feel myself falling, tumbling like a star dropping from the sky and spinning toward Earth. My heart stretches outward, becomes light and jittery.

This moment—this boy—could tear me apart and upend every-thing. But in the heat of the cottage, wind rattling the glass in the win-dows, rain pelting the roof, with our skin flecked with salt water, I don't care. I let his hands roam my chilled flesh and my fingers weave up the back of his neck. I don't want to be anywhere else. I only want him. *Him.*

Love is an enchantress—devious and wild.

It sneaks up behind you, soft and gentle and quiet, just before it slits your throat.

I wake on the hardwood floor beside the fireplace, Bo asleep next to me, his arm folded over my hip bone. He is breathing softly against my hair. My eyes skirt across the living room, remembering where I am: his cottage. The fire has turned to coals, all the logs burned down, so I shimmy from beneath his arm—his fingers twitching—and slide a fresh log into the fireplace, pushing it through the coals. It takes only a moment for the flames to reignite.

I cross my legs and run my fingers through my hair. I smell like him, his T-shirt still against my skin. I know I can't leave him alone now. Marguerite will try again. And I won't let her have him. This thing I feel for him is working its way into my bones, like water through cracks in my surface. When it freezes, it will either shatter me into a million pieces or make me stronger.

I pick up one of the books sitting on the floor next to me, flipping through the pages. There are notes in the margins, paragraphs highlighted, corners dog-eared. The ink is faded and smeared in places.

"I think they were your father's books," Bo says. His eyes are open, but he's still lying on the floor, watching me. He must have heard me sit up.

"Why do you think that?"

"They were purchased from a bookstore in town. And there's a name in the front of that one." I flip back to the front cover where a piece of paper sits tucked into the crease. Handwritten with black ink on the paper is the name JOHN TALBOT. It was a book he had special ordered, or maybe put on hold. And an employee wrote his name on a slip of paper until he came to pay for it. "Your father was John Talbot, right?"

"Yeah." Beneath the paper is a folded receipt from the Olive Street Tea & Bookhouse. It's dated June fifth, three years earlier. Only a week before he disappeared.

"He must have been researching the Swan sisters," Bo says. "Maybe he was looking for a way to stop them."

A scattering of memories crack through me, of the night I saw him moving down to the dock in the dark. The night he vanished. The rain fell sideways, and the wind ripped shingles from the roof of the house. But he would never return to repair them.

He had been collecting these books all along, in secret, looking for a way to end the Swan season.

"Are you all right?" Bo sits up, creases formed between his brows.

"Fine." I close the cover of the book and set it back on the floor. "And you've read most of them?" I ask.

He nods, stretching upright.

"And what did you find?"

"Mostly speculation about witches and curses—nothing definitive."

"Anything about how to end a curse?"

He shifts his gaze to me, exhaling. "Only the obvious."

"Which is?"

"Destroy the purveyors of it."

"The sisters."

"The only way to end it would be to kill them," he says.

"But then both the Swan sister and the girl whose body they stole would die."

He nods.

"And you still want to kill Gigi Kline?" I ask.

"I want whoever killed my brother to pay for it. And if the only way to do that is to destroy both the girl and the monster, then that's what I'll do."

I brush both hands through my hair, catching on knots that my fingers must work through before I can twist my mass of hair over my shoulder. "Does this mean you believe in the Swan sisters now?"

"I don't think I have a choice," he says. "One of them is trying to kill me." The fullness of his lips seems amplified as he pushes them together, a rivulet of tension passing over his expression. It can't be easy knowing someone—some*thing*—wants you dead.

But what's even harder is knowing it's your fault. Marguerite wouldn't want Bo so badly if he were just some random tourist. It's because of me that she's so intrigued by him. She loves a challenge. And Bo is the perfect prey.

I stand up from the floor. Otis and Olga had been sleeping on the couch, curled up together at one end. But now Olga is awake, her ears alert, head turned toward the door.

"I'm sorry you're here," I say, rubbing my palms down my arms. "I'm sorry you got dragged into this."

"It's not your fault." His voice is deep, his eyebrows angled downward, softening the hard edges of his face. "I came here because of my brother. I did this; not you."

"If you weren't on this island with me," I tell him, forcing the tears down so they don't rise up. "Then she wouldn't want you. I was wrong when I thought keeping you here on the island would make you safe. She'll find you wherever you are."

"No." He stands up too but doesn't touch me, doesn't run his hands up my arms to comfort me—not yet. "She's not in my head anymore," he says. "I don't hear her voice, feel her thoughts. You broke whatever hold she had on me."

"For now. But she'll try again. She'll come for you, here to the island if she has to. She'll physically drag you out into the water. She won't give up."

"If I'm not safe, then you're not safe."

"It doesn't work like that," I tell him. "It's you she will drown. Not me." My stomach begins to wrench and turn.

"If you can see them, and they know it, then you're in danger too."

I think of Marguerite out in the harbor, waiting for Bo, beckoning him with the promise of her lips skimming delicately over his. She is a wraith dredged up from the seafloor. She is vengeful and clever. She is single-minded in her hatred for this town. And she won't stop.

"You can't protect me," I tell him. "Just like I can't protect you."

Olga hops down from the couch and trots between us to the front door, stretching up on her hind legs to scratch at the wood. She begins to mew, and it wakes Otis.

"I can try," Bo says, moving closer, and in his eyes I see the ocean, and it draws me into him like the tide against the sand.

His hands find me in the firelight, grazing my wrists, my arms, then his palms slide up to my jaw, through my hair, fingerprints on my skin, and for a moment I believe him. Maybe he can keep me safe; maybe this thing threading between us is enough to keep all the terrors at bay. I suck in a breath and try to steady the two halves of my heart, but when his lips brush against mine, I lose all rooting to the earth. My heart turns wild. His fingers pull me closer, and I press myself against him, needing the steadiness of his heartbeat inside his chest and the balance of his arms. My own fingers slide up beneath his shirt: feeling the firmness of his torso, air filling his lungs. He is strong, stronger than most. Maybe he can survive this town, survive Marguerite. Survive me. I dig my fingers into his skin, his shoulders, losing myself to him. He feels like everything—all that's left. The world has been shredded around me. But this, *this*, might be enough to smooth the brittle edges of my once-beating heart.

The fire makes the heat between us almost unbearable. But we fold ourselves together among the pages of books and the blankets scattered across the floor. The wind roars outside. His fingers trace the moons of my hip bones, my thighs, my shivering heartbeat. He kisses down my throat, the place where my secrets are kept. He kisses my collarbone, where the skin is thin and delicate, patterns of freckles like a sailor's map. He kisses so softly it feels like wings or a whisper. He kisses and I slip, slip, slip beneath his touch. Crumbling.

His lips inch beneath my shirt, along the curves of my body. Valleys and hills. Breathing promises he'll keep against my skin. My clothes feel burdensome and heavy—clothes that belong to him, boxers and a T-shirt—so I peel them away.

My mind spins, my breathing catches then rises again. My skin crackles, set alight, and his touch feels infinite, fathomless, a wave that rolls ashore but never ends. He is gentle and sweet, and I never want his hands, his lips, to be anywhere else but against me. The morning sunlight is just starting to break above the horizon, soft pinks sifting through the windows, but I am breaking here on the floor, shattering into pieces as he whispers my name and I see only flecks of light shivering across my vision. And after, he holds his lips above mine, breathing the same air, my skin shimmering from the heat. Sweat dewing the curves of my body. He kisses my nose, my forehead, my earlobes.

I have doomed him, kept him here, made him the prey of Marguerite Swan. He is caught in the tempest of a season that could kill him. He needs to leave Sparrow, escape this wretched place. Yet I need him to stay. I *need* him.

JOHN TALBOT

O n June fifth, a week before he vanished, John Talbot entered the Olive Street Tea & Bookhouse. He had special ordered four books a week earlier, titles he had researched online that contained real-life accounts of hexes and curses that had been documented in other unfortunate towns.

It was not unusual for locals in Sparrow to take an interest in the Swan sisters. They often collected newspaper clippings and old photographs of the town from when the sisters were still alive. They shared stories at the Silver Dollar Pub over too many beers, and then stumbled down to the docks and shouted into the night about their sons and brothers who they've lost. And sometimes they even became obsessed. Sorrow and desperation can make cracks along the mind.

But John Talbot never shared his theories. He never got drunk and lamented the tragedy of Sparrow over a pint. He never told anyone about the collection of books he kept stashed in Anchor Cottage. Not even his wife.

And on that bright, warm afternoon, as he left the bookstore, there was frenzy in his shadowed eyes, lines of worry carved along his forehead. His gaze darted side to side, as if the sunlight were unbearable, and he pushed through the horde of tourists back down to the skiff waiting at the dock.

Those who saw him that day would later say he had the look of someone overcome with sea madness. The island had been known to drive people insane. The salt air, the isolation. It had finally gotten to him.

John Talbot had lost his mind.

THIRTEEN

Two days slip by uncounted.

Bo's fingers coil through my hair, he watches me sleep, and he keeps me warm when the wind tears through the cracks in the cottage windows in the early hours of morning. He slides himself beside me beneath the wool blanket and runs his fingertips down my arm. I've forgotten about everything else but this little room, this fireplace, this spot in my heart that aches to the point of bursting.

On the third day, we wake and walk down the rows of the newly revived orchard trees under a tepid afternoon sky; the leaves are beginning to unfurl and the flowers just starting to break open. This season's apples and pears might still be stunted and hard and inedible. But by next year, hopefully our hard work will produce fat, sun-sweetened fruit.

"What were you like in school?" I ask, craning my head upward to soak up the sun. Little white spots dance across my closed eyelids.

"What do you mean?"

"Were you popular?"

He reaches out a hand and touches the craggy end of a branch, small green leaves sliding through his palm. "No."

"But you had friends?"

"A few." He glances at me, his jade-green eyes spearing a hole straight through my center.

"Did you play sports?" I'm trying to piece together the person he was, the person he is, and I find it hard to imagine him anywhere else but here in Sparrow, on this island with me.

He shakes his head, smiling a little, like he finds it funny that I would even ask this. "I worked for my parents every day after school, so I didn't have much time for friends or group sports."

"Your parents' farm?"

"It's actually a vineyard."

I pause near the end of a row. "A vineyard?" I repeat. "Like grapes?"

"Yeah. It's just a small family winery, but it does pretty well." It's not exactly the farm where I imagined him toiling: hands-in-the-earth, greasy, cow-manure type of farming. But I'm sure it was still hard work.

"It's not what I pictured," I tell him.

"Why not?"

"I don't know." I examine him, eyeing his faded gray sweatshirt and jeans. "Do your parents know where you are?"

"No. They didn't want me to come here. They said I just needed to let Kyle go. That's how they coped with his death, by ignoring it. But I knew I had to come. So when I graduated this year, I hitch-hiked down the coast. I never told them I was leaving."

"Have you talked to them since you left?"

He shakes his head, pushing his hands into his jean pockets.

"They're probably worried about you," I say.

"I can't call them. I don't know what I'd say." He looks at me. "How do I explain what's going on here? That Kyle didn't kill himself but was drowned by one of three sisters who died two centuries ago?"

"Maybe you don't tell them that," I offer. "But you should probably let them know you're okay . . . tell them something. Even a lie."

"Yeah." His voice dips low. "Maybe."

We reach the end of the orchard, where one of the dead apple trees is now gone, torched down to its roots.

"When this is all over," I say, "after the summer solstice, will you go home?"

"No." He pauses to look back down the rows of perfectly spaced fruit trees. A small gray bird bursts out from the limbs of one tree and lands on the branch of another. "I won't go back there. Not now. Before Kyle died, I always thought I'd stay and work for my parents after high school. Take over the family business. It was what they expected of me. My brother would be the one to move away and live a different life, to escape. And I was okay with that. But after he died . . ." He draws in his lips and looks up through the limbs of an apple tree, buds pushing out from the green stalks. "I knew I wanted something different. Something that was mine. I had always been the one who would stay behind while Kyle saw the world. But not anymore."

"So now what do you want?" I ask, my voice soft, not wanting to crack apart his thoughts.

"I want to be out there." He nods to the western edge of the island. "On the water." He looks back at me like he's not sure I'll understand. "When my dad taught me to sail, I knew I loved it, but I didn't think I'd ever have the chance to really do it. Maybe now I can. I could buy a sailboat, leave—maybe I won't ever come back."

"Sounds like an escape plan. Like you want to start a whole new life."

His eyes flicker, and he squares his shoulders to face me. "I do. I have money; I've been saving most of my life." His stare turns cool and serious. "You could come with me."

I draw in both my lips, holding back a betraying smile.

"You don't have to stay in this town—you could escape too, leave this place behind if it's what you want."

"I have school."

"I'll wait for you." And he says it like he actually means it.

"But my mom," I say. . . . Just another excuse.

His mouth hardens in place.

"It's just not that easy for me," I explain. I feel wrenched into halves, torn between the *wanting* and the prison that is this island. "It's not a no. But I also can't say yes."

I can see the hurt in his eyes, that he doesn't understand even if he wants to. But he slides his fingers around my waist, gently, like he's afraid I'll spook like one of the island birds, and he pulls me to him. "Someday you'll find a worthy enough reason to leave this place," he says.

I once read a poem about love being fragile, as thin as glass and easily broken.

But that is not the kind of love that survives in a place like this. It must be hardy and enduring. It must have grit.

He's strong, I think, the same thought I had the other night. I blink up at him, the sunlight scattering through the trees, making the features of his face soft at the edges. *Stronger than most boys.* He could survive this place. He's made of something different, his heart weathered and battered just like mine, forged of hard metals and earth. We've both lost things, lost people. We are broken but fighting to stay alive. Maybe that's why I need him—he *feels* like I feel, *wants* like I want. He's stirred loose something inside my chest, a cold center where blood now pumps, a hint of life, of green pushing up toward sunlight.

I might love him.

And it has tilted my universe off center, the frayed edges of my life starting to unravel. Loving someone is dangerous. It gives you something to lose.

I lift up to my tiptoes, his lips hovering over mine, and I know he's looking for answers in the steady calm of my stare. But he won't find them there, so he presses his mouth to mine, as if he might press some truth out of me. But I can only give him this moment, and I climb my fingers up his chest, breathing him in, tasting the salt air on his lips.

I wish suddenly that I could promise him forever, promise him *me*. But it would be a lie.

I try to call Rose. I leave messages on her phone. I tell her mom to have her call me back, but she never does.

Where is she? Why won't she call me? But I can't leave the island. I can't risk leaving Bo alone—I'm afraid Olivia might try to lure him into the harbor again.

But after several days, I can't take it anymore. The not knowing is making me edgy and nervous.

I wake up early, hoping to slip out of the cottage before Bo sees me. Olga trails me to the door; her eyes are watery from the cold, and she blinks, as if curious about what I'm doing awake at this hour.

I pull on my raincoat hanging from a metal hook beside the door then turn the knob; a swift breeze rips into the cottage, spraying raindrops over my face. Olga zips past my feet and trots up the boardwalk. But then she stops short, ears alert, tail swishing back and forth. Something has caught her attention.

It's still an hour or so before sunrise, but the sky has turned aqueous and lucid, morning pressing down, breaking apart the night clouds and sheering the island terrain in a hue of blush pink. And in the distance, I see what Olga sees: A light is wavering across the water, and an engine is sputtering toward the island dock.

"What is it?" Bo asks, his voice a shock to my ears. I wasn't expecting him to be awake. The door is partway open, and I glance back inside. He's standing up, rubbing his face.

"Someone's here," I say.

FOURTEEN

A boat knocks loudly against the dock, motoring too fast across the water. It's Heath's boat; I recognize it as the same one we took out into the harbor to make wishes at the pirates' ship when we found the first body.

But Heath is not driving it. It's Rose.

And someone is with her: a girl.

Bo grabs my arm, stopping me from getting any closer to the boat as Rose struggles to tie a rope around one of the cleats on the dock. He recognizes the girl before I do. It's Gigi Kline.

"Rose?" I ask. And she notices us for the first time.

"I didn't have anywhere else to go," she says frantically when her eyes meet mine. She looks scared, in a state of shock, and her red wavy hair is windblown like a person who's recently escaped from an asylum.

"What did you do?" I ask.

"I had to help her. And I couldn't hide her in town, they'd find her. So I brought her here. I thought she'd be safe. You could hide her in the lighthouse or the other cottage. I don't know—I panicked. I didn't know what else to do." She's speaking too fast, and her eyes keep flicking from Gigi back to me.

"You broke Gigi out of the boathouse?" Bo asks.

Gigi is sitting silently in the boat, meekly, innocently. Her façade is well practiced as she makes slow, measured movements. Each blink of an eyelash looks rehearsed.

"I . . . I had to."

"No, you didn't," I snap. "This was a very bad idea, Rose."

"I couldn't just let them keep her locked up like that. It was cruel! And they could just as easily do it to anyone else. To me—to us."

"And they probably will when they find out what you've done."

"Penny, please," she says, stepping from the boat, palms lifted in the air. "You have to help her."

I didn't realize Gigi's imprisonment upset Rose this deeply, enough that she would break her out and bring her here. I know they were friends once, years ago, but I never imagined she'd do this. She couldn't stand to see someone she once cared about tied up and suffering. Made to be a cruel spectacle. It didn't seem right to Rose from the start. And I can't fault her for that.

"This is dangerous, Rose. You shouldn't have freed her." I lock eyes with Gigi, and with Aurora tucked inside her—watching like an animal waiting until it's safe to come out of its hiding place. She didn't have to enchant Davis or Lon to save her, Rose did it out of the goodness of her heart. But she's set loose a monster, and she doesn't even realize it.

"Maybe it's better that she's here," Bo whispers to me, out of earshot of Rose and Gigi.

I feel my eyebrows slant into a scowl. "What are you talking about?"

"We can keep an eye on her, lock her up, make sure she doesn't kill anyone else."

I know why he wants to do this: He wants to ask Gigi about his brother. And if he decides that it was Aurora—hidden inside of Gigi—who killed his brother, then what? Will he try to kill her? This is a mistake, I can feel it, but both Bo and Rose are staring at me, waiting for me to decide what to do.

This can't be happening.

"Fine. Get her out of the boat. We'll take her to Old Fisherman's Cottage. Then we'll decide what to do next."

Sometimes I think this island is a magnet for bad things, the center of it all. Like a black hole pulling us toward a fate we can't prevent. And other times I think this island is the only thing keeping me sane, the only familiar thing I have left.

Or maybe it's me that's the black hole. And everyone around me can't help but be swallowed up, drowned and trapped in my orbit. But I also know that there's nothing I can do to change it. The island and I are the same.

I lead the way to Old Fisherman's Cottage, Rose trailing behind me, then Gigi, and Bo bringing up the back. He wants to make sure Gigi doesn't make a run for it.

The door is unlocked, and the interior is darker and damper and colder than Bo's cottage. I flip on a light switch, but nothing happens. I walk across the living room, furnished with a single wood rocking chair and a burgundy upholstered ottoman that doesn't match anything else in the room. I find a floor lamp, kneel down to plug it in, and it immediately blinks on.

But the light does little to brighten the appearance of the cottage.

"It's only temporary," Rose assures Gigi. But I'm not sure what Rose thinks will happen to change the current circumstances. Kidnapping Gigi from the boathouse will only make Davis and Lon more suspicious. They will assume one of the Swan sisters broke her out, and now they'll be looking for her. And Rose and I will likely be their first suspects since both she and I were caught sneaking into the boathouse—and now I know why Rose was there. She was planning this all along.

"We'll bring you wood for the fireplace," I say to Gigi, but her eyes don't lift from the floor. She's staring at a corner of the living room rug, the edges frayed—probably chewed up by mice.

"And I'll find you some new clothes," Rose offers, looking down at Gigi's stained shirt and jeans.

I tug at the only two windows in the cottage, seeing if they'll slide up in their casings, but they don't even budge—both are rusted shut. This cottage is much older than the one Bo is staying in. And these windows probably haven't been opened in two decades. I walk back to the door, not wanting to be in the same room as Gigi any longer than I have to.

"You're safe here," I hear Rose tell her, and Bo steps through the doorway, shooting me a sideways glance. We both know what she really is, and I can tell Bo is itching to interrogate her.

"Can I have something to eat?" Gigi asks.

Rose nods. "Of course. We'll bring you food too." She has no idea who she has just invited to the island. "Try to get some rest, I'm sure you're exhausted."

Once Rose has stepped through the doorway, I shut the door and Bo drags over a warped wood board that had been stacked along the backside of the cottage. He jams it up under the doorknob, locking it in place.

"What are you doing?" Rose asks, making a move to grab the board. "She's not a prisoner."

"If you want me to hide her here, then this is how it has to be," I explain.

"You don't actually think she did anything wrong—that she's one of them—do you?" Rose might not believe in the Swan sisters, but she knows that I do.

"You don't have any reason to think she's innocent," I say. "So for now, she stays locked in there. At least it's better than the boathouse."

"Hardly," Rose counters, but she crosses her arms and steps back from the door, reluctantly agreeing to our rules.

"Does Heath know what you did?" I ask.

She shakes her head. "No. But I borrowed his parents' boat, so I'll probably have to tell him where I've been."

"He can't say anything to anyone about this."

"He won't."

"And no one saw you take her?" Bo asks.

"It was dark, and Lon was completely passed out. He probably hasn't even realized she's gone yet."

Again I'm struck by what a horrible idea this is. I'm not even sure if we're hiding Gigi from Lon and Davis or if we're holding her hostage just like they did. Whatever this is that we're doing, I'm fairly certain it's going to end catastrophically.

"Just be careful in town," I say.

"I will." And she presses her hands down deep into her coat pockets, as if she were fighting off a sudden chill. "Thank you," she adds, just before she heads down the walkway back to the dock.

Bo and I look at each other once she's out of sight. "Now what?" he asks.

Back at the house, I make two peanut butter and jelly sandwiches for Gigi, wrap them in foil, then grab a blanket from the hall closet.

When I reach the door of Old Fisherman's Cottage, the wood board has been removed and the door is slightly ajar. At first my heart jumps upward with panic—Gigi must have gotten out—but then I hear Bo's voice inside. He went to collect logs to start a fire for her while I went to make food, and he's returned before me.

I pause, listening to the crackling of flames in the fireplace.

"I know what you are," I hear Bo say.

"Do you?" Gigi answers, her voice farther away, across the living room maybe, sitting in the only chair. I touch the doorknob with my fingers then pause. Maybe I owe him this: the chance to question her about his brother. So I wait before entering.

"You're not Gigi Kline," he says coolly, his voice measured and precise. "You're something else."

"And who told you that? Your girlfriend, Penny?"

I swallow down a jagged lump.

"Did you kill my brother?"

"Your brother?" Her voice changes, dips to an octave that is no longer Gigi's but is Aurora's. "You expect me to remember your brother, one boy from the thousands who've fallen in love with me?" She says it with a laugh, as if to fall in love is the first step toward death.

"It was last summer. June eleventh," he tries, hoping this will jog her memory. But even if she did remember, she would never confess. Not to him.

"Doesn't ring a bell."

I hear footsteps move across the room: Bo's. And his voice is farther away now. "Did you drown anyone on June eleventh?"

"Hmm, let me think." Her tone takes on an upswing, like she's shifting between Gigi's voice and Aurora's, playing a game with Bo that he will lose. "Nope," she finally concludes. "Pretty sure I took that day off. A girl gets tired with so many boys fawning over her." I'm surprised she's being so candid with him, even if her answers are still veiled by untruths. She must recognize that he's not fooled by her little act. He sees right through Gigi Kline, even if he can't actually *see* the thing inside her.

"I can make you tell me," he says, his voice like a steel nail driving into wood, and I push open the door, unable to stay quiet any longer. Gigi isn't sitting like I thought—she's standing at the far wall beside one of the windows, leaning against it like she's watching the ocean for a ship sailing into the harbor that might rescue her. And Bo is only a couple feet away, shoulders drawn back, hands halfway flexed at his sides like he's about to reach forward and wrap them around her throat.

"Bo," I hiss.

He doesn't turn around right away. He stares at her, like maybe he'll see a flicker of his brother in her eyes—of the moment right before he was killed. Gigi lifts a hand, smiling a little. "Poor boy," she says in her smoothest, most condescending tone. "I can't help you find your brother . . . but I *can* show you exactly what he felt." Her fingers rise toward his face, her eyes piercing into his. "It won't hurt, I promise. In fact, you'll beg me for more." The tips of her fingers are only an inch away, about to touch his cheekbone. "I can show you things your girlfriend, Penny, can't. She's too afraid to really love you."

And just when her hand is almost to his jaw, he grabs her wrist, coiling his fingers around her skin. She winces slightly, and then he forces her arm away, where it falls to her side.

Her eyebrows rise in unison, and she glances over at me from across the room, like she wants to make sure I saw how close she was to making him hers. "I like the ones that play hard to get," she says with a wink.

I drop the blanket and two sandwiches onto the small kitchen table with a thump then turn for the door. And Bo is suddenly right behind me.

"If you miss me, Bo," she cajoles, smirking as she watches us leave, "you know where to find me." But Bo slams the door shut then slides the board back into place.

"You were right," he says. "She's one of them."

Bo and I walk the perimeter of the island like we're surveying it, watchmen on duty, scanning the boundary for marauders—as if the Swan sisters were going to swim ashore by the thousands and take over our small island. I am on edge. Fidgety. Certain none of this will end well.

Gigi Kline is locked in the boathouse. People will be looking for her. Davis and Lon want her dead; the Sparrow police are trying to locate her and return her to her parents. And we are somehow right in the middle of it.

I'm still not entirely sure what we're going to do with her.

"Do you want to come up to the house for dinner?" I ask Bo when the sun starts to set. We've spent most of our time in his cottage, alone, never in the main house.

He lifts his hat to brush a hand through his hair before placing it back on his head, lower this time, so it's hard to see his eyes. "What about your mom?"

"She won't mind. And it wasn't really a request but a demand. I'm not about to leave you alone; you might decide to go for a swim again." I say it with a grin, even though it's not funny. He smirks, looking across the island to Old Fisherman's Cottage, where Gigi is locked up. The wood board is still in place.

"All right," he agrees.

I heat a can of tomato soup and make two grilled cheese sandwiches on the stove—a simple meal. There aren't a lot of options anyway. I need to go into town for more supplies . . . eventually. But I'm not in a rush to leave the island.

We eat quickly, and then Bo follows me up the stairs. When we reach my bedroom, I can hear the fan blowing down the hall. Mom's already in bed.

"Do you think your mom knows I'm here?" Bo asks once we're inside my room.

"She knows. She senses when anyone is in the house or on the island."

"What about Gigi?"

"I'm sure Mom knows she's here too. But she won't say anything.

She hasn't talked to anyone outside the island for a couple years. I don't think she could muster the strength to call the cops about a missing girl even if she wanted to."

"Is she like that because of your dad?"

I give a swift nod then sit down on the edge of the bed while he settles into the cushioned chair beside the window. "After he vanished three years ago, she sort of lost her mind."

He nods understanding. "I'm sorry."

A light rain has started to fall, sprinkling the glass and pattering against the roof. A chorus that soothes the eaves and sharp angles of the old house. "Apparently, love is the worst kind of madness."

I go to the window and touch my palm to the glass. I can feel the coolness of the rain on the other side.

"Have you ever been in love before?" Bo braves to ask.

I look back at him, absorbing the drowsy slant of his eyes. "Once," I confess, the four-letter word spilling out. It's something I don't like to talk about—with anyone.

"And?"

"It didn't last. Circumstances beyond our control."

"But you think about him still?" he asks.

"Only sometimes."

"Are you afraid?"

"Of what?"

"To fall in love again?" His hands are resting on the arms of the chair, relaxed, but his gaze seems far more intent.

"No." I swallow down the heartbeat climbing up inside my throat. Can he see what I'm thinking, what I'm feeling? That my heart is already pooling in my stomach, that my mind can hardly think of anything but him? That when we're together, I almost believe nothing else matters? That maybe he could save me and I could save him? "I used to be afraid that I wouldn't get another chance to."

He stands up from the chair and walks to the window, pressing his shoulder against the wood frame, a hard line from his jaw up to his temple. "How did you know you were in love?"

His question makes my fingertips tingle with the need to touch his face, show him the feeling bursting from my seams. "It felt like sinking," I say. I know it might be an odd way to describe it, considering the prevailing death in this town, but it's how it comes out. "Like you're drowning, but it doesn't matter, because you don't need air anymore, you just need the other person."

His eyes flick to mine, searching them, looking to see if I'm drowning. And I am. The clock beside my bed ticks through the seconds; the rain keeps time.

"Penny," he says softly, tilting his gaze on me. "I didn't come here, to this town, expecting any of this." He looks to the floor then back up again. "If I hadn't met you, it probably would have been easier—less complicated. Maybe I would have left days ago." I frown, and he clears his throat. His words break apart then reform. This is hard for him. "But now I know . . ." He lets out a breath, eyes looking through me—turned wild and unwavering. "I'm not leaving here without you. Even if it means I have to wait. I'll wait. I'll wait in this miserable place for as long as it takes. And if you want me to stay, then I'll stay. I'll fucking stay here forever if you ask me to."

He shakes his head and opens his mouth like he's going to continue, but I don't let him. I take one swift step forward and crush my lips to his, pressing away his thoughts, his words. He tastes like a summer wind far away from here, like absolution, like a boy from a different life. Like we could make memories that belong only to us. Memories that have nothing to do with this place. A life, maybe. A real life.

I open my eyes. I trace his lips with mine. He looks at me like I am a girl brought in with the tide, rare and scarred and broken. A girl found in the roughest waters, in the farthest reaches of a dark fairy tale. He is looking at me like he might love me.

"I'm scared," I whisper up at him.

"Of what?"

"Of letting myself love you then feeling my insides collapse when I lose you."

"I'm not going anywhere without you."

Promises are easy to make, I think but don't say. Because I know he believes his own words. He believes that what we feel right now will rescue us in the end. But I know—*I know*. Endings are never so simple.

I sink back against the wall. His hand still touches my forearm, not letting me go.

"How does it end?" he asks, as if his thoughts trailed mine. "What will happen on the summer solstice?"

Memories cascade through me, all the years past, the summers that slid to a close, dead bodies left in their wake. "There will be a party, just like the one on the beach." I pull my arm away from his grip, tugging the sleeves of my sweater down over my hands and crossing my arms, feeling suddenly chilled. "Before midnight, the sisters will wade back out into the harbor, relinquishing the bodies they've stolen."

"And if they don't go into the water? If Gigi stays locked up during the solstice?"

My lungs stop drawing in air. *She will die. She will be trapped inside Gigi's body indefinitely, pushed down into the dark, dark, dark recesses of Gigi's mind. She will see and hear and witness the world, but Gigi will resume control, unaware that a Swan sister is now imprisoned inside her, buried deep within. A ghost inside a girl. The worst kind of existence. A punishment befitting the torment the sisters have caused.* But I don't tell this to Bo. Because I can't be sure it's true, since it's never happened before. A Swan sister has never stayed inside a body past midnight on the summer solstice.

"I'm not sure," I answer truthfully.

Bo's eyes have strayed to the window, he's considering something. "I have to kill her," he finally says. "Even if she didn't kill my brother, she's killed others. She doesn't deserve to live."

"You'd be killing Gigi, too," I say.

"I know, but you told me before how the town has killed girls in the past, hoping to stop the sisters, but that they always got it wrong." His eyes search mine. "This time we won't get it wrong. You can see them. You know who they are. We can find out where the third one is and we can end this for good. No one else has to die."

"Except three innocent girls."

"Better than a hundred more boys. Or two hundred. How many more centuries do they keep returning to this town before someone stops them? They never got it right in the past because they never knew for sure which girls were inhabited. But *we* know. And there's one right down there, locked up." He points to the window and his sudden urgency scares me. I never thought he'd be this serious, that he'd really want to do it. But now he's talking like we could march down there and end her life right now, all based on my ability to see what she really is.

"And you could live with yourself after that?" I ask. "Knowing you killed three people?"

"My brother is dead," he says coldly. "I came here to find out what happened to him, and I did. I can't just walk away now." He removes the hat from his head and drops it onto the chair. "I have to do this, Penny."

"You don't." I move closer to him. "At least not right now . . . not tonight. Maybe we can find another way."

He exhales then leans into the window frame. "There isn't another way."

I reach out and touch his arm, forcing him to look at me. "Please," I say, tilting my chin up at him. He smells like the earth; he smells wild and fearless and I know he could also be dangerous, but when I'm this close to him I don't care what he is. "We still have a few days until the solstice. There's time to figure something out. All those books in your cottage—maybe there really is a way to stop the sisters without killing the girls they've taken. We have to look; we have to try." My fingers slide down to his hand, the warmth of his palm burning me, setting me on fire, making me dizzy.

"Okay," he answers, tightening his fingers through mine. "We'll look for another way. But if we don't find one . . ."

"I know," I say before he can finish. *He will kill Gigi Kline just to get to Aurora.* But he doesn't fully understand what that will mean: taking a life. It will change him. It's not something he can take back.

The sun has managed to sink into the ocean in the span of time that we've been in my room, and I switch on the lamps on either side of my bed. "One of us should stay up to watch the cottage, make sure she doesn't sneak out," Bo says.

I doubt she'll try to escape, but I nod anyway, agreeing. Her odds aren't good back in town. Lon and Davis are surely looking for her. And I'm guessing she knows she's safer here—hidden in the cottage. Her mistake is that she thinks we'll protect her from them. Especially with Rose on her side. When, in fact, we're plotting ways in which to end her life.

SISTERS

Magic is not always formed from words, from cauldrons brewing spices or black cats strolling down dark alleys. Some curses are manifested from desire or injustice.

When she was alive, Aurora Swan would sometimes leave shards of broken glass or a rat's tail on the doorstep of a woman who hated her—hoping an illness might befall the woman or she might stumble on a loose stone while strolling down Ocean Avenue and break her neck. They were merely small omens, common hexes of the day to bend fate in her favor. Not real magic.

Hazel Swan could often be found whispering wishes onto a blood moon, her lips as swift as a hummingbird in flight. She enchanted the moon, wishing for things she craved—a real love to wipe all the others away.

Marguerite was more direct in her efforts. She would slide her fingers along her lovers' throats, tell them that they were hers, and if they refused her she would ensure they never loved anyone else ever again. She promised revenge and torment and the full wrath of her fury if they dared deny her. She swished through town as if she were made of the finest French silk, arrogant and imperious. She wanted power, and everyone knew it.

But their hubris would eventually catch up to them.

The sisters might have portrayed themselves scandalously, wicked and witchy. But they never practiced magic in a way that justified their demise. They were not witches, in a historical sense, but they did have a gravity about them—a thing that pulled you in.

They moved with a graceful ease, as though they were trained ballerinas from the Académie Royale de Danse in France; their hair was a hue that wavered between caramel and carmine, depending on the sunlight; and their voices had the singsong of a whistling thrush, each word a fascination.

They never stole the souls of newborn babies or cast potent spells to make the rains unending or the fish in the harbor uncatchable. Nor had they the skills to spin a curse as everlasting as the one that bound them now.

But magic was not always so linear. It was born from odium. From love. From revenge.

FIFTEEN

At two a.m. on the dot, my eyelids flutter open. The room is dark except for the angular shape of moonlight spilling across the floor from the window. The rain clouds are gone and the sky has split open. Bo is awake, sitting in the chair, finger tapping slowly and rhythmically on the armrest. He turns his head when I sit up in bed.

"You should have woken me sooner," I say drowsily.

"You seemed like you needed sleep."

I'm still fully dressed under the blankets, and I kick back the layers and stretch my arms in the air. "I'll take the next shift," I say. The wood floor is cold and creaking beneath the weight of my feet. "You must be tired."

He yawns and stands up. We bump shoulders as we try to move around one another, both of us sleepy. And when he gets to the bed, he collapses onto his back, one hand on his chest, the other stretched out at his side. He pulls his hat down over his face. I'm tempted to crawl back onto the bed beside him, rest my head on his shoulder and doze back into my dreams. It would be easy to let myself surrender to him, both in this moment and forever . . . let the days flit away until there are no more days left to count. I could leave this island with him and not look back. And maybe, possibly, I could be happy.

It doesn't take long for Bo's hands to relax, his head to shift slightly to the left, and I know he's asleep. But I don't settle into the chair. I walk to the door, opening it just wide enough to slip out into the hall. I move silently down the stairs to the front door.

A few intermittent clouds pass beneath the moon then reveal it again. A ballet of clear sky mixed with low clouds, washed in moonlight.

I wrestle into my raincoat, trying to move quickly, and then hurry out into the night, headed to Old Fisherman's Cottage.

It takes several tries before I'm able to dislodge the board from under the doorknob. My hands are wet; the wood board is wet. And when the door creaks open, the only light inside the cottage is from the fireplace across the room.

It smells like mildew and mothballs and a little like vinegar. And for a half second I feel bad for Gigi being trapped inside this place.

She is standing across the small room, awake, holding her palms over the fire for warmth. "Hello, Penny," she says without turning around. I close the door behind me, shaking the rain from my coat. "I didn't kill his brother."

"Maybe not," I answer. "But he's determined to find out who did." Instinctively, I want to move to the fire for warmth, but I also don't want to be any nearer to her than I already am. On the couch, I notice the folded-up blanket I brought her earlier. She hasn't slept at all.

"Did you come to invite me up to your house for tea and a shower? I could really use a shower."

"No."

"Then why are you here?" She pivots around, her shoulder-length, straight blond hair hanging frayed and dirty like the bristles on a broom. Again I stifle back the sensation of feeling sorry for her. She blinks, and the flickering, silvery-gray outline of Aurora Swan beneath her skin blinks too. They are like two girls transposed over top of each other. Two photo images developed all wrong, one hovering over the other. But when Gigi turns away from the firelight, I almost can't see Aurora inside her; the outlines of her face fade and turn shadowy. I could fool myself into believing that Aurora is no longer there and Gigi is just a normal girl.

"I need to talk to you."

"Without your boyfriend?" she asks, the left side of her lip arching up at the edge.

"He wants to kill you. . . . The whole town does."

"They always have; that's nothing new." In the corner of the ceiling behind her is a cobweb, partly decayed, dark specks—flies and moths—trapped in the sticky remains. Doomed. Legs and wings stuck. The spider is long dead, but the web keeps on killing.

"But this time they caught you swimming back to shore after drowning two boys. They're certain you're one of them."

Her eyebrows come together, forming a line that rises up into her forehead. "And I'm sure you've done nothing to encourage that idea." She's implying that I've said something, revealed that she is indeed a Swan sister, but I've only told Bo.

"Aren't you tired of this?" I ask. "Of killing people year after year?" This is what I had wanted to say when I confronted her at the boathouse, before Lon caught me talking to her.

She looks intrigued, and her head tilts to the left. "You say it like we have a choice."

"What if we do?"

"Don't forget," she says crisply, "it's your fault we ended up like this in the first place."

I drop my gaze to the floor. Dust motes have collected around the legs of the kitchen table and against the walls.

She smiles then rolls her tongue against her cheek. "Let me guess, you're falling in love with that boy?" Her mouth turns up again, grinning with satisfaction that she's hit on something that makes me uncomfortable. "And you're starting to think that maybe there's a way to keep this body you're in, to stay human forever?" She steps away from the fire, pushing her lower jaw out like she might laugh. "You're fucking naive, Hazel. You always have been. Even back then, you thought this town wouldn't actually kill us. You thought we could be saved. But you were wrong."

"Stop it," I tell her, my lips trembling.

"This isn't your town. That isn't your body. These people hate us; they want us dead all over again, and you're pretending that you're one of them." She lifts her chin in the air like she's trying to see me from a new angle, spy the thing inside me. "And that boy . . . Bo. He doesn't love you, he loves who he thinks you are: Penny Talbot, the girl whose body you stole." The words are spit from her lips like they taste vile on her tongue. "And now you've locked up your own sister in this disgusting cottage. You've betrayed us—your own family."

"You're dangerous," I manage to say.

"So are you." She laughs. "Tell me, were you planning on going the whole season without drowning a single boy? The solstice is coming."

"I'm done with that," I say. "I don't want to kill anymore." Even though the urge gnaws at me, tugging at my soul—the need like a thorn at the back of my throat, always pricking the skin, reminding me of what I'm here to do. But I have resisted. At times I've even forgotten. With Bo, the desire for revenge has been dulled. He's made me believe I can be someone else . . . not just the monster I've become.

"You have to. It's what we do." She twirls a strand of blond hair through her thumb and index finger, pressing her lips together into a pout. Aurora's face seems to push against the inside of Gigi's skull, like she's trying to find more space, stretch her neck a little within the confines of her body. I know the feeling. Sometimes I feel trapped in Penny's body as well—imprisoned by the outline of her skin.

"We've been living like this for too long," I say, my voice stronger now, finding purpose in the words. "Two centuries of torturing this town, and what has it gotten us?"

"You fall for some boy, who's not even a local, and now suddenly you want to protect this town?" She folds her arms over her chest, still wearing the same soiled white blouse as when she drowned those boys in the water. "And besides, I like coming back. I like making boys fall in love with me, controlling them . . . collecting them like little trophies."

"You like killing them, you mean."

"I make them mine, and I deserve to keep them," she snaps. "It's not my fault they're so trusting and gullible. Boys are weak—they were two centuries ago, and they still are."

"When will it be enough?"

"Never." She cants her head to the side, cracking her neck.

I exhale. What did I expect coming in here? What was I hoping for? I should have known: My sisters will never stop. They have become just like the sea, breaking apart ships and lives without remorse. And they'll keep on killing for another two centuries if they have their way.

I turn for the door.

"Haven't you learned your lesson, Hazel?" she says from across the room. "You were betrayed by the boy you loved once before; what makes you think Bo won't betray you too?"

I bite down on the fury boiling inside me. She doesn't know anything about what happened before—two centuries ago. "This is different," I say. "Bo is different."

"Unlikely. But he *is* cute." She smirks. "Maybe too cute for you. I think I should have him."

"Stay away from him," I bark.

Her eyes turn to slits, narrowed on me. "What exactly do you plan on doing with him?"

"I won't kill him." I won't take him into the sea and drown him. I don't want that for him—a dark, watery existence, his soul trapped in the harbor. A prisoner shifting with the tide.

"You realize that you're just going to have to leave him behind in a few days. And he will have fallen in love with a ghost and be left with the body of this girl Penny, who won't remember a thing." She lets out a short laugh. "Won't that be hilarious? He will be in love with Penny, not you."

A rattling of nausea starts to rise in my gut. "He loves me . . . not this body." But the words sound feeble and broken.

"Sure," she says, and her eyes roll in her head—such a Gigi thing

214

to do. We can't help but take on the mannerisms of the bodies we inhabit. Just as I have taken on the traits of Penny Talbot—all of her memories sit dormant in my mind, waiting to be plucked like a flower from the ground. I am playing the part of Penny Talbot, and I do it well. I've had practice.

I touch the doorknob. "I meant what I said," I say back to her. "Stay away from him or I'll make sure those boys in town get the opportunity to do exactly what they've been dying to do—kill you."

She chuckles, but then her gaze turns serious, watching me as I slip out the door and kick it shut behind me.

HAZEL SWAN

Hazel was walking swiftly down Ocean Avenue, a small package containing a vial of rosewater and myrrh perfume held delicately between her hands. She was on her way to deliver it to Mrs. Campbell on Alder Hill.

She had glanced down at the package, expertly wrapped in brown butcher paper, when she smacked right into the hard shoulder of someone standing on the sidewalk. The package slipped from her fingers and broke on the cobblestone street. The scent of rose and myrrh evaporated swiftly into the soggy, seaside air.

Owen Clement knelt down to scoop up the remains of the package, and Hazel did the same, her arm grazing his, their fingers touching and soaking up the perfume.

Hazel had always avoided the fervent affections of men, unlike her sisters. And so she wasn't prepared for the desire that twined through her upon meeting Owen Clement, the son of the first lighthouse keeper who lived on Lumiere Island. He was French, like his father, and words rolled from his tongue like a sanguine breeze.

Nightly, Hazel began sneaking across the harbor to the island—hands pressed to skin and tangled in each other's hair; bodies formed

217

as one; waking each morning in the loft above the barn that stood near the main farmhouse, the air smelling of hay and sweat. The chickens clucked from their pen below. And in the evenings, with only the moonlight to reveal their faces, they wandered the single row of young apple tree saplings that Owen's father had planted that spring. It would still be several years before they would turn a harvest. But the promise of what they would bring felt ripe and sharp in the air.

Together they explored the rocky coastline; they let the water lap against their feet. They imagined a new life together, farther south. California, maybe. They threw flat stones into the water, and they made wishes for impossible things.

But Owen's father distrusted the Swan sisters, who were rumored to be witches—temptresses who lured boys into their beds just for amusement—and when he discovered his son and Hazel folded together in the loft one morning, he swore he would make sure they never saw each other again.

It was Owen's father who mounted the inquisition into the three sisters. It was Owen's father who tied the stones around their ankles that pulled the three girls to the bottom of the harbor. It was Owen's father who was responsible for their deaths.

And year after year, summer after summer, Hazel feels drawn back to Lumiere Island, reminded of the boy who she loved in that place, who she forged promises with, and who she lost two centuries ago.

SIXTEEN

B o is still asleep on the bed when I get back to the room.

The sky turned dark on my way back to the house, rain once again blowing across the island.

His chest expands with each breath; his lips fall open. I watch him, wishing I could tell him the truth without destroying everything. Without destroying him. But he thinks I'm someone else. When he looks at me, he sees Penny Talbot, not Hazel Swan. I have carried the lie around as if it were the truth, pretended that this body could actually be mine and that I wouldn't have to return to the sea at the end of June if I believed it hard enough. Maybe this feeling blooming inside my chest will save me; maybe the way Bo looks at me will make me real and whole. Not the girl who drowned two hundred years ago.

But Gigi's laugh rings in my ear. *It's what we do.* We're killers. Our revenge will never be satiated. And I can never have Bo, not really. I'm trapped in another girl's body. I've been repeating the same endless cycle summer after summer. I am not me.

I hardly know who I am anymore.

I walk to the white dresser against the far wall and run a finger along the surface. A collection of items lie scattered like fragments of a story: vanilla perfume that once belonged to Penny's mom, beach pebbles and shells in a dish, her favorite books by John Steinbeck and Herman Melville and Neil Gaiman. Her past rests unprotected in the open, so easily stolen. I can make these things mine. I can make her life mine. This home, this bedroom—including the boy asleep on her bed.

A photograph is tucked at the bottom corner of the mirror above the dresser. I pull it out. It's an image of a woman floating in a tank of water, a fake mermaid's tail fastened at her waist to conceal her legs. Men are gathered in front of the tank, staring in at her while she holds her breath, her expression soft and unstrained. She is a lie. An invention used to sell tickets at a traveling carnival.

I am her. A lie. But when the carnival closes for the night—all the lights flicked off and the water drained from the tank—I do not get to remove my fabric mermaid fin. I do not get to have a normal life outside of the illusion. I will always be someone else.

My deception has lasted two hundred years.

I place the photo back at the edge of the mirror and rub my palms over my eyes. *How did I become this thing?* A spectacle. A sideshow curiosity. I didn't want any of this—this prolonged, unnatural life.

I blow out a breath, keeping the tears from seeping to the surface, and turn to face Bo, who's still asleep.

He twitches on the bed then opens his eyes, as if he felt me watching him in his dreams. I flick my gaze away to the window.

"You all right?" He sits up, pressing his palms into the mattress.

"Fine." But I'm not. This guilt is burying me alive. I'm choking on it, suffocating, swallowing down mouthfuls of each gravelly lie.

"Did you go outside?" he asks.

I touch my hair, wet from the rain. "Just for a minute."

"To Gigi's cottage?"

I shake my head, pulling in my lips to hide the truth. "I just wanted some fresh air."

He believes me. Or maybe he's only pretending to believe me. "I'll stay up for a bit so you can sleep," he says. I start to tell him no then realize how exhausted I am, so I crawl onto the bed, knees drawn close to my chest.

But I can't sleep. I watch him standing at the window, looking out at a world that I don't belong in.

The sun will be up soon. The sky made new. And maybe I'll be made new too.

Three days whirl by in fast-forward. Rose comes to the island to check on Gigi—her freed prisoner. She brings forgetful cakes from her mom's shop: blackberry mocha and sea salt caramel with crushed pistachio.

She tells us that Davis and Lon are searching for Gigi, that they're worried they'll get in trouble if she goes to the police and rats them out for keeping her locked up in the boathouse. Somehow no one seems to suspect that she might be on Lumiere Island, secretly incarcerated in one of the cottages.

Bo spreads out books on the floor of his cottage each evening, fire blazing, his eyes watering and tired from reading late into the night. He is searching for a way to kill the Swan sisters but save the bodies they inhabit—a pointless endeavor. I know things he doesn't.

And I, secretly, am hoping for a way to keep this body forever.

I read books too, curled up on the old couch, the wind rattling the cottage windows. But I'm looking for something else: a way to remain, to exist above the sea indefinitely—to live. There are legends of mermaids who fall in love with sailors, their devotion granting them a human form. I read about the Irish tales of selkies shedding their sealskins, marrying a human man, and staying on land forever.

Perhaps this one thing is enough—to fall in love? If love can bind something, can it also undo it?

On the eve of the summer solstice, Bo passes out beside the fire with an open book on his chest. But I can't sleep. So I leave his cottage and wander up to the orchard alone.

From the rows of trees, I can just barely make out Mom—Penny's mom—standing out on the cliff's edge, the shadow of a woman waiting for a husband who won't return. Seeing her out there, alone, her heart cleaved in half by pain, I could easily let the grief buried inside this body rise up to the surface. Not only are memories stored in the bodies we take, but emotions as well. I can feel them, resting broad and deep inside Penny's chest. If I look too close, if I peer into that darkness, I can feel the gaping sadness of losing her father. My eyes will swell with tears, an ache twisting in my heart, a longing so vast it could swallow me. So I keep it stuffed down. I don't let that part of the host body overcome me. But my sisters have always been better at it than me. They can ignore whatever past emotions have ruled the body, while I tend to feel the sorrow and grief creeping through my veins, up my throat, trying to choke me.

I stop at the old oak tree at the center of the grove—the ghost tree, its leaves shivering in the wind. I press my palm against the heart carved into the trunk. I stare up through the limbs, a theater of stars blinking back at me. It reminds me of the night so many years ago, lying beneath this tree with the boy I once loved: Owen Clement. He held a knife in his hand and carved the heart there to mark our place in the world. Our hearts bound together. Eternity pumping through our veins. It was on that same night that he asked me to marry him. He had no ring or money or anything to offer except himself. But I said yes.

A week later my sisters and I were drowned in the harbor.

INQUISITION

A gust blew in through the open door of the perfumery, scattering dead leaves across the wood floor.

Four men stood in the doorway of the shop, muddy boots and filthy hands. Stinking of fish and tobacco. Against the stark white walls and the air tinged with the delicate intermingling of perfumes, their presence was alarming.

Hazel stared at their filthy boots and not their faces, thinking only of the soap and water she would need to scour the floor clean once they had left. She did not yet realize the men's intent or that she would never see the perfumery again.

The men grabbed the sisters by their forearms and dragged them from the shop.

The Swan sisters were being arrested.

They were hauled down Ocean Avenue for everyone to see; fat drops of rain spat down from the sky; muck from the street stained the hems of their dresses; the townspeople stopped to gawk. Some followed them all the way to the small town hall that was used for town meetings, a gathering place during bad storms, and occasionally but quite rarely, also for legal disputes. A squabble over a missing goat, disagreements over dock anchorage, or property lines with neighbors.

Never before had an accused witch been brought into the building, let alone three.

A group of selectmen and town elders had already gathered, awaiting the Swan sisters' arrival. Marguerite, Aurora, and Hazel were brought before them and made to sit in three wood chairs at the front of the room, their hands tied behind them.

A bird fluttered in the rafters, a yellow finch, trapped just like the sisters.

Quickly, the women of Sparrow came forward, pointing fingers at Marguerite and occasionally Aurora, telling lurid tales of their misdeeds, their infidelity with the husbands and brothers and sons of this town. And how no woman could be so enchanting on her own—it surely must be witchcraft that made the Swan sisters so irresistible to the poor, unwilling men in town. They were merely the victims of the sisters' black magic.

"Witches," they hissed.

The sisters weren't allowed to speak, even though Aurora tried more than once. Their words could not be trusted. Too easily spells could be uttered from their lips to charm those in the room and then they could use their power to demand they be released. They were lucky, one of the selectmen said, that they hadn't been gagged.

But there was another voice, one of the elders, a man who was blind in one eye and would often be seen standing on the docks staring out at the Pacific, longing for the days he once spent at sea. His voice rose above the others: "Proof!" he called. "We must have proof."

This single demand forced silence through the courthouse, overflowing with spectators. A crowd pushed against the doors outside, straining to hear the first-ever witch trial in the town of Sparrow.

"I've seen Marguerite's mark," a man called from the back of the room. "On her left thigh, there is a birthmark shaped as a raven." This man, who had emboldened himself to speak at the urging of his wife, had shared a bed with Marguerite some months back. Marguerite's eyes went wide, and fury brewed behind them. She did in fact have a birthmark, but to call it the shape of a raven was the result of a clever imagination. The mark was more of an inkblot, but it made no difference; a mark of nearly any kind was considered the brand of a witch—proof she belonged to a coven. And Marguerite could not wipe away that which she was born with.

"What of the other two?" the half-blind elder called.

"Aurora," spoke a much quieter voice, a boy of only eighteen. "Has a mark on her shoulder. I've seen it." And he had, as he had claimed, seen the collection of freckles on her right shoulder. His lips had pressed against her flesh on several nights previous, tracing the freckles that dotted much of Aurora's skin. She was like a galaxy, speckled with stars.

Aurora's gaze met the boy's. She could see the fear obvious in his eyes. He believed Aurora might in truth be a witch as the town had claimed, and perhaps she had used dark magic on him, making his heart race whenever she was near.

"Two honorable men have stepped forward with proof of guilt for two of the accused before us," said one of the selectmen. "What of the last sister? Hazel Swan? Surely someone has spied the mark of a coven on this enchantress's skin?"

A stir of whispers carried through the room and echoed off the steep ceiling, voices trying to discern whom among them might have found themselves ensnared by Hazel, coaxed to her bed unwittingly.

"My son will tell you." A man's deep voice broke through the chatter.

Owen's father appeared at the back of the courthouse, and trailing behind him, head down, was Owen. "My son has been with her. He has seen what marks she conceals."

The air inside the room condensed, the damp walls stiffened. The yellow finch caught in the rafters fell quiet. Not even the floorboards creaked as Owen was pulled by his father to the front of the courthouse. Hazel Swan looked as if she might faint, her complexion drained of all color. Not from fear for herself, but fear for Owen.

"Tell them!" his father barked.

Owen stood stone-faced, eyes locked on Hazel. He would not.

His father marched up to where the sisters sat in a row, hands bound by rope. He drew a large knife from the sheath at his waist and placed it to Hazel's throat, blade pressing against her alabaster skin. Her breath hitched; her eyes quivered but did not stray from Owen's gaze.

"Stop!" Owen cried, stepping toward Hazel. Two men grabbed his arms and held him in place.

"Tell us what you've seen," his father demanded. "Tell us of the marks that riddle this girl's body."

"There are no marks," Owen shouted back.

"Her spell on you has made you weak. Now tell us, or I will cut her throat and you will watch her bleed out, here in front of everyone. A painful death, I assure you."

"You will kill her anyway," Owen said. "If I speak, you will accuse her of being a witch."

"So you *have* seen something?" the half-blind elder asked.

Those in the room that day would later say it was as if Hazel Swan was conjuring a spell before their eyes, the way she peered at Owen, forcing his lips to remain silent. But others, the few who had known real love, saw something else: the look of two people whose love was about to destroy them. It was not witchcraft in Hazel's eyes; it was her heart splitting in half.

And then Hazel spoke, a soft series of words that sounded almost like tears streaming down cheeks: "It's all right. Tell them."

"No," Owen answered back. He was still being held by the two men, his arms tensed against their grip.

"Please," she whispered. Because she feared he might be punished for protecting her. She knew it was already too late; the town had decided—they were witches. The selectmen just needed Owen to say it, to prove what they already believed. He only needed to tell them of one little mark; any imperfection on the skin would do.

His eyes watered, and his lips fell open, the air hanging there for several breaths, several heartbeats, until he uttered: "There is a small half-moon on her left ribs."

A perfect freckle, he had once whispered against her skin in that very spot, his lips hovering over it, his breath tickling her flesh. She had laughed, her voice bouncing along the eaves of the barn loft, her fingers slipping through his hair. He had wished on that half-moon many times, silent desires that someday he and Hazel would leave Sparrow, steal away on a ship bound for San Francisco. A new life far away from this town. Maybe if she really had been a witch, his wish muttered softly against her flesh might have come true. But it did not.

A gasp passed through the room, and his father lowered the knife from Hazel's throat. "There it is," his father proclaimed, satisfied. "Proof that she, too, is a witch."

Hazel felt her heart sink into her gut. The room echoed with murmurs. The finch resumed its chirping.

The half-blind elder cleared his throat, speaking loudly enough so that even those outside the town hall with their ears pressed to the doors would hear. "In our small town, where the ocean brings us life, it shall also take it. The Swan sisters are found guilty of witchcraft and sentenced to death by drowning. To be carried out at three o'clock this afternoon, on the summer solstice. An auspicious day for the assurance that their wicked souls will be extinguished permanently."

"No!" shouted Aurora.

But Marguerite's lips pinched shut, her cold stare enough to curse anyone who dared look at her. Hazel remained quiet, not because she wasn't afraid, but because she couldn't pull her eyes away from Owen. She could see his regret, his guilt. It wrenched him apart.

But he did not condemn her—she and her sisters were doomed the day they arrived in this town.

The men seized the three sisters before Hazel could mutter a word to Owen, leading them into a back room where five women stripped them naked of their clothes, verified the marks that had been claimed against them, and then dressed them in white gowns to purify their souls and ensure their eternal and absolute death.

But absolute, their death was not.

SEVENTEEN

The cottage rattles from the wind, and I wake, gripping for something that isn't there. I had been dreaming of the sea, of the weight of stones pulling me under, water so cold I coughed at first but then couldn't fight it as it spilled into my lungs. A bleak, lonely death. My sisters only a finger's width away as we all plummeted to the bottom of the harbor.

I rub my eyes, crushing away the memory and the dream.

It's early, the light outside the cottage still a watercolor of grays, and Bo is stoking the fire.

"What time is it?" I ask, turning over from my place on the floor where I managed to fall asleep. He's added several new logs to the fire, and the heat sears my cheeks and tingles my lips.

"Early. Just after six."

Today is the summer solstice. Tonight, at midnight, everything will change.

Bo has been unsuccessful in finding a way to kill the Swan sisters without also killing the bodies where we reside. There is nothing in any of the books. But I knew there wouldn't be.

And I know what he's thinking as he faces the fireplace: Today he will get his revenge for his brother's death. Even if it means killing an innocent girl. He won't allow Aurora to keep on killing. He will end her life.

But I've also made a decision. I'm not going back into the water tonight; I won't return to the sea. I'm going to fight to keep this body. I want to stay Penny Talbot, even if it means she no longer gets to exist. Even if it might be impossible—painful and severe and terrifying—I have to try.

Each summer, my sisters and I are given only a few short weeks inside the bodies we've stolen, making each day, each hour, precious and fleeting. And so we have a habit of lingering inside our bodies until the final seconds before midnight on the summer solstice. We want to feel every last moment above the waterline: breathe in our last gulps of air; peer up at the sky, dark and gray and infinite; touch the soil beneath our feet and savor the feeling of being alive.

Even when the draw of the harbor begins to pulse behind our eyes, coaxing us back to its cold depth, we resist until it becomes unbearable. We hold on to those final seconds for as long as we can.

And there have been summers past when we've pushed it too far, waited too long to return to the sea. It's happened to each of us at least once.

In those times, in those seconds that ticked past midnight, a flash of bright pain whipped through our skulls.

But the pain isn't all you feel; there is something else: a pressure. Like being stuffed down into the dark, into the deepest shadows of the body we occupied. When it happened to me many years back, I could sense the girl rising once again to the surface, and I was being crushed. We were swapping places. Wherever she had been—

hidden, stifled, and suppressed inside the body—I was now sinking into that very place. It was only when I returned to the sea that I slipped free from the girl's skin. The relief was immediate. I swore I would never cut it that close again. I would never risk being trapped in a body after midnight.

But this year, this summer solstice, I'm going to try. Maybe I can fight it. Resist the pain and the grinding force pushing me down. Maybe I'm stronger now, more deserving even. Maybe this year will be different. I haven't taken a single boy's life—perhaps the curse will release me, allow me this one thing.

Just like in the books I've read, about the mermaids and selkies who found a way to be human and exist above the sea, I'm going to stay in this body.

Even if Penny will be stifled indefinitely, I'm willing to be selfish to have this.

"I need to go into town," I say, my voice scratchy. Last night, sitting beside the oak tree, I realized that if I truly want to have this life with Bo—if I love him—then I need to let go of the one thing I've been holding on to.

"For what?" he asks.

"There's something I need to do."

"You can't go by yourself. It's too dangerous."

I pull down the royal-blue T-shirt that wrapped itself around my torso while I slept, tossing and turning fitfully as I battled my nightmares. "I have to do this alone." I yank on the dark gray sweatshirt I was using as a pillow then stand up.

"What if one of those guys—Davis or Lon—sees you? They might question you about Gigi."

"I'll be fine," I tell him. "And someone needs to stay here—keep an eye on Gigi." He knows I'm right, but the green of his eyes settles on me like he is trying to hold me in place with his stare. "Promise me you'll stay away from her while I'm gone."

"Time is running out," he reminds me.

"I know. I won't be gone long. Just don't do anything until I get back."

He nods. But it's a weak, uncommitted nod. The longer I'm off the island, the greater the risk that something bad will happen: Bo will kill Gigi; Gigi will seduce Bo and coax him into the ocean, where she'll drown him. Either way, someone will die.

I leave the cottage, closing the door behind me. And then another thought, a new fear rises inside my gut: What if Gigi tells Bo what I really am? Would he even believe her? Doubtful. But it might edge a sliver of suspicion into his mind. I have to go quickly. And hope nothing happens before I get back.

The harbor is crowded, fishing boats and tour barges chugging out past the lighthouse. The clouds are low and heavy, so close it feels like I could reach up and touch them, swirl them with my fingertip. But no rain spills from their bloated bellies. It waits. Just like everyone is waiting for the next drowned body to be found—the last of the season. But I'm the only sister who has yet to make a kill, and I refuse to do the thing I know both Aurora and Marguerite want me to do: drown Bo.

It's never happened before: a summer where one of us didn't make a single kill. I don't know what will happen, how it will change things—change me—if at all.

I feel the sea already, tugging at me, calling me back into the water. The need to return will grow stronger as the day wears on. It happens every year, a pulse behind my eyes, a twitch inside my ribs, drawing me back to the harbor, back into the deep where I belong. But I ignore the sensation.

The skiff motors past the orange buoys and through the marina, gliding into place at the dock.

Sparrow is teeming with tourists. Along the boardwalk kids run with rainbow-colored kites, struggling to get them airborne without any breeze; one is even tangled around a street lamp with a little girl tugging against the string trying to pull it down. Seagulls peck along the concrete for scraps of popcorn and cotton candy. People stroll the shops; they buy saltwater taffy by the pound; they take pictures beside the marina; they know the end is near. Today is the last day. The season is coming to a close. They will return to their normal lives, their normal homes in normal towns where bad things never happen. But I live in a place where bad things surround me, where *I* am a bad thing.

I don't want to be that anymore.

I move in the opposite direction of Coppers Beach and the boathouse, and I head up to Alder Hill at the south end of town. The same part of Sparrow where I was supposed to deliver a vial of rosewater and myrrh perfume the day I met Owen Clement. I never made the delivery.

Blackbirds circle above, eyes roving the ground, following me. Like they know where I'm headed.

Alder Hill is also the location of the Sparrow Cemetery.

The graveyard is a broad, grassy plot of land encircled by a partially fallen-down metal fence overlooking the bay so that the fisherman buried here can watch over the sea and protect the town.

I haven't been here in a very long time. I've avoided this place for the last century. But I find my way to the tombstone easily, my feet guiding me even after all these years, past graves covered in flowers and graves covered in moss and graves left bare.

It's one of the oldest stone markers in the cemetery. The only reason it hasn't turned to dust is because for the first century I made sure to keep the weeds from growing over it and the earth from pulling it under. But then it became too hard to come. I was holding on to someone who I would never see again. It was my past. And the person I had become—a murderer—was not who he had loved. I was someone else.

It's a simple marker. Rounded sandstone. The name and date carved into the rock have long ago been smoothed away by wind and rain. But I know what it used say; I know it by heart: OWEN CLEMENT. DIED 1823.

After the day his father caught us together in the barn's loft, Owen wasn't allowed to leave the island. I tried to see him, I rowed across the bay, I pleaded with his father, but he forced me away. He was so certain I had cast a spell on Owen to make him love me. That no boy could love a Swan sister without the sway of some hex or wicked enchantment.

If only love were so easily conjured, there wouldn't be so many broken hearts, I remember Marguerite saying once, back when we were alive.

I didn't realize what was coming—what Owen's father was plotting. If I had known, I wouldn't have stayed in Sparrow.

Clouds hung heavy over the town the day my sisters and I were led from the courthouse down to the docks. Aurora wailed, screaming at the men as they forced us aboard a boat. Marguerite spit curses into their faces, but I remained still, scanning the crowd of gathered spectators for Owen. I had lost sight of him after we were taken into a small dark room at the back of the courthouse, stripped bare, and forced into simple white gowns. Our death gowns.

They knotted rope around our wrists and ankles. Aurora continued to weep, tears making lines down her cheeks. And then just as the boat pushed back from the dock, I saw him.

Owen.

It took three men to restrain him. He yelled my name, scrambling to the end of the dock. But the boat was already drifting too far away, with his father and several other men steering us out to the deepest part of the harbor.

I lost sight of him in the low fog that settled over the water, muffling all sound and obscuring the dock where he stood.

My sisters and I sat together on a single wood bench at the bow of the boat, shoulders pressed together, hands bound in front of us. Prisoners being led to their death. The sea spray stung our faces as the boat pushed farther out into the harbor. I closed my eyes, feeling its cool relief. I listened to the harbor bell buoy ringing at long intervals, the wind and waves gone nearly still. One last moment to breathe the sharp air. The seconds stretched out, and I felt as if I could slip into a dream and never wake—like none of it was real. It's rare to know your death is approaching, waiting for you, death's fingers already grasping for your soul. I felt it reaching out for me. I was already half-gone.

The boat drifted to a stop, and I opened my eyes to the sky. A seagull slipped out from the clouds then vanished again.

The men tied burlap sacks filled with stones to our ankles—the stones likely pulled up from a farmer's rocky fields behind town, donated for the occasion of our death. We were forced to stand then pushed to the edge of the boat. Marguerite eyed one of the younger boys, her gaze clawing into him, as if she might be able to convince him to free her. But we would not be spared. My sisters and I were finally being punished: adultery, lust, and even true love would find atonement at the bottom of the sea.

I sucked in a breath of air, bracing myself for what would come next, when I saw the bow of another boat breaking through the fog. "What the hell?" I heard one of the men say behind us. It was a small boat, oars driving fast through the water.

Aurora turned and looked at me—she realized who it was before I did.

He stole a boat.

A second later, I felt the swift push of two hands against my back.

The water shattered around my body like razors, knocking the air from my lungs. Death is not a fire, death is a cold so fierce it feels like it will peel the skin away from your bones. I sank quickly. My sisters plummeting just as swiftly through the murky water beside me.

I thought death would take me quickly, a second, maybe two, but then there was movement above me: an explosion of bubbles, and a hand wrapping around my waist.

I opened my eyes and focused through the dark, speckled with bits of shell and sand and green. A haze dividing us. But *he* was there—Owen.

He grabbed hold of my arms and began tugging me upward toward the surface, fighting the cold and the weight of rocks around my feet. His legs kicked furiously while mine hung limp, tied together. His face strained, eyes wide. He was desperate, trying to save me before the water found its way down my throat and into my lungs. But the stones around my ankles were too heavy. His fingers worked at the rope, but the tension was too great, the knots too stiff.

Our eyes met, only inches apart as we sank deeper to the bottom of the harbor. There was nothing he could do. I shook my head frantically—pleading with him to give up, to release me. I tried to pry his hands off of me, but he refused to let go. He was falling too deep, too far. He wouldn't have enough air to make it back up. But he pulled me against him and kissed his frigid lips to mine. I closed my eyes and felt him against me. It's the last thing I remember before I drew in a breath and the water spilled down my throat.

He never let me go. Even when it was too late. Even when he knew he couldn't save me.

We both lost our lives in the harbor that day.

The following summer, when I returned to the town for the first time—hidden in the body of a local girl—I walked up the steep slope to Sparrow Cemetery and stood on the cliff over his grave. No one knew who I really was: Hazel Swan, come to see the boy she loved now buried in the ground.

The day we both drowned, his body eventually drifted to the surface of the harbor and his father was forced to pull his only son from the sea. A fate that he had set in motion.

Guilt seethed through my veins as I stood over his freshly dug grave so long ago. His life had ended because of me. And that guilt quickly turned to hatred for the town. All these years, my sisters sought revenge for their own death, but I wanted revenge for Owen's.

He sacrificed himself to try to save me, maybe because he felt he had betrayed me—for the trial, for confessing to having seen the mark of a witch on my skin. He believed he caused my death.

But I caused his.

I should have died that day—I should have drowned. But I didn't. And I've never forgiven myself for what happened to him. For the life we never got to have.

I kneel down beside the grave, brushing away the leaves and dirt. "I'm sorry. . . ." I begin then stop myself. It's not enough. He's been gone for nearly two hundred years, and I've never said good-bye. Not really. Not until now. I lower my head, unsure how any words will ever feel like enough. "I never wanted to live this long," I say. "I'd always hoped that someday the sea would finally take me. Or old age would bury me in the ground next to you." I swallow down a deep breath. "But things have changed. . . . *I* have changed." I lift my head and look out at the sea, a perfect view of the harbor and Lumiere Island, where Bo is waiting. "I think I love him," I confess. "But maybe it's too late. Maybe I don't deserve him or a normal life after everything I've done, all the lives I've taken. He doesn't know who I really am. And so maybe what I feel for him is also a lie." The wind brushes my cheeks, and a light rain starts to scatter over the cemetery. Confessing this to Owen's grave feels like a penance, like I owe him this. "But I have to try," I say. "I have to know if loving him is enough to save both of us."

I wipe a palm over the face of the tombstone, where his name was once etched. Now just a smooth surface. A grave without a name. I close my eyes, the tears falling in slow, measured rhythm with the raindrops.

Maybe I did die that day. Hazel Swan, the girl I once was, is gone. Her life taken on the same day as Owen's. My voice trembles as the last word slips out—I say it to him as much as to myself. "Good-bye."

I stand before my legs are too weak to carry me, and I leave the graveyard, knowing that I'll never come back here again. The people I loved are gone.

But I won't lose the one I love now.

EIGHTEEN

Memories can settle into a place: fog that lingers long after it should have blown out to sea, voices from the past that take root in the foundation of a town, whispers and accusations that grow in the moss along the sidewalks and up the walls of old homes.

This town, this small cluster of houses and shops and boats clinging to the shoreline, has never escaped its past—the thing it did two hundred years ago. Ghosts remain. But sometimes, the past is the only thing keeping a place alive. Without it, this fragile town may have long ago been washed out with the tide, sunken into the harbor in defeat. But it persists, because it must. Penance is a long, unforgiving thing. It endures, for without it, the past is forgotten.

I stop in front of the old stone building that sits squat and low on a street corner facing the sea. Rain pings off my forehead and shoulders. The sign above the door reads: ALBA'S FORGETFUL CAKES. But it didn't used to. A sign with bold black swirling letters hand-painted by Aurora once hung across the sidewalk, clattering with the afternoon breeze. This was once the Swan Perfumery. Although I've walked past it thousands of times in the summers since our death, seen countless businesses occupy it, and even watched in dismay during a fifteen-year period when it sat abandoned and crumbling before it was restored, sometimes, like today, it still strikes me that after all this time it has endured . . . just as we have.

A woman steps out through the glass door, her rain boots splashing through a shallow puddle as she walks to her red SUV holding a pink pastry box surely filled with tiny frosted cakes intended to wipe away some sticky memory caught in her mind.

I spent nearly every day inside that shop, concocting new scents made of rare herbs and flowers, my hair and fingers and skin always bursting with scents that couldn't be washed away. The oils soaked into everything they touched. Marguerite was the saleswoman, and she was good at it, a natural peddler. Aurora was the bookkeeper; she paid bills and tallied profits from a small, wobbly wood desk behind the front counter. And I was the perfumist, working out of a windowless back room that should have been a storage closet—a place for brooms and metal buckets. But I loved my work. And in the evening my sisters and I shared a tiny home behind the shop.

"It doesn't even look like the same place," a voice says beside me. I flinch. Olivia Greene is standing next to me, a black umbrella held over her head to protect her sleek, charcoal-black hair from the rain. My eyes pass through her fair skin to Marguerite underneath.

"The windows are the same," I say, looking back to the building.

"Replicas," she answers, her voice more somber than usual. "Everything it used to be is now gone."

"Just like us."

"Nothing that lives this long can stay the same."

"Nothing *should* live this long," I point out.

"But we did," she says, as if it were an accomplishment to be proud of.

"Maybe two hundred years is enough."

She blows out a quick breath through her nostrils. "You want to give up eternal life?"

"It's not eternal," I say. Marguerite and I have never viewed our imprisonment the same way. She sees it as our good fortune, a lucky draw of the card that we should live on for centuries, indefinitely perhaps. But she didn't lose anything the day we were drowned. I did. She wasn't in love with a boy who loved her back—not real love, like what Owen and I had. With each passing year we spent beneath the waves, each summer we rose again to claim our revenge on the town by taking their boys and making them ours, we lost a part of who we once were. We lost our humanity. I watched my sisters' cruelty grow, their ability to kill sharpen, until I barely recognized them.

My wickedness grew too, but not to a place I couldn't come back from. Because there was a thread that bound me to who I used to be—that thread was Owen. The memory of him kept me from slipping completely into the dark. And now that thread ties me to Bo. To the real world, to the present.

"We've spent most of our lives trapped in the sea," I say. "Cold and dark and miserable. That's not a real life."

"I block it out," she rebukes swiftly. "You should too. It's better to sleep, let your mind drift away until summer arrives."

"It's not that easy for me."

"You've always made things harder for yourself."

"What does that mean?"

"This thing you have with that boy, Bo. You're only dragging out the inevitable. Just kill him and get it over with."

"No." I turn to look at her, a shadow settled over her face beneath the domed umbrella. "I know you tried to lure him into the harbor."

Her eyes twinkle, as if delighted by the memory of almost drowning the boy I love. "I just wanted to help you finish what you started. If you like him so much, then take him into the sea, and you will have him for eternity."

"I don't want him like that. His soul trapped down there just like ours."

"Then how *do* you want him?"

"Real. Here—on land."

She laughs loud and full, and a man and woman strolling past us turn to look at her. "That's absurd and not possible. Tonight's the last night to make him yours."

I shake my head. *I won't do it.* "I'm not like you," I say.

"You're exactly like me. We're sisters. And you're just as cold-blooded as I am."

"No, you're wrong about that."

"Have you forgotten about Owen? How he betrayed you? Maybe if he hadn't spoken up about the mark on your skin, you wouldn't have been found guilty. You wouldn't have drowned with us. You might have lived a normal life. But no"—her lips curl up at the edges, a wolf baring her teeth—"boys cannot be trusted. They will always do whatever they can to save themselves. They are the cruel ones, not us."

"Owen wasn't cruel," I snap. "He had to tell them about the mark."

"Did he?"

I bite down on the rage building in my chest. "If he hadn't, they

245

would have believed he was one of us, helping us. They would have killed him."

"And yet he died anyway." One of her eyebrows arches upward.

I can't stand here anymore, listening to Marguerite. She's never known real love. Even her infatuations with men when we were alive were all about her: the attention, the pursuit, the satisfaction of winning something that wasn't hers to start with. "Owen tried to save me that day, and he lost his life. He loved me," I tell her. "And Bo loves me now. But you wouldn't know what that's like because you're incapable of love."

I turn away from her and start up the sidewalk.

"Did you hear?" she calls after me. "Our dear sister Aurora has been sprung from her jail in the boathouse. It seems someone decided she was innocent after all."

I look back at her over my shoulder. "She's not innocent," I say. Marguerite squirms inside Olivia's body. "None of us are."

The dock is slick from the rain. Waves push into the marina at steady intervals, a ballet choreographed by the wind and tide. I climb into the skiff and start the motor. A few persistent rays of sun break through the dark clouds, spilling light over the bow of the boat.

Tonight, the summer solstice party will happen on Coppers Beach, marking the end of Swan season. But I won't be there. I'm staying on the island with Bo. I'm staying in this body—whatever it takes, no matter how painful, I'm going to fight it.

Yet I have the acute, anxious feeling that something bad is stirring out on those waters, in that approaching storm, and none of us will be the same after tonight.

SHIP

The *Lady Astor*, a 290-ton merchant ship owned by the Pacific Fur Company, left New York City in November of 1821 for its five-month passage around Cape Horn and up the west coast to Sparrow, Oregon.

It carried mostly supplies and grain to be delivered to the rugged western coastline, but it also carried two dozen passengers—those brave enough to venture west to the wilds of Oregon, where much of the land was undeveloped and dangerous. Aboard the ship were three sisters: Marguerite, Aurora, and Hazel.

Four months into the voyage, they had encountered mostly storms, dark seas, and sleepless nights when the ship rocked so violently that nearly everyone aboard, including the crew, was ill with seasickness. But the sisters did not clutch their stomachs and heave over the side of the boat; they did not press their palms to their eyes and beg the ocean to cease its churning. They'd brought herbs to sooth their swirling stomachs and balms to rub into their temples. And each evening they walked the deck even in the rain and wind to stare out across the Pacific, yearning for the land that would eventually rise up on the horizon.

"Only a month remains," Aurora said on one of those nights as the three sisters stood at the bow of the ship, leaning against the railing, the stars spinning bright above them in a clear, boundless sky. "Do you think it will be how we've imagined?" she asked.

"I don't think it matters what it's like, because it will be ours," Hazel mused. "A new town and a new life."

They had always craved to leave the hurried panic of New York City, to leave behind the reminder of their callous mother, to start anew in a land so far away, it could have been the moon. The west, a place said to be uncivilized and brutal. But that's exactly what they wanted: a territory so unfamiliar that their hearts raced and their minds whirled with fear and excitement.

"We can be anyone we want," Marguerite said, her wild, dark hair unspooling from its pins and cascading out behind her.

Aurora smiled, feeling the salt wind on her cheeks, and closed her eyes. Hazel stuck out her tongue to taste the sea, imagining a perfume that smelled just like the open ocean—crisp and clean.

"And no matter what," Marguerite added, "we'll be together. The three of us, always."

The sisters leaned into the railing, urging the ship forward as it pushed on into the night, through gales and strong currents and unfavorable winds, the moon chasing them. They saw something out in that vast sea, in the dark as the ship speared across the Pacific: the promise of something better.

They didn't know their fate.

But perhaps it wouldn't have mattered even if they had. They would have come anyway. They needed to see it, to step onto soil that was rich and dark and all theirs. They had been unmoored since birth, brave and fearless and wild just like that boundless unknown land.

They wouldn't have changed course even if they'd known what was awaiting them. They had to come. It was where they belonged—in Sparrow.

NINETEEN

Puddles have collected in the overly saturated soil, and my feet slap against the bent and warped wood boards of the walkway. I hurry up to the main house and fumble out of my boots.

I feel rattled after seeing Marguerite, after returning from the graveyard, knowing what I'm about to do. I need to settle my nerves before I go back to Bo's cottage.

I pace across the kitchen floor in my bare feet, weaving my hands into knots. My head pounds, crackling like Penny's body is trying to rid itself of me already. Trying to reclaim control. And there's another sensation building inside me: like a string being pulled from the very center of my chest. It's starting already, the gnawing beneath my fingernails, the desire weaving up my spine—the sea is calling to me. It wants me back. It beckons me; it begs.

But I'm not going back, not tonight, not ever.

The phone rings from the wall, clattering the bones down every limb of my body.

I pick it up without even registering the motion.

"They're coming!" Rose barks from the other end.

"Who?" My mind careens back into focus.

"Everyone—they're all coming to the island." Her voice is panicked, on the edge of breaking. "Olivia and Davis and Lon and everyone who got the text."

"What text?"

"Olivia said the summer solstice party is happening on the island this year. She texted everyone." Rose is flustered, and her *S*'s slur into *Th*'s. An old habit sneaking back in.

"Shit." My eyes dart around the kitchen, settling on nothing. *Why would Olivia do this?* What does she have to gain by bringing everyone to the island . . . and risking Gigi being found?

"We can't let them find Gigi," Rose says, echoing my thoughts.

"I know."

"I'm coming to the island right now. Heath will bring me."

"Okay." And she hangs up the phone.

I hold the receiver in my hand, squeezing it until my knuckles turn white.

I hear the back door bang shut, and I nearly drop the phone. There's the sound of feet shuffling slowly across the hardwood floor, and then Mom appears on the other side of the kitchen doorway, her robe hanging loose over her silt-gray pajamas, the belt dragging across the floor behind her. "People are coming," she says, her right thumb and index finger tapping together at her side. "They're all coming."

"Yeah, they are," I agree.

"I'm going up to my room until it's over." She won't look at me.

"I'm sorry," I tell her . . . for more than I can explain.

Memories of my real mother—Fiona Swan—shiver through me.

A quick burst of images. She was beautiful but vicious. Captivating and cunning and deceitful. She flitted through New York City in the early 1800s with an infectious attraction that men could not resist. She used them for money and status and power. My sisters and I were born to three different fathers who we never knew. And when I was only nine, she abandoned us for a man who promised to whisk her off to Paris—the city she had always envisioned would be her home someday. Where she would be adored. I don't know what happened to her after that: if she did cross the Atlantic to France, when she died, or if she had other children. My sisters and I have lived long enough to forget about her almost entirely. And I close my eyes briefly to squeeze back the memories of her.

Penny's mom pauses in the doorway, her fingers trembling where her left hand is holding tightly to the collar of her robe. Her voice comes out shaky but exact, a pinprick of words that have resided in her chest for too long. "I know you're not my Penny."

My eyes snap to hers, my heart drops down into my kneecaps. "Excuse me?"

"I've known all along."

I start to clear my throat but can't; my entire body has dried up and petrified. "I . . . ," I begin, but nothing else comes out.

"She's my daughter," she adds, her voice settling into a cool pace that wavers against the threat of tears. "I knew the moment she became something else . . . when she became you."

She's known the whole time. I find myself struggling for air.

But of course she's known. This is her talent—her gift. She's always sensed when people are on the island—strangers who've come unannounced—so she must have sensed when *I* arrived. Yet she's allowed me to pretend to be her daughter, to live on this island with her, knowing that at the end of this month, upon the summer solstice, I would leave.

"She's all I have left." Her blue-green eyes lift, penetrating mine, more lucid than I've ever seen them before, like she's just woken from a thousand-year dream. "Please don't take her from me."

She must sense that I have no intention of leaving. That I plan to steal this body permanently and make it my own. I'm not going back into the sea. "I can't promise that," I answer truthfully, a cloud of guilt growing inside me. She has been the closest thing to a real mom I've ever had—even with her madness. And maybe it's foolish to feel this way, desperate even, but I've allowed myself to think that this is my home, my bedroom up those stairs, my life. And that she could be my mom.

I recognize in her a part of myself: the sadness that darkens her eyes, the heartbreak that has unraveled the loose threads woven inside her mind. I could be her. I could slip into madness and let it overtake me just like she has. Turn into a shadow.

She and I are the same. We've both lost people we love. Both crushed by this town. Both know that the ocean takes more than it gives.

I wish I could undo her misery, the pain skittering behind her eyes. But I can't.

"I'm sorry," I tell her now. "I'm sorry for what's happened to you. You deserved a better life, far away from here. This town destroys everyone eventually. Like it destroyed my sisters and me. We weren't always this way," I say, wanting her to understand that I was good once, decent and kind. "But this place destroys hearts and throws them into the sea.

We are all at the mercy of that ocean out there—we'll never escape it."

We stare at each other, a streak of broken sunlight falling in through the kitchen window, the truth sliding like a crisp winter breeze between us.

"Go back into the water tonight," she pleads, tears slipping down her cheeks. "Let her have her life back."

I cross my arms, rubbing my hands down the sleeves of my coat. "But I deserve a life too," I counter, hardening my gaze on her.

"You've already had a life. You've had the longest life of anyone. Please."

I have stolen her daughter, the last thing she has left in this entire world—even her sanity has slipped away from her—but I can't release this body. It's my only chance at a real life. Surely she can understand that. Surely she knows what it is to be trapped, to be willing to do anything to escape, to crave normalcy in this tormented, messed-up town. To finally feel settled.

This is my second chance. And I'm not going to let it get away.

"I'm sorry." I back step through the kitchen, knowing she isn't strong enough to stop me, and I dart through the doorway into the hall, nearly bumping into a side table, then out the front door.

I pause on the front porch, hoping that Rose was wrong. A wall of black clouds has materialized several miles out at sea, dense and wide, laden with rain and maybe lightning.

But still no sign of boats converging toward the island.

I hurry down the porch steps, my heartbeat thudding against my ribs, and I move toward Old Fisherman's Cottage, where Gigi is still locked up. When I reach the door, I yank the board out of the way and step inside. Gigi's standing at the window, staring down toward the dock.

"People are coming to the island," I tell her, breathing heavily. "The summer solstice party is happening here. Olivia invited everyone. You need to stay inside and lock the door."

"First I was locked in, now you want me to lock you out? This is a very confusing situation for a prisoner."

"If any of them find you in here . . ."

"Yeah, yeah," she interrupts. "They want me dead. I get it."

"I'm serious."

She lifts her palms in the air. "You think I want to be hanged or strangled or shot? Trust me, I don't want them to find me either. I'll stay put like a good evil sister."

I tilt my head at her—I don't find her funny right now—but she smirks. I open the door a crack, letting in a sliver of wind that brushes my dark hair off my shoulders, and I'm about to step back outside when she asks, "Why are you helping me?"

"You're my sister." I gulp down the word, knowing that no matter what she and Marguerite have done, they will always be my sisters. "I don't want you dead . . . at least not like this."

She crosses her arms and looks back to the window. "Thank you," she answers, and then, in a voice that reminds me of Aurora when she was younger, tiny and sweet, "Will you be back before midnight to let me out?"

I nod, meeting her stony blue eyes—like snow under moonlight— sister to sister, letting her know that I won't abandon her. And I only hope I can keep my promise.

* * *

Once you've experienced death, living never feels quite the same.

The divide between the dark wretched sea and the bright places above the waterline begin to saturate your mind, until all you can think about is clawing your way to the surface, where you'll suck in deep, choking breaths of air. Feel the sun on your cheekbones. The breeze against your eyelashes. And never suffocate again.

I head straight for Bo's cottage, open the door, and step inside. But he's not here.

I start to turn back for the door and then a hand is on my shoulder. I whip around, nearly clocking him in the face. "What's wrong?" he asks, standing just outside the doorway, recognizing the panic in my eyes.

"They're coming," I say.

"Who?"

"Olivia and . . . everyone."

"They're coming here?"

"Olivia told them the summer solstice party is on the island. I don't think we have much time until they get here." Bo glances up the path to Old Fisherman's Cottage. "I already told Gigi to lock herself inside."

"If they find out she's here, they'll think you're protecting her . . . that you're one of them." Hearing him say this—knowing that he's so certain I couldn't possibly be a Swan sister—sends sharp pangs straight into my heart. He would defend me if he had to; he would probably bet his life that I am not one of them. And he would be wrong.

"They won't find her," I say to assure him, but I have no reason to think they won't. I can only hope she stays holed up in the cottage. Keeps quiet. And doesn't do anything stupid. But it's Aurora, and she's always taken risks—like drowning two boys in the harbor at once.

"We have to do it now," Bo says, his temples pulsing. "Before they get here."

I shake my head out of reflex and grab his arm, holding him in place. "No," I say.

"Penny, we might not have another chance. Tonight she'll go back into the ocean; then it'll be too late."

"We can't do it," I say weakly. "We can't kill her." *She's my sister, and even after everything she's done, I can't let him take her life.*

"We have to. She's drowned innocent people," he says like I've forgotten. "And she'll keep doing it unless we stop her." And then the worst crime, the one that nags at him for revenge. "My brother is dead, Penny. I need to end this."

The echo of quick footsteps rattles the air, and Bo and I turn at the same time. Rose is scrambling up the walkway, Heath a few paces behind. "There's still time," I say in a hush to Bo. "We'll figure something out before midnight." But it's only to stall him.

Rose is out of breath when she reaches us, her cheeks a fevered pink and her hair sticking out from under the hood of her raincoat, ruddy-red curls bursting to be set free. "They're coming," she says, the very same two words she told me on the phone, but this time she points out over the water. "They're piling into boats back at the marina. And there's a lot of them."

Heath reaches us and nods at Bo, a quick hello. His dusty blond hair is plastered to his forehead, but he doesn't make a move to brush it away.

"What are we going to do?" Rose asks, still sucking in air between each word.

"Keep Gigi hidden and act normal, whatever happens." I look straight at Rose. "And you can't tell anyone that you brought her here. If they find out you're responsible, they'll suspect you of being one of them."

She nods, but her lips start to tremble, like she's just now realizing the seriousness of what she's done by freeing Gigi from the boathouse and bringing her here.

The sun is coasting low over the water, forming dazzling slivers of light that play against the choppy sea, and then I spot them: a parade of boats sputtering across the harbor, making their way to the island.

The boats thump against the dock and some anchor just off shore, casting their lines down to the stony bottom.

And then there are voices. Dozens. Excited and pitched as they file up the boardwalk. Many of them have never been to the island before, and there is a sense of curiosity that permeates the air. And leading the mob, raven-black hair whipping out behind her, is Olivia Greene.

They carry cases of cheap beer and bottles of wine stolen from their parents' cellars. Without permission, they construct a bonfire just outside the old greenhouse, and under Olivia's command they take over the glassed-in structure, removing potted plants and replacing them with stacks and stacks of beer. Music begins to thump from inside, and as the sun begins to vanish past the horizon, a string of lights illuminates the interior—Christmas lights that someone brought and strung along the eaves. The bonfire sparks and grows larger as more and more people converge on the island.

We watch from Bo's cottage, keeping our distance, wary of anyone who strays away from the party.

Luckily, Gigi's cottage is tucked away on the north side of the island, the farthest structure from the main house and the dock and the greenhouse. Someone would have to go investigating to stumble across it. But from Bo's cottage we can see everything. And as Olivia waves her arms in the air, instructing a group of boys where to place several logs, which were taken from he woodshed, around the bonfire, I can't handle it anymore.

"What are you doing?" Bo asks when I open the cottage door.

"I have to talk to Olivia."

Rose stands up. "I can't stay in here anymore either. I'm going to check on Gigi."

I want to tell her it's better if she doesn't, that she should keep her distance, not draw attention to Gigi's cottage, but she and Heath are already out the door and hurrying up the path to Old Fisherman's Cottage.

Bo eyes me, then follows me outside and up to the bonfire.

Olivia spots us as we approach, and she saunters over. "Bo," she says in a singsong, reaching out to touch him, but I smack her hand away. She rubs it with her other hand and makes a pouty face. "Very protective, aren't you, Penny?" she says. "And perhaps a little jealous, too." She winks at Bo, like she's trying to give me something to really be jealous of. But Bo's gaze remains stiff and unwavering. He doesn't find her amusing—not after what she did to him. In fact, he looks like he wants to murder her right here, in front of everyone.

"What are you doing?" I ask.

"Decorating," she says with a flourish, sweeping an arm over her head. "I've always loved throwing parties—you know this." I do know, but I don't acknowledge it.

Behind her, Lola Arthurs and two of her friends are making cocktails in red plastic cups using a makeshift table constructed of plywood set on top of two empty flowerpots. They generously slosh vodka into each cup, followed by a splash of club soda. They've set up a full bar, and people are going to get drunk fast.

"Why here—why did you bring everyone to the island?" I ask her, making sure to stare through Olivia and down to Marguerite, her real eyes unblinking as they keep sliding over to settle on Bo. This is the last night, her last chance. But I won't let her have him.

"It's just a party," she says with an air of superiority, her bright blue eyes shimmering like she is taunting fate to bring our secret crashing down around us. With so many people here, how will she slip into the sea unnoticed? How can she be sure Gigi won't be discovered? "You used to love parties." She winks then puckers her lips together, a sly, furtive gesture. She wants Bo to figure out the truth, she wants him to know what I really am. She won't say it out loud, yet she'll gladly sprinkle hints along the razor's edge.

"This isn't going to end well," I whisper to Olivia, my eyes meeting hers, then penetrating deep to focus on the wispy mirage of my sister nestled down beneath Olivia's skin.

"We'll see," she counters.

A wind slides over the surface of the island, seeming to push a new group of uninvited guests up the gentle slope to the greenhouse.

TWENTY

It was high tide when the party began. When beers were pounded and shots guzzled into warm bellies, when the music started at a medium volume and conversations were had without the occasional hiccup. But as the tide recedes, so does the party. People stumble over the bonfire, melting the rubber from the bottom of their shoes; girls spill their drinks between their cleavage; boys vomit in the beach grass down near the dock. And Olivia grins from her place at the entrance to the greenhouse, like a queen overseeing a gala held in her honor.

And as it nears ten o'clock, only two hours until midnight, decisions will have to be made. Sacrifices allotted. Like Cinderella, at the stroke of midnight all magic will be revoked. And these bodies we inhabit will have to be given back. Or maybe, if my plan works, I'll keep this one for eternity. It's never been done before. We've never attempted to stay in a body indefinitely—I'll be the first to try. When the clock ticks past midnight, I won't wade out into the sea; I will resist the urge, the beckoning call of the ocean. I will endure whatever pain rips through me; I will fight the transition. I will stay in this body.

And I will watch the sunrise as Penny Talbot.

Rose and Heath reappeared a few minutes after checking on Gigi. Now they stand next to Bo and me near the bonfire, Rose's eyes always flashing across the island to the path that leads to Old Fisherman's Cottage. She's anxious, her fingers tapping against her thigh, afraid someone is going to find Gigi. And like the rest of us, she wishes everyone would just leave the island and go home.

But the party wears on. Boys are enticed down to the water's edge by the girls, dared to enter the harbor one last time before midnight. At the Swan party several weeks earlier, it was the girls who were braving the waters, risking being stolen by a Swan sister. Now it's the boys being persuaded to wade out into the sea, where they risk being drowned by a Swan sister looking for a final kill. It's a game to them.

But I can feel the sway of the sea, the changing tide, the magnetic draw of the harbor. It wants me back; it wants all three of us back. I know my sisters feel it too. I press my fingers against my temples, trying to silence it, keep it at bay. But at times it pulls against me so fiercely I feel dizzy.

"It's getting late," Rose says beside me, worry lines cutting deep into the space between her eyes. The countdown to the end drawing near.

Gigi will need to be let out of the cottage by midnight if she's going to sneak back into the sea. I will need to do it without Bo seeing, without anyone seeing.

And I will need to slip away, find somewhere to be alone, to fight the rising force of Penny, who will start to take back her body come midnight. I can't go to the main house because Penny's mom will hear my screams of pain. I had thought I could hide among the orchard rows, or perhaps the far rocky shore of the island where the crashing waves would conceal my cries. I will need to decide soon.

I turn to Bo.

Earlier, I promised him we would decide what to do with Gigi before midnight. Now there's only an hour left, and I need to tell him something, some reason why he can't take her life. *Because taking a life comes with consequences.*

But when I shift my gaze, Bo is no longer standing beside me. I scan the crowd of faces, searching for him. But he's nowhere within the ring of firelight. He's gone.

"Fuck," I say out loud. *How long has he been gone? How did I not notice when he slipped away?*

"What's wrong?" Rose asks, dropping her hand where she had been chewing on a fingernail.

"I—I think Bo went back to his cottage. I'm going to go check," I lie. I don't want her to know where he really is, what I realize in a sudden flash that he's gone to do: kill Gigi. He couldn't wait any longer, he couldn't let me talk him out of it, so he snuck away.

It might already be too late.

"I'll come with you," Rose offers quickly.

"No. You guys stay here, keep an eye on everyone."

Heath nods, but Rose doesn't look so sure.

I spin around, about to cut through the mob of people gathered around the bonfire, when I'm hit with both relief and horror. Gigi isn't dead, at least not yet, because she's strutting up the pathway, heading straight for the bonfire and the party. She got out.

My lungs cease to draw in air. My heart ratchets up so that it's beating against the back of my throat.

"Holy shit," I hear Heath say behind me.

And then Rose asks, "What is she doing?"

She's come for revenge.

Gigi escaped the cottage.

She must have broken through a window or forced her way past the barricaded door. She was tired of waiting for me to come release her. She's already feeling the pull of the tide, just like me. The sea in our blood, in our minds, begging us to sink into the darkness and be purged from these bodies. It will only get harder to resist.

But now Gigi's free. She's out. And she's surely really pissed off.

But where's Bo? Maybe he didn't go to kill her after all. Maybe I was wrong.

Gigi strides into the group, hair falling out of her ponytail, plain blue T-shirt and white drawstring pants one size too big because they're clothes that Rose brought for her to wear. Most people don't notice her as she pushes past them; they're already too drunk. But as she winds her way through the dwindling crowd, I can tell she's looking for something: someone.

Davis and Lon are standing just inside the doors of the greenhouse, hovering where the cases of beer and a nearly empty keg have been placed. Gigi spots them, mouth leveled into a sharp, determined line. She cuts swiftly up to the greenhouse. Davis sees her first, then Lon catches sight of her and actually takes a step back. He's wearing one of his loudest, most obnoxious shirts tonight: pink and teal with rainbow-colored peacocks and hula girls. It's actually hard to look directly at it.

Davis and Lon are the only ones in the greenhouse, and they could make a run for it, sprint out through the door on the far side of the glassed-in building. But they seem frozen, stupefied into inaction, which is exactly how I feel.

Rose and Heath, still standing near me, stare at Gigi with their mouths slightly agape.

Gigi slides in between Davis and Lon, fluttering her eyelashes up at Lon and tilting her head to the side. She grazes a finger around the rim of his cup, smiling, licking her lips. Still, the rest of the party has no clue what's happening: that Gigi Kline has suddenly reemerged. A few drunk girls on the other side of the fire pit giggle loudly then stumble backward, arms looped together. Another guy who is standing the closest to the greenhouse has a cigarette between his lips and is taking long drags as if he were actually smoking, but the cigarette isn't even lit. He's too trashed to notice anything around him.

I can see Gigi's lips moving, but she's whispering so softly, I can't make out the words. Her voice is slipping into Lon's ears; she wants to take him with her, one last kill before she retreats into the sea for the winter. She wants her revenge for what he and Davis did to her. Then her gaze snaps to Davis, biting her bottom lip. She wants them both.

But before she's able to brush her fingers across his cheek, he grabs her wrist and bends it away. "You fucking witch," I hear Davis bark. Lon already looks entranced, staring at her meekly, like a dog waiting to be told what to do. But Davis has stopped her before she's infiltrated the cracks in his mind. "I knew you were one of them," he says, loud enough that we can hear. He towers over her, broad meaty shoulders, holding her arm locked at her side. But she doesn't seem afraid. She smiles from the left side of her lips, amused. Her gaze penetrates his, and with his hand around her wrist, it's enough to seduce him into falling desperately in love with her. I watch as his expression melts, turns sappy at the edges until his thick, bushy eyebrows fold downward, and he releases his hold on her. She runs her fingers up his jaw then lifts onto her tiptoes. She brushes her lips against his ear, whispering things that will make him hers.

And when she's done, she threads her fingers through both Davis's and Lon's hands and begins leading them from the greenhouse. As she meanders past us, around the bonfire, her eyes glide over mine, but I don't move.

Rose looks baffled. She doesn't fully understand what's happening. "Gigi?" she says when Gigi and Davis and Lon stride past. "What are you doing?"

"Thanks for saving me," Gigi says to Rose, her tone guileful and distant. She's already thinking about the sea, about leaving Gigi's body and becoming part of the Pacific. "But they were right about me. . . ." She nods to Davis and Lon, standing obediently behind her. "See you next summer."

"Gigi, don't do this," I hiss, and her eyes snap to mine. Our real eyes meet, beneath these human exteriors. And there is a warning in hers, a threat that I can read in my sister's expression: If I try to stop her, if I do anything to prevent her from taking Davis and Lon, she will reveal who I really am. Right here. Right now. In front of everyone.

She tugs against Davis's and Lon's hands, pulling them toward the dock. But then a voice bellows from behind me. "It's Gigi!" I look over my shoulder, and Rose has taken several steps away from the firelight, pointing down the path to where Gigi has stopped, Davis and Lon standing obediently on either side of her.

The crowd encircling the fire stalls their conversations in almost perfect unison. They stop laughing and slurping beers and swaying dangerously close to the flames. And instead, they all turn to look at Rose, following her outstretched arm down to Gigi.

There is a pause, a delayed moment while everyone processes what's happening, their brains chugging forward at half speed. And then a girl shouts, "She has Davis and Lon!"

As if choreographed, several guys standing around the bonfire drop their beers into the flames then break into a sprint after Gigi. They know what she is—at least they think they do. And seeing her leading Davis and Lon down toward the water, on the last night of the summer solstice, after she's been missing for weeks, is proof enough that they've been right all along.

Gigi waits a half beat; her gaze sweeps over the crowd then back to me as she registers what's happening, and then her hands release their hold on Davis and Lon. She won't be able to take them with her. She has to run now. And she does.

Her blond hair shivers against the moonlight as she veers down the path to the dock. The boys shout after her, darting past Davis and Lon, both numbed to the commotion. And when the small mob reaches the dock, there is more shouting, and what sounds like people clamoring into boats and engines rumbling to life. Gigi must have dove straight into the water. It was her only escape.

She will have to swim; she will have to hide. Or maybe she will dip safely beneath the surface of the harbor, quickly relinquishing the body she's stolen to spend another winter in the cold and dark.

By morning, the real Gigi will wake as if from a hangover, floating in the harbor perhaps, forced to swim ashore and pull herself onto land. Only foggy images will surface in her mind from the last few weeks, when she was no longer Gigi Kline but was Aurora Swan. But we will all know the truth.

And that's assuming the crowd chasing after her doesn't catch her first.

Rose shakes her head in disbelief, staring down the path where Gigi has fled, where the rest of the party has descended to climb into boats and assist in the search for Aurora Swan.

I feel a wave of sympathy for Rose. She thought she was doing the right thing by rescuing Gigi. She thought she could see what was right in front of her—the truth—but she can't. She's blind, just like everyone else in this town.

She doesn't even know what I am.

Her best friend has been turned into something else. And for a sliver of a split second, I consider telling her the truth. Getting it over with. One night to shatter her entire world—to tear apart her reality.

But then I remember Bo.

He wasn't with Gigi in the cottage. He didn't go to kill her after all.

And then I realize . . . Olivia is nowhere in the crowd. She wasn't even here when Gigi appeared.

They're both missing.

"Where are you going?" Rose asks. She and Heath and I are the last remaining people standing beside the bonfire. Everyone else has gone in pursuit of Gigi.

"To find Bo," I tell her. "You guys should go back to town."

A slight rain has begun to fall, and a wall of bruise-black clouds pushes beneath the stars and blocks out the moon.

I walk to Rose. I hope this isn't the last time I'll see her, but just in case, I say, "You did the right thing helping Gigi. You didn't know what she really was." I want her to understand that even though she was wrong about Gigi, she shouldn't doubt herself. She wanted to protect Gigi, keep her safe, and I admire her for it.

"But I should have known," she says, her eyes turning glassy with tears, her cheeks flushed. And in this instant, I know I can't tell her what I really am. It will destroy her. And after tonight, if I'm still Penny Talbot, I will continue pretending to be her best friend. I will let her believe I am the same person she grew up with. Even if the real Penny Talbot will be gone—lost in the trenches of a body and mind that I have stolen.

"Please," I say to her and Heath. "Go back to town. There's nothing more you can do tonight. Gigi's gone."

Heath reaches forward and touches Rose's hand. He knows it's time to go.

"Call me tomorrow?" she asks. I hug her, smelling the sweet cinnamon-and-nutmeg scent that lingers in her wavy hair from her mother's shop.

"Of course." No matter what, if I'm still Penny tomorrow, I'll call her. If I'm not, I'm certain the real Penny will call her anyway. And Rose will hopefully never know the difference.

Heath pulls her away, back to the dock, and my chest aches watching them leave.

A deluge of rain begins falling from the dark, funeral-black sky, making the bonfire pop and sizzle.

I pick my way through the sharp beach grass and large boulders, the rain blowing steadily now. I will check Bo's cottage first and then the orchard. But I don't even make it that far when I notice something atop the lighthouse. Two silhouettes block the beam of light as it sweeps clockwise around the lantern room.

Bo and Olivia. It has to be them. They're in the lighthouse.

The metal door into the lighthouse has been left open by whoever was the last to enter, and it taps lightly against the wall behind it, the gusting wind blowing rain onto the stone floor.

Otis and Olga are standing just inside, mewing softly up at me, eyes watery and wide. *What are they doing out here?* I pause beside the stairwell, listening for voices. But the storm beating against the outer walls is louder than anything else. Bo must be inside. Otis and Olga have been attached to him since he arrived, following him around the island, sleeping in his cottage most nights. I think they've known I'm not really Penny since the start; they sensed the moment I took up residence inside her body. And they prefer Bo over me.

"Go back to the house," I urge them, but the two orange tabbies blink away from me, staring out into the gloomy night, uninterested in leaving the lighthouse.

I take the stairs two at a time, my breathing ragged. I use the railing to propel myself up the interior of the lighthouse. My legs are on fire. Sweat ripples down my temples. But I keep going. My heart feels like it's burning a hole through my chest. But I reach the top in record speed, pulling myself up over the last step and sucking in deep, quick breaths.

I inch along the stone wall, trying to steady my crazed heartbeat, then peek around the corner into the lantern room. Bo and Olivia are no longer inside. But I can see them through the glass. They are standing outside on the narrow walkway that encircles the lighthouse. Bo has something in his hand. It glints as he moves closer to Olivia.

It's a knife.

TWENTY-ONE

The small door that leads out to the walkway bangs open when I turn the knob, sucked out by the wind. Both Bo and Olivia jerk around to face me.

"You shouldn't be out here, Penny," Bo yells over the storm, his gaze quickly whipping back around to Olivia. Like he's afraid she might vanish into the air if he doesn't keep an eye on her.

The walkway hasn't been used in decades; the metal is rotted and rusted, and it creaks as I shuffle out onto it. "You don't have to do this," I say. The wind is blinding, rain stinging my face and eyes.

"You know that I do," he answers, his tone calm, resolute.

I'm trying to piece together the series of events that brought the two of them up here—who ambushed who? "Where did you get the knife?" I ask. The blade is large, a hunting knife, and not one I immediately recognize.

"Dresser drawer, in the cottage."

"And you're just going to stab her with it?" I ask. Olivia's eyes widen, and beyond the thin surface of her skin, Marguerite seems to be squirming.

"No," Bo answers. "I'm going to force her over the edge."

Eighty feet below us, rocky outcroppings lie in jagged, toothy mounds. A quick, abrupt death. No final gasps. No twitch of a finger. Just lights out, for both Olivia Greene and Marguerite Swan. At least it'll be painless.

"How did you get her up here?" I ask, inching closer to Bo. Olivia is leaning against the metal railing, and the entire walkway shudders when I take a step.

"I didn't. I saw her walking to the lighthouse." He swallows and grips the knife tighter in his hand, held firmly out in front of him. The blade glints with rainwater. "I knew it was my only chance." So it was Marguerite who lured him. Maybe she thought she could seduce him, prove to me that she could have him if she wanted. But instead Bo hunted her. She never had a chance to even touch him. And now he's going to force her over the ledge. It will look like suicide, like sweet, popular Olivia Greene took her own life by flinging herself from the town's lighthouse.

"Please," I say, stepping closer to Bo. The walkway shivers beneath me. "Doing this won't bring your brother back." At this, Olivia's expression changes. She didn't know about Bo's brother, that he was drowned in the harbor last summer, but her eyes light up and her lips tease into a smile.

"Your brother?" she asks inquisitively.

"Don't fucking talk," Bo snaps.

"Your brother was drowned, wasn't he?" she prods.

I can just barely see the side of Bo's face, and his temple pulses, rain spilling off his chin. "Was it you?" he asks with gravel in his voice, taking a single, swift step forward and pressing the blade against Olivia's stomach. He might just gut her right here if she gives him the wrong answer. He wants his vengeance, even if it means spilling her blood instead of forcing her over the railing. Murder instead of suicide.

Again Olivia smiles, eyes swaying over to me as if she were bored. She can see it in my face, in the tense outline of the real me hovering beneath Penny's skin. Marguerite is my sister, after all—she knows me, can read the truth better than anyone. "Of course not," she answers sweetly to Bo. "But you should ask your girlfriend; maybe she knows who it was."

I feel my chest seize up, ribs closing in around my heart and lungs, making it hard to draw in air and pump blood to my brain. "Don't," I say too softly, hardly loud enough for her to hear.

"You probably want to know why I brought all those people to your island, why I wanted the summer solstice to happen here."

I don't respond, even though I do want to know.

"I wanted you to see that no matter what we do, no matter how many times we steal a body and pretend that we are one of them . . . we never will be. We're their enemies. They hate us. And if given the chance, they will kill us." She nods her head at Bo, as if he were the proof. "You have been playing house for too long—too many summers in that body. You think you have friends here; you think you could make a real life in this town. You think that you can fall in love—as if you were entitled to it." She sneers, left eyebrow raised. And even though the rain cascades down her face, she still looks beautiful. "But they only like you because they don't know what you really are. If they did, they would hate you. Despise you . . . they'd want you dead." She says this last word as if it tastes like metal. "He"—she flashes her gaze at Bo—"would want you dead."

The knife is still pressed to her belly, but she leans into it, staring at Bo. "Ask your girlfriend what her real name is."

My heart stops completely. My eyes blur over. *No. Please*, I want to beg. *Don't do this. Don't ruin everything.*

"She's been lying to you," she adds. "Go ahead, ask her."

Bo turns just enough to look me in the eye where I'm pressed up against the wall of the lighthouse, palms flattened against the stone.

"It doesn't change anything. . . ." I start to say, trying to keep the truth from spilling up to the surface.

"Doesn't change what?" he asks.

"How I feel about you . . . how you feel. You know me."

"What the hell are you talking about?"

Olivia's smirk reaches her eyes. She's enjoying this. This is what she's wanted all along: for me to realize that we can't change what we are. We're killers. And I can never have Bo. Not like this, in this body. The only way a Swan sister can truly keep someone is by drowning them, trapping their soul in the sea with us.

"My name isn't Penny," I say, the confession ripping at my insides. My lips quiver, rainwater dripping over them and catching on my tongue.

The knife in his hand starts to lower, and his gaze cuts through me. The realization of what's coming next is already settling into his eyes.

"My name is Hazel."

He shakes his head a fraction of an inch. The knife is now low-ered at his side, his mouth forming a hard, unyielding line.

"Hazel Swan," I concede.

His eyes sway briefly and his jawline tightens, and then he goes perfectly still, like he's solidified into a statue right in front of me.

"I should have told you before. But I didn't know how. And then when I found out why you came here, I knew you'd hate me. And I just couldn't—"

"When?" he asks matter-of-factly.

"When?" I repeat, not sure what he means.

"When did you stop being Penny Talbot?"

I try to swallow, but my body rejects the motion. As if Penny's body and mine are battling each other. Fighting for control. "The first night we met." I brush a wet clump of hair away from my forehead. "After the Swan party on the beach, Penny brought you back to the island. That night, she woke from sleep and came down to the dock before sunrise. It was a dream to her. She waded into the water, and I took her body."

"So that night on the beach, when we talked by the bonfire and you told me about the Swan sisters . . . that was Penny? Not you?"

I nod.

"But everything after that night . . . has been you?"

Again I nod.

"But you remembered talking to me on the beach, and things about Penny's life."

"I absorb the memories of the body I inhabit. I know everything about Penny."

"That's not the only reason," Olivia chimes in, happy to fill in the holes I'd like to avoid.

I close my eyes then open them. Bo has turned fully away from Olivia and is now staring at me. I'm the threat now. I've hurt him. Lied to him. Made him trust me and even love me. "I've taken Penny's body every summer for the last three years," I confess.

A blast of wind barrels into us, sending a surge of rain against the windows of the lighthouse.

"Why?" Bo manages to ask, though his voice sounds strangled.

"I like her life," I say, the first time I've admitted it aloud. "I like being here on the island."

"Oh, Hazel, if you're going to tell the truth, you might as well tell him everything," Olivia interjects.

I shoot daggers at her, wishing she'd just shut up. I should have let Bo push her over the edge. I shouldn't have stopped him. But now here she stands, bringing up every lurid detail of my past. And calling me by my real name.

"I used to come here when I was still—"

"Alive," Olivia finishes for me, raising both eyebrows.

"You lived here before?" Bo asks.

"No." I don't want to tell him about Owen. About my life before. It doesn't matter now. I'm not that girl anymore. That girl drowned in the harbor two centuries ago . . . and this girl is here, alive, right in front of him.

"The first lighthouse keeper had a son," Olivia fills in for me. "His name was Owen Clement. He was handsome; I'll give him that. But I never understood what she saw in him. He had no money, no estate, no lucrative future. Yet she loved him anyway. And she was going to marry him. That is, if his father hadn't accused us of being witches and drowned us in the harbor."

I cringe at her sharp account of Owen and me. As if it could be summed up so crisply. A single breath to tell our story.

"Now Owen is buried up on Alder Hill in the Sparrow Cemetery. That's where she went this morning—to his grave." She says it like an accusation, like I have betrayed Bo with this single act. And maybe I have. But it's not the worst offense, not by a mile.

Bo looks stunned. He's staring at me like I have ripped his heart from his chest, squeezed it between my clawed fingers, and crushed it until it stopped pumping.

Where he once saw a girl, he now sees a monster.

"It wasn't like that," I say. "I went to say good-bye to him." But my words seem frail and ineffectual. They don't mean anything anymore. Not to him.

"So you see, Bo," Olivia continues, hair whirling about her face, Marguerite Swan grinning and swaying beneath her skin as if she were suspended in midair. "Your sweet Penny is not who she says she is. She is a murderer like me, like Aurora—her sisters. And she only comes back to this island because it reminds her of the boy she used to love. And if you think you care about her, love her even, you might want to consider that she is a Swan sister, and seducing boys is what we do. You might only love her because she has spun a spell to make you think you do. It's not real." Olivia licks her lips.

"That's not true," I bark.

"Oh, no? Perhaps you should tell him about his brother. Tell him how good you are at seducing unsuspecting outsiders."

My knees buckle, and I dig my fingernails into the wall of the lighthouse to keep from collapsing. *I can't do this.*

"What was your brother's name?" Olivia ponders. "Doesn't matter. I'm sure you resemble each other, and how could my sister resist the chance to seduce two brothers? It's just so perfect."

"Stop it," I tell her, but Bo has taken a step back against the railing, and it rattles beneath him. His hair is soaked, his clothes soaked.

We all look like we've been swimming in the ocean, drenched, the three of us trapped together on this walkway, caught by the wind and whatever fate has brought us here to this point. Centuries of deceit now tearing me apart. The truth more painful than anything I've ever felt. Even more painful than drowning.

"Was it you?" Bo asks, and the way he says it feels like he's just thrust the knife straight into my gut.

"I didn't know at first," I say, fighting through the heat of tears that push against the rim of my eyes. "But when you told me what happened to your brother, I started to remember him. You look so much alike." I clear my throat. "I didn't want to believe it. I was different last summer. I didn't care whose life I took—I didn't care about anything. But I do now. You helped me see that. I don't want to hurt anyone anymore, especially not you."

"This entire time, you knew I was trying to figure out who killed him. . . ." He gets tangled up on the words. Then he finds them again. "It was you?"

"I'm sorry." Another breath.

He looks away, not even listening to me anymore. "This is why you could see what Gigi really is, and Olivia?" His eyes shift to look at Olivia and then me, like he's trying to see what lies inside us. "You could see them because you're one of them?"

"Bo," I plead, my voice sounding weak.

"You drowned my brother," he says, and he takes one quick step forward and locks his body around mine. His breath is low and shallow, and he brings the knife up to my throat, pressing it just beneath my chin. My eyelids flutter. I lean my head back against the wall. His gaze tears through me. Not with lust but rage. And I sense in the fury pumping through his stare, through his fingertips where they hold the knife, that he wants to kill me.

Olivia's eyes flash to the doorway. This is her chance to flee. But for some reason she stays. Maybe she wants to see him slit my throat. Or maybe she just wants to see how this plays out.

"How many have you killed this year?" Bo asks, like he's looking for another reason to slide the blade across my throat and let the life drain out of me.

"None," I mutter.

"My brother was the last one?"

I nod, just barely.

"Why?"

"I don't want to be that person anymore." My voice is a whisper.

"But it's what you are," he spits back.

"No." I shake my head. "It's not. I can't do it anymore. I won't. I want a different life. I wanted it with you."

"Don't do that," he says.

I try to clear my throat, but I'm shaking too badly.

"Don't act like I changed you. Don't act like you care about me," he says. "I can't trust anything you've said. I can't even trust how I feel about you." These last words sting the worst, and I grimace. He thinks I made him love me, that I seduced him just like Olivia did. "You lied to me about everything."

"Not everything," I try to say, but he doesn't want to hear it.

He drops the knife from my throat. "I don't want to hear anything else." His eyes are like stone, rimmed with hatred for what I am. Mine are pleading for forgiveness. But it's too late for that. I killed his brother. There is nothing more to say.

I have made myself his enemy. And now he recoils from me.

And just as the beam of light from the lighthouse passes over his face, he turns away, the rain slamming against his back, and ducks through the door into the lighthouse.

His shadow moves through the lantern room and disappears down the stairway. "He doesn't love you, Hazel," Olivia says, as if to console me. "He loved what he thought you were. But you've been lying to him."

"This is your fault. You did this."

"No. *You* did this. You thought you could be one of them—human—but we've been dead for two hundred years—nothing will change that. Not even a boy you think you love."

"How the hell would you know? You've never really loved anyone in your whole life. Only yourself. I don't want to be miserable like you, stuck in that harbor for eternity."

"You can't change what we are."

"Watch me," I say, and I push away from the wall and dart back into the lighthouse.

"Where are you going?" she shouts after me.

"I'm going after him."

TWENTY-TWO

The bonfire outside the greenhouse is a smoldering heap of coals, unable to survive in this downpour. And everyone who had come to the island for the summer solstice is now gone. A party cut short by the return of Gigi Kline.

The shadow of Bo is already headed down the path to the dock, and the wind and rain between us makes it seem like he's miles away, a mirage on a desert highway. I open my mouth to yell down to him but then clamp my lips closed. He won't stop anyway. He's determined to leave this island . . . and me. For good.

So I start to run.

At the dock, the cluster of boats and dinghies that had been clotted together only a few hours earlier are now all gone. Only the skiff and the sailboat remain, thumping against the sides of the dock, the wind battering down on them like an angry fist.

Out on the water, several lights sweep through the dark, still searching for Gigi, unable to locate her, while the others must have given up and returned to the marina. She might still be out there somewhere, hidden. Midnight inching closer. Or maybe she's already gone beneath the waves, Aurora dissolving back into the deepest dark

283

of the harbor. But if I know my sister, she will find a way back to shore so she can wait out the last few minutes until midnight. Savor these fleeting moments until she has to return to the brutal sea. And Marguerite will do the same. Maybe she will stay atop the lighthouse, staring out over the island, watching the storm push inland over the Pacific, until she's forced down to the water's edge in the final seconds.

Bo is not in the skiff, so I scan the sailboat. He appears near the front starboard side, throwing the moor lines.

"Where are you going?" I shout up at him, just as he tosses the last bowline. But he doesn't answer me. "Don't leave like this," I plead. "I want to tell you the truth—tell you everything."

"It's too late," he replies. The auxiliary motor rumbles softly, and he walks to the steering wheel at the stern of the sailboat. It sounds just like I remember from three years ago—a gentle sputter, the wind aching to push against the sails once the boat reaches the open ocean and can grasp the Pacific winds.

"Please," I beg, but the boat begins to drift forward from the dock.

I follow it until there is no more dock, and then I don't have a choice. Two feet separate me from the stern of the sailboat where the blue script letters painted on the back read WINGSONG. Three feet. Four. I jump, my legs catapulting me forward, but I fall just short. My chest slams against the side, pain lancing across my ribs, and my hands scramble for something to keep from falling into the water. I find a metal cleat and wrap my fingers around it. But it's slick, and my fingers start to give way. Seawater splashes up against the backs of my legs.

Then Bo's hands tighten around my arms and pull me upward

onto the boat. I gasp, touching my left side with my palm, pain shooting through my ribs with each deep breath. Bo is only inches away, still holding on to my right arm. And I look up into his eyes, hoping he sees me, the girl inside. The girl he's known these last few weeks. But then he releases my arm and turns away, back to the helm of the sailboat. "You shouldn't have done that," he says.

"I just need to talk to you."

"There's nothing else you can say."

He steers the boat not toward the marina, but out to sea, straight into the storm.

"You're not going to town?"

"No."

"You're stealing a sailboat?"

"Borrowing it. Just until I get to the next harbor up the coast. I don't want to see that cursed fucking town ever again."

I press my fingers to my ribs again and wince. They're bruised. Maybe cracked.

The sailboat heaves to the side, the wind fighting us, but I shuffle to where Bo is holding tight to the steering wheel, maneuvering us right out into the heart of the storm. The tide swells; waves crash over the bow then spill out the sides. We shouldn't be out in this.

"Bo," I say, and he actually looks at me. "I need you to know. . . ." My body shakes from the cold, from the knowing that I'm about to lose everything I thought I had. "I didn't force you to care about me. I didn't trick you into loving me. Whatever you felt for me was real." I say it in the past tense, knowing that whatever he felt is probably now gone. "I'm not the monster you think I am."

"You killed my brother." His gaze peels me open, severs me in half, crushes me down to nothing. "You fucking killed him. And you lied to me."

This I can't make right. There's nothing that can change it. It's unforgivable.

"I know."

Another wave slams into us, and I grab on to Bo instinctively then let him go just as quickly. "Why did you do it?" he asks. I'm not sure if he's asking about his brother or asking why I lied about who I am. Probably both.

And the answers are tied up in each other. "This town took everything from me," I say, blinking away the water on my lashes. "My life. The person I once loved. I was angry . . . no, I was more than angry, and I wanted them to pay for what they did to me. I took your brother into the harbor like I've taken so many boys over the years. I was numb. I didn't care whose life I stole. Or how many people suffered."

I grip the wood helm beside the steering wheel to keep from being thrown sideways by another wave. This storm is going to kill us both. But I keep talking—this might be the last chance I get to make Bo understand. "This summer, when I took Penny's body for the third time, I awoke in her bed just like the last two years, but this time a new memory rested in her mind: a memory of you from the night before. She was already falling for you. She saw something that made her trust you. But I was in her body now. And you were on the island—the boy she brought across the harbor and let stay in the cottage. And for some reason I trusted you too. It was the first time I've trusted anyone in two hundred years." I brush away a stream of tears with the back of my hand. "I could have killed you. I could have drowned you that first day. But for some reason I wanted to protect you. Keep you safe. I wanted to feel something again for someone—for you. I needed to know that my heart wasn't completely dead, that a part of me was still human . . . could still fall in love."

Rain and seawater spill over the hard features of his face. He's listening, even if he doesn't want to.

"No one should exist for as long as I have," I say. "Only getting small glimpses of a real life each summer, tormented by dark waking dreams the rest of the time. I've spent most of my two hundred years down there, at the bottom of the sea, a spook . . . an apparition moving with the tide, waiting to breathe air again. I can't go back there."

Not alive—not dead. A phantom trapped as the months tick by, every hour, every second.

"So you'd keep this body forever?" he asks, squinting into the storm as we near the end of the cape and chug out into open water.

"I'm not sure what I want now."

"But you stole it," he answers sharply. "It's not yours."

"I know." There is no justification for wanting to keep this body. It's selfish, and it's murder. I would be killing the real Penny Talbot, tamping her down as if she never existed at all. I wanted to believe I was a different person because of Bo, because I haven't killed this summer. But I'm no different from who I've been for the last two hundred years. I want something I can't have. I am a thief of souls and bodies. But when will I stop? When will my torment on this town be enough? My revenge satiated?

Penny deserves a full life—doesn't she? The life I never got to have. And in a burst of realization, I know: I can't take it from her.

All my thoughts surface at once. A deluge of memories.

They snap like little firecrackers in my mind. Explosions along every nerve ending. I can fix this. Remedy the injustices. Give Bo what he wants.

"I've only been on this sailboat once before," I tell him. He frowns at me, not sure what I'm talking about. "The first summer that I took Penny's body, her father was suspicious of me. He figured out what I was. I think that's why he collected all those books in your cottage: He was trying to find a way to get rid of me without killing his daughter—the same thing you were searching for. Except he found a way." Bo turns the boat south down the coastline, and the wind shifts direction too, hitting us from the starboard side. "That summer," I continue, "he left the house one night after dinner and walked down to the dock. I followed him. He said he was taking the sailboat out and asked if I wanted to go along. Something didn't seem right. He seemed off—anxious—but I went because that's what Penny would have done. And I was pretending to be her for the first time. We didn't get very far out, just past the cape, when he told me the truth. He said that he knew what I was—a Swan sister—and that he was giving me a choice. He had found a way to kill me without destroying the body I inhabited—Penny's body. He had discovered it in one of his books. But it involved sacrifice. I draw in a shallow breath, locating the words lodged at the base of my throat. If I jumped into the sea," I say, trying to steady my voice, "and drowned again, like I did two hundred years ago, I would die, but Penny would not. I had to repeat my death. And he believed it would also kill my sisters, effectively breaking our curse. We would never return to the town of Sparrow again."

Bo tilts his head to look at me, his hands white-knuckled and braced around the steering wheel, fighting to keep us from being blown to shore or capsized completely. "But you didn't do it?"

I shake my head.

And then he asks what I knew was coming. "What happened to Penny's father?"

"I thought he was going to push me overboard, force me to do it. He came toward me, so I grabbed the mooring hook and I . . . I struck him with it. He wobbled for a minute. Off balance as the boat rolled with each wave." I choke back the memory. I still wish I could go back and undo what happened that night. Because Penny lost her father, and her mom lost her husband. "He went over the side. And he never came back up to the surface again." I look out at the sea, midnight blue, churning and pockmarked with rain, and I picture him sucking in water, drowning just like I did so many years ago. "There was a book sitting on the deck of the boat, the one where he had read how to break our curse, so I threw it overboard. I didn't want anyone else finding out how to kill us." I had watched it sink into the dark, having no idea that there was an entire cottage filled with books he had collected. "The boat had slowly been drifting toward shore," I explain. "The sails were down, thankfully, and the motor still running. So I steered it away from the rocks and somehow made it back to the island. I tied it to the dock and crept back up to the house. And there it has sat, until now."

"Why are you telling me this?" Bo asks.

"Because I know what I need to do now. I should have done it that night. I should have changed the course of everything. Then your brother would still be alive, and you never would have come here. I was selfish then, and a coward. But I'm not anymore."

"What are you talking about?" He releases one hand from the steering wheel.

"I'm going to give you what you want—your revenge."

I turn away from him and walk to the starboard side of the sailboat, facing out to sea. My grave—the place where I belong. Lives have been lost. Deaths counted. It started with my sisters and me when we were drowned in the harbor all those years ago, but we have caused more suffering than can ever be measured.

"What are you doing?" Bo's voice is still hard, but I sense a hint of uncertainty in it.

"I wanted to stay in this body and live this life . . . with you. But now I know that I can't . . . for so many reasons. You will never be able to love me knowing what I've done, who I am. I'm sorry for your brother. I wish I could take it back. I wish I could take back most of the things I've done. But at least now I can end it. Make right this wrong." I close my eyes briefly, drawing gulps of air into my lungs.

"Penny," he says, a name that isn't mine. He steps away from the wheel, the motor still rumbling, the sailboat crashing through the waves without a captain to pilot it. He doesn't touch me. But he stands in front of me, rocking side to side with the heaving sailboat. "Hazel," he tries instead, but there is still the burning of anger in his voice. "You ruined my life; you took my brother from me. And then I fell in love with you—I fell in love with the person who killed him. How am I supposed to deal with that? What do you want me to say? That I forgive you? Because I can't." His eyes waver away from me. *He can't forgive.* He never will. I can see the struggle in him. He feels like he should try to stop me, but a part of him, a bitter, vengeful part of him, also wants me dead.

"I know you can't forgive me," I say. "I know I hurt you—I ruined everything. I wish it were different. I wish *I* were different. But . . ." I choke down on the words I need to say. "But I did love you. That was real; everything between us was real. I love you still."

I hope to see a glimmer of something in his eyes, recognition that a part of him still loves me too. But he can't see through what he now knows I am. I am only the girl who drowned his brother—that's all.

When he doesn't speak, I glance over to the steering wheel, where a small clock is mounted to the dash. Eleven forty-eight. Only twelve minutes left until midnight, and then it'll be too late. I can't stay in this body, not now. I can't steal another life. But if I plunge into the icy sea, if I don't allow my soul to escape but instead let this body drown with me inside, I will be the one to die. Not Penny. I will drown just like I did two centuries ago. And hopefully, if Penny's father was right, she will survive.

"In years past, when we've returned to the sea," I explain, the wind blowing my hair straight out behind me, "we leave the bodies we've stolen before the clock reaches midnight. But I think, for this to work, Penny's body has to drown with me inside it. I will die, but she can be brought back. You will have to save her. I will be gone, but she can live."

He looks through me, like he doesn't want to believe what I'm saying.

I turn toward the railing. The sea spraying my face, the dark sky like a funeral. This will be my last breath. My last glimpse of the life I could have had. I close my eyes, knowing I can't turn back.

But then Bo's hands grab me, spinning me around to face him. "No," he says. His eyebrows are tugged together, lips cut flat. There is torment in him. He doesn't know what to feel, what to do. And this is why I'm taking the decision away from him. I'm ending this once and for all so he doesn't have to. He speaks anyway, says what he thinks he should: "It doesn't have to end like this."

I smile a little, shaking my head. "You know there's no other way. My sisters will just keep on killing. And I don't want to go back into the sea for another two hundred years. I can't. It's not a life. And I'm tired."

He slides his hands up to my cheeks and into my soaking-wet hair. And even though there is love in his eyes, a pain that I recognize, there is also hate. Deep, undeniable, entrenched hate. I took his brother from him. And there's no going back from that.

But even with loathing in his dark green eyes—which still remind me of the place where the sea meets the sky after a storm—he pulls me to him, pressing his warm lips to mine as the rain continues to fall between us. He kisses me like he won't let me go, even though I know he will. Desperate and angry. Loving me and hating me. And his fingers pull against my hair, drawing me even closer. My fingernails dig into his chest, trying to hold tight to this moment. This feeling. I could take him with me, like both Olivia and Aurora suggested. I could drown him now, and he would be trapped in the sea with me for eternity. But I don't want him like that—confined to a watery prison. It isn't real. And he doesn't deserve it.

His lips lift only an inch away from mine, and I draw in a tight breath of air.

"Thank you for giving me these days with you," I say. Tears push forward, and I don't try to stop them.

I close my eyes and rest my forehead against his chest, breathing him in, wanting to remember his scent forever. But right now he just smells like the sea. A boy drifted in on the tide. Like a dream, like a memory I hope I'll never forget.

I drop my hands from his chest, turning to look out at the ocean. Wild and turbulent. The bottomless black Pacific beckoning me into its cold interior. It's nearly midnight, and lightning spiders against the clouds in the distance, drawing closer. "When I jump in," I say to Bo over the crashing waves and wind, "after I've drowned, you need to pull her body back out."

He doesn't nod. No response. He can't comprehend what's happening. But he knows he has to let me go.

I meet his forest-green eyes for the last time, seeing myself reflected back in them. "Don't tell her what happened to her father," I say. "Don't tell her about me. I think it's better if she doesn't know."

Thunder snaps down from the sky. He nods.

I will leave the good memories inside Penny's mind, and I will take the bad ones with me. She will remember images of Bo, of his warmth beside her in the cottage, of his hands on her skin, his lips on hers. She will remember days when her heart felt about to burst with love for him. She won't recall going to the cemetery to say good-bye to Owen; she won't remember speaking to Marguerite in front of the old perfumery. She won't remember talking to Gigi Kline as if she were her sister. She will only recall that she provided sanctuary for Gigi from the boys who had been hunting her. She will live the life I wish I could have. She will miss her father, but sometimes missing is better than knowing. I will give her the gift of good memories. The gift of Bo—the last boy I loved.

The boy I love still.

I step over the wire railing. The deck is slippery, and I almost lose my footing. My heart begins to pound, fear and doubt seizing me. My fingers grip so tightly to the railing that they begin to throb.

I don't take my gaze off him. "I told you that love is like falling, like drowning. This will be the same. I just have to let go." My lips quiver. "Don't forget me."

"Never," he answers. And his face is the last thing I see before I jump over the side and hit the water. And everything turns black.

The world is instantly made silent. The storm churns and crashes above the waterline, but down here, everything is calm and quiet.

I swim hard. I pull myself into the deep, closer to the bottom of the sea. The cold turns my hands and feet numb almost immediately—the cold that will slow my heart and preserve Penny's body. The darkness is absolute, blotting out the surface of the ocean so that I can't tell which way is up. But I don't want to change my mind—I don't want any chance of swimming back up and sucking in a breath of air.

I plummet like a coin sinking down to the pirate wreckage in the harbor. I think about the penny I tossed into the water the night with Bo and Rose and Heath. We each made wishes. Some tangible. Some likely not. My wish was to be human again. To live a normal life. But it didn't come true. I fall deeper, darker, colder. But maybe this, what I'm doing right now, is the most human I've ever been. To die. To sacrifice yourself so others don't have to. To make a choice.

And I fell in love. What's more human than that?

The cold seizes my extremities so that I can no longer move my fingers and toes, arms and legs. And the dark makes shapes that I know aren't really there. Death plays tricks on me.

I think I see my reflection in the water, which is impossible. But there are two images: Penny's face and mine, masked deep beneath her skin, the real reflection of me—Hazel Swan. Dark hair, wide green eyes, lost. Alone. But not really alone. I've known love—deep, foolish love. And that has made it all worth it.

I squeeze my eyes closed.

I open my mouth, gulping down the sea. It tastes like salt and absolution. Like letting go. And then, drawing inward from the cold, is massive warmth. My body is no longer numb. It feels like I'm lying in a hollow of beach grass under an afternoon sun, watching clouds bounce lazily across the sky. The warmth is so real that I open my eyes again, and then I'm swallowed by it.

PENNY TALBOT

I have forgotten the day. The hour. But I feel bitterly cold and I draw in a breath like it's the last and the first. My ribs ache.

Arms around me, tugging me onto a boat. The wind racks my ears, the rain makes me shiver. I'm huddled at the stern, a blanket over my shoulders. "Where am I?" I ask, and a faint voice shouts over at me, words I can't seem to understand. The dark sky spins above me.

The dock beneath my feet.

The long march up the walkway.

And then the cottage I haven't been inside of in years. A fire starting low and then growing warm and bright. I sit on the floor. Books everywhere. Again a voice and a face I don't recognize brings me hot tea, and I drink it carefully, warming my insides. *How did I get here?* Everything is a dream I'm not sure I want to remember.

But then I do remember. The boy crouched beside me, his face. I do know him. From the marina, looking for work. And then the party on the beach. He saved me from Lon Whittamer, who tried to pull me into the water. And then we sat beside the bonfire and talked. His name is Bo. He's cute. And the singing from the harbor chased us all the way back to the island. I told him he could stay here in the cottage, that I'd give him work for the summer. And here he is. Drenched, worry lines punctuating his face.

"Did the singing stop?" I ask.

"The what?" he says.

"The Swan sisters. The singing. Have they all returned yet?"

He pauses a moment, his expression pulling at the edges of the scar by his left eye. *Where did he come from?* I wonder. There is kindness in his eyes. But he shouldn't be here in Sparrow. It's too risky. "Yeah," he finally answers. "The singing stopped. And I don't think we'll ever hear it again."

I fall asleep on his couch. A blanket tucked over my shoulders. And each time I open my eyes, he's still awake, staring into the fire like he's looking for something, or waiting for someone.

"What happened to me?" I ask as dawn inches through the windows.

He turns around, sorrow scribed into the features of his face. The coolness of morning slips through the cracks in the doorway, making me shiver even with the fire roaring behind him.

He squints at me, like it pains him just to look at me. A deep, wretched heartache. But I'm not sure why. "You've been asleep for a while," he tells me. "Now you're awake."

I look down at my hands, curled together in front of me. On my left index finger is a pink scar, nearly healed. At least a week or two old. But I don't recall how I got it. I can't seem to find the memory in the trenches of my mind. So I tuck my hands back inside the blanket and push the thought away.

I know there is more meaning in his answer than what he's willing to reveal. But my head still feels foggy, my body wanting to drag me back into my dreams. So I ask one more question before I drift off. "What happened to you?"

"I lost someone I loved."

THE HARBOR

Some places are bound in by magic. Ensnared by it.

The town of Sparrow may have possessed slivers of magic long before the Swan sisters arrived in 1822. Or maybe the three sisters brought it with them across the Pacific. No one would ever know for sure. Their beauty and unluckiness may have been its own kind of spell, spun together in a rugged place like Sparrow, Oregon, where gold washed down from the mountains and the sea pulled ships under when the moon was full and the tide vengeful.

Magic is a tricky thing. Not easily measured or metered or weighed.

Even though the Swan sisters will never again return to torment the small town, their enchantment still resides in the sodden streets and the angry winter winds.

The morning after the summer solstice, a local fisherman steered his boat out into the harbor in search of crabs rolling along the seafloor. The tourists had begun their exodus from the bed-and-breakfasts, loading into cars and boarding buses. Returning home.

The Swan season had ended. But what the tourists and locals didn't yet know was that there would never again be another drowning in the town of Sparrow.

Olivia Greene would wake the following morning atop the lighthouse on Lumiere Island. She would recall only fragments of the party the night before and assume she drank too much and passed out on the cold stone floor, her friends having abandoned her.

Gigi Kline, who had been missing for several weeks but reappeared unexpectedly at the summer solstice party, would wake up on the rocky shore of Lumiere Island, her feet halfway submerged in the water and three toes swollen and frostbitten, unable to be saved. After having fled into the harbor the night before, Aurora circled back around to the shore, easily evading capture from the mob of mostly drunk Sparrow High students. She was watching the boats drift farther away, her arms hugging her chest, soaking wet, about to slip back into the water and relinquish the body she had stolen, when she collapsed right there on the rocks.

Neither Aurora nor Marguerite Swan ever made it back into the water. Because at eleven fifty-four, their sister Hazel Swan dove into the sea and drowned herself, severing the two-centuries-long curse in a single act of sacrifice.

Aurora and Marguerite vanished from their stolen bodies like a wisp of sea air, a rivulet of smoke finally extinguished for good.

But still, unknowingly, the following morning a local fisherman navigated his boat among the wreckage of sunken ships, drifting over the very spot where the three Swan sisters had been drowned two hundred years ago. And in that place, bubbles rose up to the surface. Usually caused by crabs knotted together, moving among the silty bottom. But not this time, not on this morning.

What he saw was something else.

Three bodies, dressed in gossamer-white gowns that clung to

their ashen skin, drifted together with the current. He pulled them aboard his boat, unaware of what he had just discovered. They were not skeletons, not chewed apart by fish and salt water; it was as if they had been drowned that very morning.

The Swan sisters' bodies had finally been recovered.

And when they were carried ashore and laid on the dock in Sparrow, people gasped. Children cried and women cut off locks of the sisters' hair for good luck. They were beautiful. More stunning than anyone had ever imagined. More angelic than any portrait or story had ever described.

The curse of the Swan sisters had been broken.

It took several days for the locals to decide what should be done with the perfectly preserved bodies. But eventually they were buried in Sparrow Cemetery atop Alder Hill, overlooking the bay. It was only fitting.

People still come to take pictures beside their gravestones, even though the Swan season has never returned. No songs whispered from the deep waters of the harbor. No bodies stolen for a brief few weeks in June.

But there is one who comes to the cemetery every week, a boy who lost a brother, who fell in love and then let her slip into the sea. Bo Carter kneels down beside the grave of Hazel Swan, he brings flowers, he tells her stories about the island and the tide and the life they never had. He waits for the sun to set before he stands and walks back down Ocean Avenue to the docks.

He still lives in the cottage on Lumiere Island. He is the keeper of the lighthouse. In the summer, he harvests apples and pears, bringing crates into town to sell. And during a storm, he takes the sailboat out alone past the cape to the open sea, battling the wind and the waves until the morning sunlight breaks over the horizon.

But he is not alone on the island. Penny Talbot wanders the orchard rows with him, her memories slowly returned in the days after the summer solstice—memories that were plucked just for her, only the good ones. On calm, sunny days, Bo teaches her how to sail. She eats forgetful cakes in the afternoons—gooseberry and cinnamon spice—brought to the island by Rose, who worries about her more than Penny can understand.

Her mom bakes apple pies and fresh pear tarts; she hums while she works; she makes cups of tea and invites locals out to the island to foretell their futures. She watches her daughter—who is herself once again—and she knows she's lost many things, but she didn't lose Penny. Her mind settles; her grief eases. She stacks smooth rocks beside the cliff overlooking the sea. A marker, a grave for the husband she lost. He belongs to the Pacific now—like so many others.

In the evenings, Penny reads tea leaves at the kitchen table, blinking down at her future and her past, recalling something she once saw in their smudged remains: a boy blowing in from the sea. And she thinks that maybe her life has been predestined from the start.

But even when they kiss between the apple trees, Bo seems caught in a memory, carried away to another time she can't see. And late at night when he folds her in his arms beside the crackling fire and kisses the space just behind her ear, she knows he's falling in love with her. And maybe he's loved her long before this, long before he pulled her from the water on the night of the summer solstice—the night that is a blur in her memory. But she doesn't ask. She doesn't want to know about the before.

Because she loves him now, with the wind seeping through the cracks in the cottage windows, Otis and Olga curled up at their feet, the world stretched out before them.

They have eternity. Or even if it's just one life, one long, singular life—that's enough.

LAND AND SEA

Graveyard of the Pacific: That's what locals call the waters off the coast of Sparrow. Not only because of the hundred or so shipwrecks dotting the seafloor, but because of all the lost souls drowned in the ocean over the last two centuries.

Some days the sea is calm, lapping gently against the shores of Sparrow, seagulls diving among the rocks and tide pools in search of trapped fish. On these days it's easy to forget the history of what happened here.

But on stormy days, when the wind whips violently against the town and the tide rises over the seawalls, you can almost hear the song of the sisters blowing in from the deep—an echo of years past, the ocean unwilling to forget.

When the sky is gray and mournful and the fishermen push out beyond the cape through the fog, they will look up to the island and say a prayer—for good winds and full nets. They say a prayer to her, the girl they often see standing on the cliff's edge, the girl who was drowned long ago but returned again and again, white gown catching in the wind.

And during harvest in early spring, when the island smells sweet and bursting with sunlight, a figure can be seen wandering the rows, examining the trees. *She* is still there. An apparition caught in time, the ghost of a girl who lived longer than she ever should have, who dared to fall in love. Who lingers still.

Not because of revenge. Not because she's looking for atonement in the seams and shadows of the town.

But because this is where she belongs, rooted where she first came ashore two centuries ago. This land is hers. Damp and moss green and salt winds. She is made of these things. And they are made of her—the same sinew and string. Death cannot strip her of this place.

She belongs where the land meets the sea.

She belongs with him.

In those quiet moments when she stirs the new spring leaves on the apple trees, when she watches Bo moving down the rows, his eyes bent away from the afternoon sun, his hands rough with the soil, she leans in close—so close she can recall the warmth of his skin, his hands against her flesh—and she whispers against his ear, *I love you still.*

And when he feels the wind flutter against his neck, the scent of rosewater and myrrh in the air, a hush sailing over him like a memory he can't shake . . .

He knows. And he smiles.

ACKNOWLEDGMENTS

Magic resides in many things, and most certainly in humans. Without the following magical people, this book would still just be a few scribbles on tea-stained paper.

For her tireless work, encouragement, and badassery, I thank the inimitable Jess Regel. You have been my ally, my agent, and now you are a friend.

To my extraordinary editor, Nicole Ellul—you see hidden meaning in the margins, spells in the spaces between words, and I adore you for it. I couldn't have asked for anyone more skilled or clever or magnificent to shepherd this book into the world.

Thank you Jane Griffiths at Simon & Schuster UK for your enthusiasm and belief in the book. And for seeing exactly where the forgetful cakes belonged.

Everyone at Simon Pulse, you have given this book a home and championed it in so many ways. Mara Anastas, Mary Marotta, Liesa Abrams, Jennifer Ung, Sarah McCabe, Elizabeth Mims, Katherine Devendorf—how you ladies juggle it all, astounds and impresses me! Jessica Handelman for designing a perfectly spooky cover and Lisa Perrin for the bewitching artwork. Jessi Smith—thank you for reading the book numerous times! To the crusaders who stand on apple boxes and shout about all the books that need to be read: Catherine Hayden, Matt Pantoliano, Janine Perez, Lauren Hoffman, and Jodie Hockensmith. You all deserve daily cake and tea.

To my inspiring, fearless, unbelievably talented writer friends—you know who you are—who have been on the other end of my phone calls when my characters wouldn't behave or I wanted to burn it all. I thank you for being rocks and also warm blankets.

To Sky, I think I'll keep you forever. Your support and belief in me are more than I deserve. Someday we'll write the Lightkeeper's Apprentice story. I heart you.

My parents, you filled our home with books, and you let me believe I could write them someday too. I thank you for it all. More than I can measure.